THIS BOOK BEL

Elemental Ascension

Hardback ISBN: 978-1-7399188-7-3
Paperback ISBN: 978-1-7399188-6-6

Images from Pixabay, used with permission under the CCO license. Cover image credit to Pixabay: variandigital
Internal images: Pixabay

Edited and formatted by Curious Cat Books, UK

Fonts free for commercial use:
FoglihtenNo04, AvQest, Wizzta, Times New Roman

A copy of this title is available through the British Library.

First Edition.
Also available as an e-book.

Published by Curious Cat Books, UK
www.erachaelhardcastle.com
www.curiouscatbooks.co.uk

Elemental Ascension

E. RACHAEL HARDCASTLE

Also by E. Rachael Hardcastle

Elemental Ascension

Finding Pandora: The Complete Collection

Aeon Infinitum: Run For Your Life

Noah Finn & the Art of Suicide

Noah Finn & the Art of Conception

Forgotten Faith

(Non-Fiction)

The Universe Doesn't Give A Sh*t About Your Book

(with David Hardcastle)

Bluetooth & the World Wide Web

Dedicated to Oscar

INTRODUCTION

THE BIRTH OF MAGIC

Introduction: The Birth of Magic

When the Land was young, five Gods were born of the spirit realm Akasha to live and rule over Man. Their father, the God of Magic, instructed them to remain in Akasha and influence Man from afar, for if any were to perish at Man's hand, their collective magic would diminish and die.

His children watched Man for thousands of years but soon fell victim to curiosity. One by one, they descended to the Land as animals, playing games and tempting Man to do their bidding. To impress their father, each grew desperate to prove their power and influence was the greatest.

The eldest of the children, the God of the Land, was destructive and disrespectful. He delivered natural disasters interwoven with devastating storms, the scale of which the Land had never seen. He shook Man with mighty earthquakes, drowned them with enormous tidal waves, and burned their crops to dust. At their suffering, he laughed.

His sister, the God of the People, wished to counteract her brother's evil. She injected hope, leadership and community, encouraging Man to defend themselves against his brutality, despite their brother, the God of Universal Energy, seeing this as an act of defiance. He believed the strongest men should rule the Land as royalty, so he waged war on his siblings. Through his influence, Man became violent, greedy, and dishonest.

Even the logical influence of their fourth sibling, the God of Emotion, was not enough to extinguish Man's pain and suffering. So for many years, the Land was a cold, frail vacuum.

Until the fifth and final sibling, the God of the Senses, moved quietly between boundaries, listening to their hunger for war. Afraid of the repercussions, she asked her father to bestow magic upon the people so they could govern and protect themselves instead.

Angered by their meddling, he agreed, but in return demanded their magic for himself, weakening and imprisoning his children in Akasha, where they could no longer intervene in Man's affairs, but where they would be safe from Man's craving for revenge.

The God of Magic descended upon the Land, leaving behind five delicate Dragon eggs to represent his children's magic, which he sat atop a fire pit fuelled by his rage. He told Man to keep them safe and warm, for one day when they sensed a truly innocent soul, they would each birth wise, harmonious creatures that could erase the Gods' mistakes, bringing peace.

Before he returned to Akasha, he promised that for as long as the fire burned so the Dragons lived on, Man would never have reason to fear his children again—they would be forever imprisoned.

As four of the Dragons hatched and their magic flourished, spreading peace across the Land, those still worshipping the God of Universal Energy grew jealous of the beasts' status. They believed the creatures were an abomination. Soon, they began to hunt and kill the Dragons until eventually, the creatures and their offspring ceased to exist, leaving only their followers—the Dragonborn Guardsmen—to hide the fifth and final egg, and keep the fire and its magic from going out.

PROLOGUE

KITE AND REVERIE

Prologue: Kite and Reverie

Nestled in a sunken stone cottage in the quaint little hamlet of Broad Wells, there lived a lowly Hydromancer named Kite and his young wife, Reverie.

Unlike her Seer neighbours, Reverie was a gracious, comely Human; one who, despite being without Alchemy, saw beauty and potential in the Land wherever she went. Ordinarily, her kind was unheard of in Broad Wells. Despite their divergence, most who crossed their path accepted and adored the couple.

What Reverie most relished was their time together at home, warm beside an evening fire, watching thousands of golden embers twinkle like fireflies. Whenever Kite caught the glow in her periwinkle eyes, he thought of their wedding day, proud he'd won her hand through his archery skills.

Each morning during her walk to the well, children would wave while skimming stones and running barefoot in the stream. Reverie imagined one day she might cradle a baby of her own; a daughter to whom she could teach the way of the Land, but it was not to be.

Unable to predict a birth in their future through his tea leaves, Kite soon feared losing Reverie to an interminable depression, so he sought the advice of Echelon: Shaman of the Deeds. Echelon was a blind, ill-tempered old Soothsayer, who made his living brewing unbalanced home remedies with plants from his marshlands. But, his unstable Alchemy was all Kite could afford.

In exchange for a single debt to be repaid in Reverie's fourth month of pregnancy, Echelon gave Kite a delicate onyx flower that grew amongst the swamp's wild rice and water-lilies. He told Kite the plant was a Necrosis, and if he boiled the petals in a soup for Reverie to drink that eve, the potion would heal her.

Kite left without asking what the debt entailed.

Time went by. Reverie awoke each day excited for motherhood, and on the first morning of the fourth month, she kissed Kite through his matted locks of silver hair and left him to sleep before her morning stroll. She fastened her boots and went outside to find hundreds of stale Necrosis petals on their doorstep, tumbling in the breeze.

As she reached down and caught one, her husband opened his grey eyes to blindness.

In exchange for Reverie's pregnancy, Echelon had stolen Kite's sight and made haste for the Gravelands—an active volcanic mountain range enclosed by brimstone and a blistering desert—where Kite and Reverie would never dare venture. Kite knew there was only one kind of Alchemist capable of healing one as poor as he. They would have to beg for the nearest Oracle's mercy.

That night, Reverie and Kite left Broad Wells to travel through the Sleeping Reeds Valley, heading for Blackheart Dock where, in a darkened corner of the Lawful Hand Tavern, they would find their drunken Oracle.

CHAPTER ONE

ASH THE ELEMENTAL

Chapter One: Ash the Elemental

Between curses and stumbles, Ash the Elemental browsed the Blackheart Dock marketplace for something to eat, occasionally rubbing his foggy head. He was beginning to feel queasy as he rummaged in a worn leather satchel to pay an elderly Soothsayer for some apples when a thief knocked him aside and lifted the sack of fruit at his feet.

"Stop that man!" someone shouted, but nobody in the vicinity pursued.

Ash glowered as the man fled downhill toward the shipyard with his breakfast. He wouldn't usually have risked his life to save a bag of apples, but the stall owner—a Soothsayer who had wide, tear-filled eyes and waxy skin—was alone, blind, and too frail to chase the man himself. They stood facing one another, shocked, until an odd sensation washed over Ash. He hadn't felt such deeply rooted anger on behalf of another's livelihood since returning from those ten long years in the criminal-infested Open Country, back when caring for naught was second nature. Ash only vouched for Ash these days. But, sighing, he ducked through the crowd anyway, leaving the stall owner to be comforted by his other customers.

Two hundred feet ahead, Ash spotted a runner weaving through the mass of horses and peasants. As the marketplace was on a thin dirt track that snaked along a steep hill, Ash picked up uncontrollable speed. The only way he could stop now would be to trip and tumble, crash into the water, or catch the thief. If he did, all six feet of him, leather, weaponry, and muscle would flatten both the escapee and the fruit.

Ash dreaded any outcome. They would all further his pain —aggravate his pounding headache, tighten his aching limbs, and weaken his already deteriorating Elemental abilities.

"Out of my way!" he shouted, knocking innocent bystanders aside.

Adrenaline pumped and through thick, brown gloves, his fingers pulsed and tingled with sparks of Salamander magic. Beneath his matching doublet, his heart beat with passion.

Suddenly, Ash had to swerve around a small boy who had knelt to tie his laces. He ploughed through a cart of hay, leaving choking yellowish dust behind. Now forced off course, he propelled his body across an empty wooden stall. Before finding his target again, Ash stole a glance at his breeches, worried he had torn them, and feeling light-headed, he cursed at his graceless landing.

Critical gazes were following the pursuit. A group of shopkeepers shouted abuse at him when he dashed through their conversation. But at the base of the hill, supportive townsfolk were pointing and cheering. Ash followed their gestures and ran toward the Cerulean Grace, a rickety merchant ship about to depart. In the absence of a wooden ramp, he scrambled up the rope ladder and onto the deck. Stood in his way was a burly tradesman with dark chocolate skin, two heavily tattooed sleeves visible beneath his white cloth shirt, and a closely shaven head. He towered almost a full foot above Ash.

"Identification papers," he demanded with his arms folded.

Ash peered around the man's wide frame in search of the thief. "I'm not a passenger."

"No permit, no passage."

He took a single step forward, forcing Ash to take one back. It was then Ash spotted the thief, struggling to climb the mainsail with the sack of apples in one hand and his life in the other. Ash wondered how he had avoided being stopped by this mountain of muscle, or any of the other deckhands.

"Stop, thief!" Ash shouted and skirted around to give chase when the man turned his head.

The tradesman grabbed a boy with a mop and bucket of water by his collar and ordered him to fetch the Captain. Ash ignored them both and started to climb, careful to avoid catching his satchel or belt on the way up. He didn't want to lose his physical weapons; there were no open flames close by to fuel Ash's Elemental fire, so what little Salamander magic he could conjure would be useless in their absence. Steel was all he could rely on.

The thief kicked Ash away as he reached for his ankle and wriggled free. He wobbled and almost fell; his legs were shaky, his vision beginning to blur. It wasn't long before Ash lost his temper and drew a dagger from inside his boot. He slashed at the man's legs and cursed with each failed attempt until, at last, he pierced the leather.

The thief shrieked and tumbled, grabbing Ash on the way down. In what seemed like slow motion to them both, they plummeted through the quarterdeck into a tight, dimly lit room, casting an explosion of dust, splinters, and other debris up through the hole. The entire ship rumbled.

Although in agony, feeling dizzy and flustered from the impact, Ash managed to separate the wailing thief from the sack before drawing his longsword with one hand and punching the man in the jaw with the other. He flexed his gloved hand and swore, but continued to beat the man until he drew blood.

The Captain finally interfered. "Who are you and *what* are you doing on my ship?"

Recognising the Captain's voice, Ash turned his face from

the sunlight. He warned the thief to stay down with the tip of his sword, then out of respect for the Captain and their history, he quickly sheathed it and picked up his dagger.

"Apologies, Captain Deerbolt," Ash mumbled, then scooted past and made haste for the deck.

The Captain was a flushed, leather-clad young woman with long black hair and narrow hazel eyes. She dragged the injured thief on deck without aid and threw him forward, then gestured the handsome rogue be stopped whilst disembarking. The burly tradesman outstretched an arm across Ash's chest before he could reach the ladder.

"You put a hole in my ship," she called out. "You owe me your name at least."

Ash rolled his eyes and slowly turned to face Captain Deerbolt with a wide, cheeky grin across his lips that lifted his hazelnut eyes and brow.

"Why? Ten years later, I'm still waiting for yours."

Her expression quickly changed from delirium to that of exhausted expectation, intermingled with surprise.

Ash dipped his shoulders and smirked. "Nice to see you again, Captain Deerbolt. You changed the name of your ship, I see. Bad luck to change the name of a ship." He tutted.

She threw back her head and released an anticipative laugh. "*Well, well, well!* Ash the Elemental! I should have known—selfish and reckless as always. Desperate times, I'm afraid, but welcome back aboard the now Cerulean Grace, *Scoundrel.*"

Haven't been called that *in a while*, Ash thought.

He lifted the sack above his head and winked to acknowledge her memories of their time together—few of them (but the best of them, Ash remembered) were positive, despite never learning her given name. The entire crew's judgemental eyes were upon them until she snapped her fingers and barked an order. Without speaking, they continued about their business.

Some of the Captain's most loyal men had travelled with Ash previously from the Isle of Dragonborn to the Northern

Trading Post ten years ago, a trading point north of Blackheart Dock. Between it and the dock sat nothing but barren Open Country where Ash had been living since.

Deerbolt tucked away a stray lock of hair and watched Ash's nervous twitches. He shuffled and itched, occasionally shivering or shaking his head to erase the whistling in his ears. His condition had worsened since their voyage from Dragonborn; she and the crew who knew of him expected he'd be dead by now. It was obvious he didn't have long left.

Deerbolt's curiosity overcame her fury, and she demanded to see what he'd risked her ship for. As he was in no position to protest, the tradesman snatched the sack and emptied it for inspection.

Deerbolt leaned down. Her mouth fell agape. "All *this* for a sack of apples?"

She selected one and polished it on her thigh.

Ash grumbled. "They were *my* apples."

"*Were*," she repeated, then bit into the juicy red fruit. Between bites and breaths, she said, "Got... a... death... wish... *Scoundrel*?"

Before Deerbolt could offer the rest of the apples back, Ash spun on his heel and jumped over the side of the ship, vaulting into the air. He crashed beneath the surface and disappeared into the murky water. The crew rushed to see if he'd drowned, shouting and pointing at erupting bubbles and ripples sloshing against the side of the ship. After a few moments, Ash reappeared gasping for breath, and swam to shore, all the while beaming with delight.

"Foolish Elemental," said the tradesman. "He'll get himself killed."

Deerbolt shook her head in disbelief, stifling a grin. "Aye, he will, Sarronious, and soon." She waited until Ash had reached land before she shooed her crew back to work. "How soon can you fix my deck? Can she sail?"

"At least a day, Captain." Sarronious's eyes lowered and shifted between the open sack of apples and the unconscious thief Ash left behind. “Everything in its place,” he said. “Allow me to throw out the trash?”

“Aye,” she said. “Call the Constable and have him remove this filth from my deck.”

Besides returning empty-handed to a thwarted stall owner, Ash had no reason to perform the dreary, shameful walk back up the hill, but he did so. From head to toe, he was sodden; his dark brown hair was flat to his skull and his satchel dripped, leaving a trail from the dock to the stall. People were no longer cheering or smiling, but avoiding Ash like a savage plague.

As it should be, he thought.

In the marketplace, wriggling beneath a worn grey tunic, was the Soothsayer's beckoning finger. Ash squelched over and leant on the wooden table to empty his boots.

“Heard me coming, huh? I'm sorry about your apples,” he said, unable to meet the man's vacant stare.

“I hadn't expected you to return with them.”

Ash was taken aback. He slammed each boot down hard to squash his swollen feet back in, then bent to re-buckle them. “But you expected *me* to return?”

He tapped his head, though his gaze drifted past Ash and into the market square. “Aye, to discuss your future.”

Ash shrugged off what he assumed was an offer to tell his fortune. Peering from the man's pocket was a berry-coloured silk cloth and wrapped within would be a deck of tatty-looking cards—the Soothsayer was a Cartomancer: a Tarot reader.

Ash wrung his hands and opened his satchel to pay for the lost fruit with a handful of clear jewels.

"I know my future," he said, "and I deserve naught for my failure. Sorry I couldn't retrieve your apples. Please allow me to pay for them."

The man reached for Ash's shoulder and halted him. At their touch, he was once again angry for the Soothsayer's loss. Replacing it, however slowly, was now an intense feeling of loyalty, trust and significance, like they were old friends—a feeling Ash hadn't experienced during those lonely years in Open Country.

Ash flinched. "So *that's* how you got me to retrieve your apples." He rolled his narrowed eyes. "Made me feel sorry for you by touching me? I didn't know Cartomancers could use Psychometry. Sneaky."

"Evidently, there is a lot you don't know. I didn't touch you, but—"

Ash laughed. "This ought to be good."

"You can be forgiven, Ash. Your pain vanquished. Your honour restored."

Unsettled, Ash pulled back further. "What, can you read minds too? How do you know my name? Redemption for my crime is impossible, so I wouldn't waste your gift on me."

"I can offer other ways to validate my visions. Chiromancy? Hydromancy? Though, what use are palms and tea leaves when the cards do not lie?"

"Oh, you're an Oracle," Ash replied.

It explained the man's wider skill set. Hopeful, he allowed the Oracle to examine every crease of his palm. He was silent. After several minutes, the old man confirmed there was no mistake—the sun was setting on Ash's poor luck. He fished the cards from his pocket and unravelled them carefully. Ash cleared a space on the table for the Oracle's cloth to lay, then as his frail hand fanned the cards in a semi-circle, Ash selected one at random, remembering exactly what to do from his last encounter with a Cartomancer. First came the signifier card—one Ash connected with.

Before Ash could turn the card over, the Oracle identified it. As he dug deep into his abilities, the old man's dominant hand twitched, and his eyelids flickered as he studied the information flooding through his sixth sense.

"*The Fool.*"

And it was. Upon the smooth surface, an artist's depiction of a foolish Alchemist hung from a delicate branch atop a cliff, balancing on a crumbling rock whilst holding a precious stone. It was shiny and round, but otherwise plain and colourless like the Land's currency. Despite his surroundings and predicament, *the Fool* was laughing.

"Your signifier. This card represents innocence. Card zero of the major arcana: a blank slate. Many believe *the Fool* to be reckless, but he is blissfully ignorant, awaiting the turmoil of life to stimulate him."

Ash's voice quivered when he replied because he resonated with *the Fool*. His gut grumbled with untrusting, suspicious butterflies.

"Tell me more."

The Oracle calmly said, "You are free, but you have been on the run, hated by two groups, who hate one another. You could risk the life you have now for a new beginning, though you are unsure it is possible. Yet, you will do so anyway. The truth dangles precariously. Why? I wonder. You already hold the answers, but are careless with them."

He admitted reluctantly, "You're correct that I have nothing to lose now—anything I can do to fix my plight is worth a try. So I take the odd task here and there. I don't think I have been foolish, necessarily."

"*The Fool* is the card before the cards," he replied.

Ash selected a second card from the deck and flipped it, startled by the image of another major arcana card, which he knew to represent life events.

The Chariot.

Remaining silent to test the blind Oracle's authenticity, Ash awaited an explanation.

"Ahead of you, there are two paths, pulled by horses as is represented here." The Oracle tapped the sketch with a crooked nail, sensing the card's meaning without needing to see the image. "The black horse leads you on a dangerous adventure and the white horse to a continuation of your current existence. Each road has its perils. You are to be held accountable not only for actions you take that affect *your* life, but for what happens to others because of your decisions."

Ash was unresponsive and deep in thought.

He added, "*The Chariot* represents determination and travel. You will embark upon an important quest."

He brushed *the Fool* aside and placed *the Chariot,* Ash's first official card, in the centre of the cloth. The determined driver of the carriage glowered, connecting with Ash's short-sighted soul.

Around them in the marketplace, passers-by gave the working Oracle a wide birth. They scowled at him as they actively avoided the stall's perimeter. Ash pulled another card, beginning to trust his wisdom.

"*The Hanged Man* crosses your path," the Oracle immediately added. "Your world is inverted at the moment. You are hanging around, wasting time. You are wanted, too, Ash the Elemental, and could move on, but are waiting for a sign."

He planted the card horizontally, facing up across *the Chariot* to signify this temporarily blocking his call to adventure.

Ash replied in a whisper, "I have been waiting for ten harrowing years."

"What interrupts—no, *prevents*—your voyage is your reluctance to surrender. Trepidation curses the opportunity for a glorious victory—you are apprehensive of the ultimate sacrifice and this shall delay your decision to allow the black or the white horse to take the reins. Do you remain upside down, or risk seeing the world in a new light?"

Ash knotted his fingers as he admitted aloud that trepidation was not his curse. *His* curse led to jitters for a future he was persuaded he'd never see. He had only allowed his discomfort to progress because he thought he deserved it; his world had been upside down for so long, and this was his reality now. For ten years he'd seen his face on wanted posters, and Ash was convinced nothing could undo the Land's hatred of him.

"You cannot prevent the outcome, only walk your chosen path to its end and trust in..."

The Oracle pulled Ash's next card for him, interrupting any thoughts or questions he pondered, and placed it to the left of the others.

"...*Justice*."

"A card I pulled back when they *hanged* me—*Justice* is in my past," Ash told the man. He swallowed hard. "Ideally, before I leave the Land, justice is what I want again. But there is none in my future for those who wronged me. Justice for *my* mistakes is still ongoing, and I feel the punishment no longer fits the crime."

Ash scowled at the cards on the stall and then at his shaking fingers—none of this was news, but his cards so far were reminding Ash to look within. He'd avoided contemplating his future for so long. But now the curse wiggled through his veins and sent each digit into spasm. His future reading was two cards away, but he already predicted he'd pull another major arcana card there... *Death*.

Frustrated, he shook his wrists and reached for another card. The Oracle slapped at him.

"No more." He gathered the cards to tidy the stall.

"That's it? All you've given me is the state I'm in now, and where I once was. It's a potential problem and an outcome I've longed for since my life went to hell! I have six cards left to pull; I know how this works!"

"No. More. Cards."

Ash protested, but the Oracle wrapped the cards and tucked them back in his pocket.

"We are out of time."

"But, you can't—"

"In three days you will meet a young Human woman at the Lawful Hand Tavern," the man said. He gestured at the far side of the market square, despite being unable to see it. "She needs help, so get her safely to Dragonborn. The fate of magic, and the future these cards speak of, rests in their hands."

Ash's eyes widened at this order. "*Dragonborn*?" He shook his head, sending droplets of sea water flying from his hair. "You're an Oracle, you ought to know I'm banished, cursed, and assumed dead! I'll be killed for treason if I return to the Isle. You have the wrong Elemental, my friend."

The old man swayed as black Necrosis petals scattered across his mind's eye; flashbacks of hopelessness and torment overwhelmed him. If he told Ash of the mystery woman's pregnancy or the young man's recent blindness, he'd deem the quest impossible, flee Blackheart Dock, and turn his back on the girl as he had with the rest of the Land's inhabitants.

Ultimately, Ash would die. But, he would let Ash discover his options in three days.

The Oracle blinked away many more disturbing images of the Shaman's cruelty and steadied his balance against Ash's frame.

"My gifts make me weary," he said, "but there is no mistake. You can resolve this endless struggle for power and control across the Land. The fate of magic has been foretold. When you follow the black horse, you, Ash the Elemental, are at my prediction's centre."

Ash's eyes were wide and fearsome. "I don't—*cannot*—believe in ancient stories. It's too late for me to be following black horses and going on adventures."

"Then follow the white horse."

Ash felt instant remorse for the altercation. "Look, I'm sorry but I can't."

"You are a *good* man with a strong heart," the Oracle said.

He tapped Ash's arm and directed his gaze to a cloaked figure carrying his sack of apples, moving at a fair pace through the marketplace. She lowered her black hood. Ash rolled his eyes and turned from the Oracle, stunned by his abilities.

"You're following me, Deerbolt. Don't you have a ship to sail or a thief to imprison?"

"Aye, but I have plenty of strong men to do my bidding." She winked. "As we're a day behind schedule now, I have some time on my hands. Can't think why." She paused as if to change her mind, then deposited the sack at his feet. "You don't deserve these, but they are not yours to waste."

The Captain nodded to acknowledge the Oracle's presence, who smiled despite being unable to appreciate her beauty. She flicked up the hood, then disappeared without a word more.

"*Humans* for you!"

With a sharp tone to his voice, the Oracle corrected him. "Captain Deerbolt is a *Velocal*."

"To be a *Velocal* she would have to be experienced in the laws of Alchemy or have suffered severely at the hands of an Alchemist," Ash countered. "In sailing, she is a fast-learning genius. But in magic? No. Why would you have me escort one to Dragonborn on a quest to be beheaded or something equally... *final?*" Ash gulped.

"I will look past your discriminatory views and lack of charm when I repeat you are a good man," the Oracle said, bending to collect the sack. He offered it to Ash and chortled. "I can predict your future, Ash the Elemental, but I cannot walk it for you. I withheld your reading because I knew we would be interrupted, but also because you cannot yet be trusted to do the right thing. The Equos departs for Land's Edge tomorrow eve. Believe you are capable, though you do not have long. To make it to Dragonborn in time, follow the black horse and book your passage. Use these apples, if they would help."

"No, no," he grumbled, "Deerbolt's ship is the Cerulean Grace now—she changed its name from the Equos, which means..." Ash laughed and shook his head. "It means '*the Steed*'."

The Soothsayer shooed Ash away. "Hurry now, pest. Be on your way. It appears this black horse waits for no one."

Ash took two apples from the sack and bit into one. Then he returned the rest to the Oracle. "You're wrong about me," he said through a juicy mouthful, stowing the other apple in his satchel for later. "Lucky for you—and this mystery Human woman—I have nothing left to do around here but wait to die, anyway." He grinned and set off walking. "My *chariot* awaits."

CHAPTER TWO
THE LAWFUL HAND TAVERN

Chapter Two: The Lawful Hand Tavern

The Lawful Hand Tavern was teeming with drunken, middle-aged men. Some were on leave from the marketplace's demands, while others purposefully avoided their neglected housewives. Most, however, had walked uphill from their work in the shipyard.

A few of the Cerulean Grace's Human repairmen recognised Ash from his reckless jump overboard, and they raised a tankard as he entered beneath the tavern's sign—a clenched fist and thick iron letters, swinging above the creaky wooden door. He scraped between their filthy bodies to avoid bumping any shoulders; if he were to be blamed for a brawl and thrown out, Deerbolt would refuse his passage to Land's Edge the next day. He didn't want to waste his valuable ticket, and there was no use lingering here any longer.

The men's barking laughter and a heavy mist of tobacco smoke, intermingled with the harsh drift of week-old body odour, violated his senses. The candlelight did nothing for his orientation. He coughed and had to squint to find a quieter place to sit.

Once taverns such as the Lawful Hand were Ash's only sanctuary on return from Open Country. Its sharp aroma of ale and dark confines provided shelter, hot broth, and warmth from chilly winter eves, back when he was a sworn Dragonborn Guardsman on the run with snow-filled boots and a bounty on his head. Those days were now far enough behind him to escape, but never forget. These days, such taverns were cauldrons for conflict and disarray, especially in the summer, where the richest and most powerful of the Land did business. The Order was now more of a government than a clan, and only those with Astral Alchemy were members. Ash had always thought of them as a cult. They fought for control against those less fortunate than themselves. More often than not, the Order won. Ash noticed them gathering behind the bar, planning their next conquest. Here, they birthed unfair taxes, and brutal laws, negotiated property purchases, and nursed development opportunities.

Ash kept himself to himself in such places. Any stranger who recognised his face or name still held the right to execute him for treason, and Ash would have no means to defend himself against the men seeking information about, or revenge for, something they could *never* understand—the Isle of Dragonborn, and its ruthless, yet loyal, Guardsmen.

A barmaid walked by and delivered his drink. Ash ignored her unlike other men in the room and found an empty stool further from the noise. The tankard was cool to touch, but he cradled it, scanning the mass of locals for an out-of-place Human woman. His knees juddered anxiously as he anticipated her arrival. Then, from the cool evening air, a young blonde girl hurried inside, hand-in-hand with a male about the same age. They moved in Ash's direction but their target seemed to be a man sitting at the next table. A man Ash recognised as an Oracle. But, he wasn't just any Oracle; he was *the* Oracle in these parts—best known to the public for regular performances for jewels.

Ash considered intervening. In person, he hadn't dealt with

this Oracle in many years, but the hot-headed senior was living proof looks were deceiving, and he was famous for it. Whatever this woman's reason was for interrupting his solitary supper, Ash knew it had better be good.

Eager to learn more about the couple's troubles, he decided to remain seated and eavesdrop. Ash learnt her name was Reverie and her companion, Kite sat uninvited at the Oracle's table. Ash soon realised Kite was her husband, and he, like the marketplace Oracle, was completely blind.

"We've travelled from Broad Wells, through the Sleeping Reeds Valley and Open Country, to ask for your help," she began. "We lost everything on the journey. My husband was a Hydromancer before our local Shaman, Echelon, stole his vision and with it, his gift, to give me this child. Without Kite's abilities as a Seer, we won't know of any complications, and he will never lay eyes on our baby. Please, can you help us?"

Ash froze. The Oracle had not mentioned Reverie would be accompanied by her husband, much less an invalid, and he hadn't mentioned she'd be carrying an unborn baby. This impairment would surely add several days to their already perilous journey across the sea to Dragonborn, and Ash had declared as little to Deerbolt. But Ash felt empathy for the couple after hearing Reverie's story of how Echelon: Shaman of the Deeds had taken advantage of Kite's desperation for a child. Her pregnancy was showing, and although it was unlikely, he hoped the Oracle would take pity and agree to help heal him, if only for their child's sake.

"The removal of another's curse is difficult. Twenty jewels," said the Oracle without looking up.

Reverie's brow furrowed. Her fists clenched. "But, you're the most powerful Seer we know of! We're poor, and—"

"So too would I be if I helped every sob story for free," he said.

Ash leaned back to hear her plea and was stunned when, mid-bargain, Reverie fell silent. Arguing with those more fortunate was always to no avail. The Land had seen the effects of a ruling, rich majority in the way most Astrals of the Order behaved. Their circumstances were no different.

She inhaled profoundly, fighting back tears, and squeezed Kite's hand. "Sorry to have wasted your time."

She aided Kite to a stance and guided him toward the door, ignoring his protest to return and demand that the Oracle help them. Ash watched with his mouth agape as Reverie passed by. He had expected the couple's prayer to be jilted, but not for lack of only twenty jewels.

They truly are *poor.*

Frankly, Ash was disgusted because even after payment, the Oracle's magic was no match for a curse like that. He readied his tongue and temper to deal with the Oracle himself, when the old man turned as if to address him, then thought better of it, and raised a hand.

"There is *one* other way."

Ash took a deep breath and lowered his head. Reverie glanced over her shoulder as the Oracle dug inside his tunic and produced a large, ale-stained map of the Land. He unravelled and flattened it, placing a tankard at either end. His unsteady finger pointed to the Isle of Dragonborn, due north-east of Land's Edge, where a fearsome winged reptile roared above a lava-covered mountaintop.

And then he sang:

"Bless all who watch o'er the flame,
Where loyal guards are duly sworn,
For here they are re-birthed to new name,
So unto pledge their hearts to Dragonborn."

The Oracle's words sat heavily upon unwanted ears as the room fell silent and interested eyes glinted in the candlelight from every corner. In particular, a red-headed woman in Captain's leathers now stared at the couple across the bar. She nudged her First Mate and gestured at Ash's table, pulling a beaten parchment from her pocket and studying the two. They had recognised Ash from an old wanted poster.

Time to go.

He swigged the last of his ale. Desperate to escape their gaze, he stood quickly and knocked over his stool, then ushered Kite and Reverie into a corner by the door, using his thick arms as a plough. All the while, he held firm to the female's forearm as she grumbled and protested, dragging the blind and confused man behind her.

"Come with me," he told them, "for your safety."

Reverie scowled and yanked her arm free. "We'll take our chances. If you will excuse me, the Oracle and I—" She turned to locate the old man, but he was no longer at the table.

"Look around," Ash said, lowering his voice to a growl.

He gestured over his shoulder at the attention they'd attracted. Men were drawing their longswords and downing the remaining ale in their tankards.

"You have an audience."

Reverie followed his motion. "Kite and I are used to other Alchemists staring."

"Oh, it is not your husband's love for a Human they are staring at. There are souls here who know more of the Oracle's song than you. Myself included."

To identify the mysterious strangers and speak to the outlaw she recognised from the poster, the Captain made her way toward the threesome. Her First Mate drew his longsword too and followed her through a mass of merry patrons. Ash didn't want to be anywhere near the Lawful Hand when the Captain's intent was revealed.

He was positive he already knew what was going to happen, though. People were about to die.

"You need to trust me," Ash said. His eyes were wide. He bounced impatiently on the spot, then groaned and flung open the door. "You'll thank me later."

"*What* do you think you're—"

Ash pushed Kite and Reverie into the chilly street and

slammed the wooden door behind them. They had thirty seconds, and his gaze darted across the market square.

"There. The alley. Go!"

"What's going on? Who were those people?" Kite asked.

Reverie led her husband away, realising how serious their situation was through Ash's firm and concerned expression. They broke into a sprint and hid in time for the tavern door to fly open. Ash was leant beside a burning torch with one boot against the wall, rubbing his gloved hands together and whistling a sea shanty. The marketplace being so high up, any breeze could be biting when the sun went down, though during the day it was pleasant.

He jumped as the door smacked the stone beside him and yelled, "Oi, watch it!"

A bunch of drunken tradesmen stumbled off down the hill, swinging their blades and missing Ash as he lingered in the shadows. But the Captain, her First Mate, and two other heavily armed men surrounded him. As they moved into the light of the window, Ash noticed the First Mate had a second shadow, and it moved against his own—an Astral, most likely of the Order.

Prior to following Ash outside, the Astral had selfishly invoked the use of a tortured spirit, pulling it from the Lingerverse—a terrifying void between the Land and Akasha where lost and cursed souls roamed—to feed his own power and do his bidding. From the shadow's sporadic movement, the Astral's dominance weighed heavily on the soul's remaining energy. If he held it against its will much longer, it would dissipate from existence completely.

Astrals were a powerful breed of egotistical energy-suckers. Such Alchemists considered themselves Demi-Gods, and therefore dominated most of the Land's towns and villages as the government they called 'the Order', under the watchful eye of the God of Universal Energy. In truth, their God had long since been imprisoned with his siblings (if you believed the ancient creation stories) and his followers were rogues and pillagers who unlawfully taxed and stole from peasants, despite owning most of the west coast's castles and monuments. They despised all magic besides their own, including that of Elementals like Ash and of Seers like Kite, and all who took a pilgrimage to its birthplace, the Isle of Dragonborn, intent on pledging their service to the Guard.

Through an Astral's eyes, any magic beneath their own was a loathsome handicap, so they made it their purpose to cleanse the Land of its influence. In its place, they imagined they would rule like Dragons once did. Recently, however, resistance as riots and protests against the Order had been on the rise.

Beside the Astral stood the Captain. Her dagger's hilt was engraved with a tight spiral, which Ash recognised as the Order's seal. With their knowledge and experience, it wasn't unusual for Velocals to aid the Order, either. Mostly, under false promises. If this Captain *truly* understood the Oracle's song, she would have Ash, Kite, and Reverie killed. If not by her own hand, then by another in the name of her government.

Twin dagger-wielding henchmen brought up the rear, both light on their feet and eager to plunge head-first into an unnecessary conflict. Ash thought they were Humans like Reverie, fleeting when hindered by responsibility, but appreciative of the Land's beauty. Ash couldn't understand why potentially decent brothers, though not quite Velocals, would support the narcissistic Order.

They have their hand in everything, these days.

But no matter Ash's opinion of his foes, without his Elemental abilities at full strength, he was greatly outnumbered.

"What was your business with the Oracle?" asked the Captain.

Her enormous emerald eyes met Ash's brown, daring him to avoid the question. Ash shrugged and told her the Oracle's business was his own, but at the snap of her fingers the twins were on him. With force, they pinned his shoulders to the wall and raised daggers to his exposed throat in perfect, practised unison.

"Let us not play games, *Ash the Elemental,*" she said, pulling his poster from her pocket.

The corner of Ash's lips upturned. "The resemblance *is* uncanny," he remarked. "Though, I think they got my nose wrong."

"What of the peasant girl and the blind man?" she growled.

"I spared them from death. We both know the Oracle does not respond well to interruptions." Ash yanked himself free of the twins and adjusted his doublet. "They were beggars, pathetic thieves. I saved their lives. They're welcome."

On the Captain's nod, the twins lowered their weapons and stepped back. The First Mate's shadow was fading as Ash's story seemed probable, but the Captain's eyes were still narrow and suspicious. Ash exhaled a sigh of relief on behalf of the spared soul, who would soon be allowed to return to his unfinished business.

"I'm Captain Lehana Hazel of the Order. This is Aldwin, my First Mate, and two of my deckhands," she said. "Tell me, which way did the Humans go?"

She had a brogue accent, suggesting a north-western origin. Ash thought he recognised it from out by Serpent's Sea or further north to the Gravelands.

"A Velocal in leadership within the Order? What did you do to gain such favour, I wonder?" He grinned, then added, "What's in it for me?"

Lehana Hazel laughed and, in a movement too swift for the eye to see, whipped out a dagger of her own and poked the tip against Ash's groin.

"How about I *don't* hand you over for the fruitful bounty on your head? Or, even better, for offending me so?"

He nodded, feigning fear. "Aye, deal. They went that way."

Ash pointed uphill at a path which eventually led to the border of Open Country. Only bandits, outcasts and desperate travellers moved there. It authenticated his lie.

"You two, check it out." She jabbed her thumb in the direction Ash had mentioned and sheathed her dagger, fluttering her lashes. "See, that wasn't hard now, was it?"

The twins sheathed their weapons too and jogged uphill away from the alley. They checked every doorway on their ascent. From the determination on the Captain's face, their hunt would continue through the night, leaving scarce opportunities for Ash to smuggle Kite and Reverie aboard the Cerulean Grace. Eventually, they'd be discovered, and through further interrogation, they'd decide to turn him in, too.

The twins were a few hundred feet ahead, leaving Lehana and Aldwin temporarily vulnerable. Ash waited until Aldwin had wandered to investigate downhill, then conjured his first Salamander Elemental incantation in weeks. He used a nimble but fluid circular motion to whip the torch's flame from the wall into a cone—designed to nip and poke, torment, and anger a foe, as it temporarily trapped them within. Before Lehana could scream, Ash flung the searing tornado across the square and held his breath as it completely encompassed her instead. Her shrieks pierced the air, scattering two rats and a flock of seabirds all at once.

Ash gasped. He hadn't intended to engulf her, nor kill her, which he expected this would.

Where did that *come from?* He stared at his palms.

Aldwin set off running and bellowed for the twins' help, so Ash drew his sword as his attacker uttered a dark incantation to re-summon the enslaved spirit. Metal could not penetrate it. To separate the Astral from his ghostly captive, Ash would have to shock the host's system into letting go of the soul and its energy. Their swords clashed first.

The twins arrived at the dying Captain's side. Regardless of Ash's strength, the tornado would cremate every limb it touched. He stole fleeting glances at her torture with a guilty knot in his abdomen. There was little they could do to ease her suffering besides kill her themselves now.

The distraction caused Ash to step too close to Aldwin's

shadow as he swung relentlessly at Aldwin. The breath was sucked from his lungs. Now, he was suffocating. Adrenaline drained from his bloodstream as the spectral warrior ingested each joule of energy as effortlessly as its Astral master breathed air, feeding it to Aldwin to fuel the fluidity of every swing and pounce. The soul fed on Ash's motivation, inspiration, and his few happy memories in an attempt to replace what Aldwin had already stolen from it.

Ash teetered on the edge of consciousness. He dropped his sword and clawed at his throat, certain his lips were turning blue. Painful pressure built behind his eyes, and his temples pounded; he was drowning beneath the unrelenting force, clawing for a place in the physical world.

Neither man saw the arrow coming. Black as the surrounding shadows, it soared through the marketplace and pierced Aldwin's chest with a *shooo-uck,* knocking him off his feet. The distance forced the spirit to release its choke hold. Pacifying air re-filled Ash's lungs. He collapsed in the dirt, slowly feeling his energy rebuilding.

Confidently, Ash's saviour appeared as if from nowhere and eliminated the twins with two skilful arrows fired in a single shot. In unison, their heads hit the ground seconds before Ash's Elemental magic wore off and the Captain was left to writhe in what remained of her clothing. Her screeching sliced the night air, gaining the attention of the remaining patrons inside the tavern.

The cloaked stranger passed Lehana Hazel and released an arrow to put her out of her misery.

Ash thanked them and pinched the bridge of his nose to alleviate the pressure in his skull. It was reckless to use so much of his energy in a single attack, but they'd left him no choice and he hadn't meant to encase her. His body's corrosion was accelerating; he could feel the old curse wriggling through his veins, causing his limbs to twitch and his balance to waver, so he assumed it caused his incantation's rogue intent.

He called for Reverie and Kite to come out of hiding, but only Reverie reappeared. His eyes examined the hill for traces of her husband until the stranger lowered his hood.

"But... you're *blind.*" Ash gasped and shuffled back.

Kite hid his weapons beneath his cloak and waited for Reverie to wrap her arms around him. She cradled his torso with such relief that Ash was instantly jealous of their unique bond.

"I could hit a bullseye before I could walk," Kite said. "Hitting one with my eyes... uhm... closed? Oh, come now!" He smirked.

"But in the tavern, your wife led you."

"It would have been foolish to reveal our strengths to the Oracle."

Reverie aided Ash to a stance and dusted him off, then they hurried downhill together to the dock, all the while looking back in fear of being followed.

They reached the Cerulean Grace at the first sign of sunrise, but it would be at least twelve hours before Deerbolt's crew could sail her. Ash suggested they get out of the street and climb onboard before any of Lehana Hazel's crew or other angry locals spotted them.

"Not yet," Reverie said, tugging Kite to her side. "What happened at the tavern? Who *are* you, and who were those people? What do they want with us?"

Frustrated by her lack of appreciation, Ash took a long, patient breath and gestured they move behind a stack of empty wooden crates alongside the ship. In the water, a shoal of multi-coloured fish swam out to sea. For a moment, Ash wished he was care free and among them.

"My name is Ash. I'm a Salamander Elemental," he said. "The Oracle did you no favours; that song is of Dragonborn and it should *not* have been sung off the island."

"That woman was of Dragonborn too, then?" Reverie asked.

"No. Honestly, I don't have time to explain just now. If you board the ship with me, we can talk when we're out of danger."

Reverie glowered. "You're a stranger—an outlaw, *right*? I saw that tattered poster in her hand. What's in this for you?"

"Redemption." Ash gestured at Reverie's stomach. He strained his stiffening neck from the day's antics. "I overheard your story. The Oracle *could* have helped you, though not completely. He chose, instead, to encourage a war. That song was intended for *me*—he knew I was eavesdropping. I owe you a debt because I put you in danger. Although I saved your life, I believe it's *my* duty to get you both, safely, to the Isle of Dragonborn. There is an Oracle and Guardsmen there who can help you... both of you."

"How do you know of our Oracle's visions?" Kite asked. "You're a Salamander, not a Seer."

"Another Oracle told me when he read my fortune three days ago," Ash told them. "He said if I do this, my mistakes will be forgiven. Maybe you should've asked him for help instead of that grumpy old man."

"Do you believe him?" asked Reverie.

Ash paused and exhaled, considering his options. Finally, he shrugged. "After everything, I have no reason not to, and nothing to lose if he's lying. You're my last chance and you need help, right?"

"Why did the Oracle sing for *you*?" Kite asked Ash.

"That song is performed in the oath ceremony. It is how Guards swear their allegiance and promise they are not of an Elemental birth."

"Why Elemental?" she asked.

"Because, there is fear an Elemental will one day extinguish the sacred flame and with it, Man's magic in its entirety. The Guardsmen believe with the deliverance of an innocent, unborn child to symbolise purity, *that* child can be born alongside the fifth Dragon as its rider, a ruler: the saviour of the Land."

Kite was taken aback and for a moment, both he and

Reverie glared at one another.

Finally, he said, "You want to extinguish the ancient flame? *You* want to use our unborn baby to hatch a long-lost, mythical egg?"

Ash tugged down his glove to reveal his Salamander brand on the back of his hand; a perfect, uncoloured circle identifying his easy manipulation of fire, and *only* fire. Not all Elementals bore the same mark. Some manipulated other elements, like the Undines and water. Their mark had a horizontal line down the centre of the circle instead, whereas a brand surrounding a small dot represented Slyphs, who manipulated only air. The fourth and final variation had a cross through the circle. It identified Gnomes, the earth Elementals.

"It will take more magic and energy than I have left in me to extinguish that flame," he replied honestly. "They need an Elemental with a mark that looks like a target. I have no way of knowing if your child will be a match for their... needs."

"So, you're not a threat to them, then?"

Reverie added, "Or us?"

"I'm incapable of what the Oracle suggests; he was trying to wind me up."

"It worked." Reverie raised her brow. "You're here."

Well, the banishment of magic would *mean the banishment of my curse*, Ash thought.

With his body deteriorating at its current rate, Ash knew he would also be dead long before any prophecies to remove the Order from power could be fulfilled by his hand anyway (even if he *was* capable!). He believed the Oracle saw potential for an ancient theory to be tested, however, with the presence of Reverie's baby on the island. No doubt he'd sent hundreds of expecting couples before them on that same quest and wound up other Elementals similarly, claiming they were destined to do so and singing that song.

This time, though, the tavern's Oracle was not the only one to encourage Ash's involvement. And this made Ash curious.

He tucked his boots in as a deckhand walked by. He hoped the boy hadn't heard their conversation above his whistling or recognised him from his accident earlier that week.

He lowered his voice to a whisper. "It would take a *very rare* Elemental with the ability to manipulate all four elements to extinguish that flame. Tetrads are born Salamanders like me, but they learn additional skills in adolescence. On the Isle of Dragonborn, Salamanders are observed, and so few of us are ever welcomed in as Guardsmen." Ash inhaled deeply. "When I pledged, I did not sing that song. I'm the only one in history."

"Do you want to extinguish the flame or something?" Reverie asked him.

"I am a weak, but very normal Salamander. I have little interest in the flame's fate and less of a belief in such prophecies. They accepted *me* because I already had a friend there who could vouch for me. He died of disease a few weeks later."

"If you are useless to them, why send you?" she asked without thinking.

Ash scowled, then said, "Because I have nothing to lose either way, and I know the territory. I used to live and work on that island. The Oracle must believe you're carrying a special child."

"We don't want to extinguish the flame either," she said, "and I certainly don't wish to place such a burden on my unborn child. A rider of Dragons? Nonsense!"

Ash placed his shaking palm against her stomach without asking, hoping he'd somehow be able to feel such a prophecy, despite being an Elemental and not a Seer.

"They'll assume the opposite when they see you. I promise they can heal your husband if you're willing to risk it, though."

This is absurd, thought Kite, but he knew Reverie's heart may already have overruled her head. Her baby was unique from the moment of conception: a genuine, magical miracle.

He couldn't blame her for wanting to protect their son or daughter from the Guards' slavery as the next and *only* Dragon rider.

It was slavery. There was no other word for it.

After a short silence, Reverie uttered, "The men of Dragonborn would *never* help Kite if they think we're there to commit treason. Their sole purpose is to protect the flame. If they see I am pregnant, they might lock me away and steal my child. If not, they might think we're here to put out the flame. Surely your presence will hinder our goal?"

Ash nodded. "Aye, maybe, but I guarantee you'll not get there without me. Though extinguishing that flame would remove Alchemy from the Land and therefore remove the Order's power, Dragonborn Guardsmen value Alchemy's continuance above all else, so if they think there's a chance you're carrying a ruler, they'll let us in. What they do with you then, I can't predict." He continued, "Guardsmen will carefully assess all who take pilgrimage to the island before they reveal the flame's location. They will kill us if they suspect foul play. The Land is safe as it currently stands, but if we don't try, then we will never know."

"Then we go only to redeem your sins and restore my husband's eyesight," she announced. "I can hide my pregnancy beneath layered clothing, I am sure, and you can take us as far as you're able before you're recognised."

Locals were gathering in the square. Lehana Hazel's charred remains had been found. Mixed with the men from the tavern, Ash knew her crew would be hunting her killer. He hoped his old wanted poster had gone up in flames, too.

"Do we have a deal, Ash the Elemental?"

He gestured they board the Cerulean Grace to find somewhere safe to hide. "We have to hurry."

Reverie folded her arms. "I asked you a question."

"Fine. Aye. We have a deal. Now, let's get a move on." He led Reverie to the ship's ladder. "Ladies first."

CHAPTER THREE
THE CERULEAN GRACE

Chapter Three: The Cerulean Grace

The Cerulean Grace was an overwhelming thirty feet high and over one hundred and thirty feet long, with dark brown wooden panels and off-white sails. Reverie had to guide Kite safely up the rope ladder, and although Ash was supporting his weight from behind, he still had to act as their lookout. He incessantly glanced over his shoulder at the marketplace, where a large mob were scouting the upper end of Blackheart Dock for Lehana Hazel's murderer. Ash insisted they hurry, but Reverie said those moving black dots were not only too far away to see them, but they now had no way to immediately identify him. With Hazel's poster in pieces, Ash's only giveaway was his Salamander brand, so he tightened the cuff of his leather glove, and continued to climb.

One particularly noisy group of local traders was approaching the ship as Ash reached the last rung. Honest lower and middle-class working men like the tinker and cutler, barber, and blacksmith had volunteered to join the search party, and all were armed with a tool from their home or workplace. Ash had planned to sneak away and trade with the fletcher to re-stock Kite's arrows prior to sailing. Kite was a lethal weapon with such tools. But, the fletcher was among the mass of mercenaries.

At the head of the pack, of course, was the Constable and the Sheriff—both Astrals of the Order—whose scruffy black dog was following their scent. He felt guilty for being such an inconvenience to Deerbolt, who had granted Ash passage if he agreed to some uncomplicated terms. He had already promised not to break anything else onboard. She'd laughed, but he meant it.

Her first term: there would be a non-negotiable search for illegal cargo such as unregistered weaponry. Unless the law had changed, Ash knew these to be protoswords, halberds, scimitars and similar (basically, weapons not approved for personal use by the Order, or anything not in the company of its forger). They would not face quarrels with Kite's arrows or Ash's longsword.

Documentation would be checked and baggage for the transportation of substances such as ale or tobacco, and there would be a thorough search to check for less popular recreational drugs. Ash had neither on his person, so he'd agreed.

Finally, a physician would inspect new passengers for lice to prevent the spread of disease.

Deerbolt explained this was all to ensure she kept her overseas trade permit. The Order was quick to judge and punish Alchemists who they deemed beneath them, therefore merchant ships crewed and captained by lower and middle-class Alchemical folk were huge targets, often harshly penalised. Deerbolt was a Velocal, but members of her crew were not Human.

Ash owned very little, so he had no concerns; everything he possessed was within regulation, including his dagger. As for the lice, Deerbolt said there had been an outbreak of disease over the past two months, hence the invasive examination of all bodily hair. Merchants had reported distinctive rashes and high fevers, so these extra measures were in place to avoid transporting what Deerbolt referred to as 'ship's fever' across the sea to Dragonborn.

Ash quickly located some old barrels, behind which Kite and Reverie could hide. If they had been filled with ale or oil, his biggest worry now wouldn't be so pressing, but they were all empty.

"I need to find something to mask my scent, then speak to Captain Deerbolt. Wait here," Ash said, then hurried out of sight.

He ran along the quarterdeck, ignoring his fatigue. He stopped briefly, suddenly overcome by dizziness, then stumbled along to the Captain's cabin and hammered on the door. Footsteps approached, but they were too heavy to be Deerbolt's.

"You!" Sarronious filled the doorway.

Ash raised both hands. "She's expecting me. We have an arrangement."

The beefy tradesman was still wearing his white cloth shirt, revealing tattoos, which Ash could now see were variations of anchors, sails, and although half-hidden beneath his sleeve, a shark's head. His size blocked the candlelight but not the warmth, nor the sweet scent of rose petals from escaping. It was exactly as Ash remembered: inviting, feminine, romantic.

"The Captain is running errands."

Ash was feeling sick and would soon need something nourishing to eat, water, and plenty of sleep. But not before Deerbolt had safely stowed his friends—one she wasn't yet aware of. He bent, resting his elbows on his knees and took a sharp breath inward. His chest tightened. Pins and needles attacked his fingers. Sarronious clasped Ash's shoulder and led him inside to sit atop a cargo box containing the Captain's belongings. Ash wobbled and stumbled, but remained upright.

"Are you alright?" He crouched and checked Ash's arms and neck.

"Aye, it's not the sickness," he said, panting. "No rash."

"Should I quarantine you?"

"You can't catch what *I* have," Ash assured him.

Sarronious scowled as he sniffed Ash's tunic with disgust. He passed him a clean white rag and directed him to an open crate filled with clean clothes and a basin of cold water. It turned out most of the men onboard were smaller across the chest than Ash, but, there was plenty of soap and a blanket to dry himself with.

"The Captain should be back within the hour," Sarronious advised, gesturing at the provisions.

"There are two others with me," he said. "Hiding on deck."

"Alright, I'll find them and have someone check you all for lice."

Once alone, Ash was pleased with the peace, and, of course, the floral-scented soap. If the dog came on board, seawater and the sweat in his pores would give his earlier escape away. For now, the Cerulean Grace was restful and unmanned. Ash stripped naked and scrubbed his skin with soapy water, splashed his face and dunked his hair, then soaked his clothing until he could no longer smell fish, smoke, or Hazel's flesh. After his brief freshen-up, he wrapped his lower half in the blanket and slung his undergarments out the window, overboard.

Sarronious found Kite and Reverie hiding where Ash left them. He ushered them quickly downstairs, then hammered until Ash opened the door, bare-chested.

"Is she back?"

Sarronious nodded. "Our legal checks will have to wait."

He ushered everyone inside the cabin, leaving the door ajar. Ash was about to object when Deerbolt stepped in and closed it herself. Since their earlier meeting, she had changed into some casual clothing and plaited her dark hair. With or without a uniform, Ash thought she looked beautiful.

"Still misbehaving, *Scoundrel*?" she said, grinning at his stark legs.

The little hair on his chest which formed a line to his belly button was still wet and defined. Deerbolt swallowed hard and turned away.

"I had to wash my clothes." Ash blushed and cleared his throat. "Captain Deerbolt, this is Reverie and her husband, Kite."

Deerbolt shook their hands, welcomed them aboard, then walked to the window and peered through the curtains.

"Two others. One blind and one pregnant. You didn't think to tell me this before I agreed to help you?"

Ash rolled his eyes. "I didn't really know then."

Her hazel eyes narrowed as she watched the rabble of local tradesmen frantically search for the harboured criminals.

"And you're a *murderer* now?" She waved Ash to the window. "Captain Lehana Hazel of the Order and two Astrals were set on fire and shot last night. Were you desperate?"

"I set the redhead on fire and Kite shot the others with an arrow. We had no choice."

"Aye," Kite admitted. "It was us or them."

Deerbolt gave the mob a second glance. The Constable had organised them into smaller groups, sending them to probe the crew of each docked ship. The Cerulean Grace was next on their list, led by the Sheriff. Ash's pulse quickened at the thought of Deerbolt and her crew being wrongly imprisoned, but what else could he do? To protect her, he'd have to hand himself in; Kite and Reverie could deny knowledge and escape with Deerbolt to Dragonborn, but it would be the end of him for sure. Determined to reach the island alive and help the couple as the Oracle instructed, Ash would have to lie and beg for Deerbolt's cooperation instead.

He held his head high and squared his shoulders.

"You're going to turn us in?"

"I haven't decided," she said without looking at him, but she cast a jealous and examining glance at Reverie.

"Deerbolt, you said it yourself, we're desperate. Kite was protecting Reverie and his baby."

Deerbolt waved off his worry. "Just tell me what happened."

Ash relaxed his frame. Exhaustion was overriding his limbs. His eyelids were heavy and his head cloudy. He'd felt dreadful so far today, but now wasn't the time to succumb to the curse's symptoms. Opening his palm and curling each finger from left to right, Ash stole the flame from the nearest candle and brightened it in his palm.

"It was supposed to be a distraction, but my plan went wrong. They had us cornered."

Deerbolt rolled her eyes and blew out his palm, sending a pleasant shudder down his arm.

"Is that the truth?" she muttered.

Reverie assured her, "I saw the whole thing. They attacked us because of the Oracle's song."

"I would imagine that was intended for you," Deerbolt said, directing her question at the only Elemental onboard.

"Aren't *I* lucky?"

Sarronious hushed them and pressed a heavily pierced ear against the door. On deck, unfamiliar voices and romping footsteps were growing nearer. He drew his longsword and backed away.

"We have company. Captain, your orders?"

Kite and Reverie awaited her reply with bated breath. Ash perched on the end of Deerbolt's bed.

Never had he begged for his life. He would not start now.

She sighed. "This won't take long."

Sarronious barred the door with his shoulder after Captain Deerbolt left. The cabin fell silent. For a dying outlaw she'd never wholly trusted and a poor couple from a nowhere hamlet in the Sleeping Reeds Valley, she was about to lie to the Order, birthing a debt they could never repay.

"Most of my men are on day leave," she told the Constable as he politely questioned her. "Unforeseen repairs delayed our departure. My men are overworked. I needed them rested."

"Where is this vessel to dock, Captain?"

"The abandoned First Watchtower," she replied, "ultimately heading for Land's Edge. We are carrying food and permitted weaponry—please, check our manifest."

"That will not be necessary. Anyone else currently here besides yourself?"

"Sarronious is a market tradesman returning to the Northern Trading Post." She lowered her voice. "He's otherwise engaged with seasickness, though the ship is yet to move. I trust him—he's an old friend. Neither of us has seen anyone else today so far."

"I see." He looked past her as the dog sniffed the base of the cabin door. "Those with weak stomachs should not be sailors. Are you sure it is not the sickness?"

She continued, ignoring the dog. "Aye. Sarronious trusts I'll get him home safely."

"Have you seen anyone suspicious?"

"We have not been aroused, Constable. If you wish to more thoroughly search my ship, I can ask Sarronious to assist once he returns."

The dog, seemingly disinterested, moved away.

"Thank you, Captain, but I'm satisfied."

After a few more minutes of small talk and well wishes, the search party left. The dog never made a sound. Deerbolt returned to the cabin and gestured for her guests to sit, leaving Sarronious to guard the door. Now comfortable, calmer, and less embarrassed about his nakedness, Ash explained everything. He began with his chase of the apple thief, shared the foretelling, recited the Oracle's song, and eventually detailed the fight outside the Lawful Hand Tavern.

Kite entwined his fingers. "Without my sight, I'm a liability. I'll slow us down."

"No more than I," Ash whispered.

Deerbolt's eyes widened as she met his gaze. Not an hour into their journey and Ash's tongue had already slipped. They'd agreed several days prior that until the ship was well on its way to the First Watchtower, Ash's full history should remain a secret so as not to put her crew in danger. Revealing his past now, even if by accident, might tarnish the couple's trust in him too. Only a handful of the serving deckhands would remember him, anyway.

"No need to incite fear. No need to cause panic." Those were *his* words.

Not that he deserves their trust yet, she thought. *Not after what he did to* me.

But they were both ten years more mature, and she hadn't thought of Ash romantically for at least nine of them.

Some men are not capable of change.

Kite leaned forward. "What do you mean, Ash?"

He shuffled and cleared his throat, unconsciously opposing Kite's inviting posture. "I'm a wanted man," said Ash, "and because of malnourishment from living in Open Country, my Elemental magic has been unpredictable lately."

"Are you... dangerous?"

There was a pause, during which Deerbolt held her breath and kept her gaze lowered.

"I made a mistake ten years ago." He narrowed his fingers, pinching them together to suggest the mistake was minor. "It angered some important people in high places and they have been on my tail since. Many thought I was dead."

"You didn't answer my question."

Ash sighed. "As is any Salamander, I'm dangerous when I need to be."

"I think your antics with Lehana Hazel proved that," Sarronious grumbled.

"You knew her?" Ash asked him.

Sarronious shook his head. "I did not."

"She deserved what she got."

"You can still get Kite and I safely to Dragonborn?" asked Reverie.

Deerbolt leaned across the table and grasped Reverie's hand, cutting Ash short of a confident response.

"Sarronious and I will get you *all* to the First Watchtower as soon as possible. We owe Ash that much. What happens then is up to you."

Ash stood abruptly, knocking over the table. Its contents crashed at their feet, prompting a gasp and silent stare from the others.

"Excuse me," he said, "I think my clothes are dry."

They were still damp to the touch, but he re-dressed, anyway. He had been too eager to escape the conversation.

After pulling on the first leg of his breeches, he lost his balance. A searing pain attacked the back of his eyes and he momentarily blacked out, collapsing against the wall and smashing a framed painting of the Cerulean Grace as he did so. Reverie ran to his side, kicking the table's contents out of her way. She took his temperature with the back of her hand.

"Don't touch him, Reverie. It could be the sickness," Kite said urgently.

Deerbolt towered over them, stern-faced. She kicked an empty trunk along the wooden floor in time for Ash to empty his stomach.

"He's not sick," she said, sighing and defeated, "he's *cursed*. By the people he angered."

Ash looked up through narrow, tear-filled eyes, then across to Reverie.

So much for keeping a secret.

Deerbolt rummaged through her personal items for a clean cloth, which she dampened and passed to Reverie. She dabbed at Ash's face and neck, hushing his groans and grunts of discomfort. Drained of all colour, he was now a waxy, lifeless figure against Deerbolt's deep mahogany walls.

"What is it doing to you?" Reverie asked. "How long do you have?"

Ash writhed beneath his blanket, with his clean breeches and hope of regaining some dignity discarded.

"There's nothing else I can tell you. I'm fine, I'll *be* fine."

"Cursed men tell no tales," Deerbolt said. She folded her arms. "Nor do the dead."

As dusk settled upon the Cerulean Grace, so too did the events of the day on Ash's energy. Alone in the cabin, he allowed the muffled sounds of a cheerful fiddle intermingled with his friends' joyous laughter to soothe his fears that he didn't have long to live. Even as he rested, his limbs were shaking and tingly, his eyesight failing, and his guts rejecting most of what he consumed. It didn't stop him drowning his sorrows in a tankard given to him by Sarronious behind the Captain's watchful eye, though (*most likely,* Ash thought, *out of pity*). It numbed his pain enough to examine his flesh from head to toe.

His once toned, tanned skin was a canvas of sores and bruises, some of which resulted from his fight with Lehana Hazel and others with the thief. In places, he was bleeding. From older Guardsman days, he was scarred. Most of his current injuries, however, were signs of Ash neglecting his hygiene or symptoms of the curse.

The good news, however, was he did not have lice. Nor did his friends.

Time was fleeting. What a brutal, carefully crafted curse it had been. With no cure for its poison, the Dragonborn Guardsmen gifted Ash the slow and excruciatingly painful death that, in their opinion, he deserved. Ash had always denied the allegations that he was a Tetrad. He'd had no intention of extinguishing the flame; it was far beyond his abilities as a mere Salamander and he wasn't cunning enough to be a spy for the Order. He hated their arrogance. Before his illness, Ash had rather enjoyed using Salamander Alchemy and thought it beneficial to the Land. Why would he spoil his existence and the benefits it offered?

After suffering their wrath, though, Ash now *craved* revenge on the Guardsmen. Perhaps not violently or to his ego's satisfaction, but enough to free his soul. If snuffing out the flame and therefore Man's magic could save his life *and* remove the Order from power, Ash would guiltlessly extinguish it given the opportunity. If *only* his magic would allow that!

Dragon or no Dragon, seeing the Guard fall would bring a smile to his wrinkling face. If he *was* a Tetrad, he could simultaneously help Kite and Reverie on their quest, *and* make the Guardsmen regret ever crossing him. But he wasn't —he was a useless, dying soul.

Ash considered the Seer's prophecy as he impatiently examined a few nasty cuts and swellings. What actually was Ash's purpose if not just to act as an experienced escort, and an unreliable one? Was he really as powerless to change his fate as he suddenly felt, despite the Oracle stating he was at the core of Alchemy's continuance?

Ash flinched when someone rapped on the door. He dressed quickly and opened it to face Sarronious's wide chest, and what Ash hoped was a genuine smile.

"Thought you might be hungry. Now we're on our way, some of us are gathered on deck."

He handed Ash a plate of mixed fruits, cheeses and half a bread loaf to compliment Deerbolt's finest wine. He stood aside and gestured for Ash to join the festivities.

Without moving, Ash swayed and stammered, "Wamt are youu c-celebrating?"

The Cerulean Grace would soon be at the First Watchtower where Ash might spend his final days. Most men would be eager to celebrate a life well lived.

Not Ash the Elemental, and not tonight.

"We're alive," said the tradesman. "That should be enough."

"I'd r-rather be anlone," Ash uttered, taking the plate with a nod of thanks and staggering to set it down on the table. He hesitated, then added, "Howm are Kite and Remeveri doing?"

Sarronious smirked. "Are you drunk?"

Ash shrugged and slumped on the bed's edge. "Sororry for myself, if amything," he slurred.

"They are anxious for tomorrow. There is excitement for the birth of their baby, and they have been discussing names."

"Did they tellm you of t-the Oracle's vinsions," Ash asked and hiccuped, "that an Elemental could cweate a future w-without Astrals of the Order dominninating the Land, using their b-baby for the Dragon elg?"

"That idea is implausible."

"Only b-because of mue."

He curled his lips inward and turned away, examining his empty tankard. Angered by his physical and mental weakness, and his inability to action such a prosperous future, he lit a tiny orange flame in the palm of his hand and stared at it, amazed he'd conjured *any* form of fire incantation so far into the curse's wrath.

Would anyone really miss him if he just...

After glancing over his shoulder at the curious tradesman, Ash immediately thought better and extinguished it.

CHAPTER FOUR
THE TRADEWAY APPROACH

Chapter Four: The Tradeway Approach

The Cerulean Grace bounced across the water, kicking up spray as waves smacked its bow. It ventured into the Tradeway's cobalt waters where hundreds of merchant ships travelled the channel every month, many intent on pillaging and plundering from coastal villages or from other well-stocked ships. Both Ash and Captain Deerbolt were familiar with these waters and their dangers, and as he dozed in her cabin—his head resting on the borrowed pillow as his friends celebrated on the poop deck—he recalled the last time he'd heard the creek of the Grace's keel and felt the corresponding queasiness.

Almost to the day ten years prior, Ash had escaped the Isle of Dragonborn with his life. He'd been running through a shower of fiery and poisoned arrows from a hoard of armed Guardsman—men he once called brothers. He was exhausted when he stumbled across Deerbolt's ship and close to passing out in the midday sun. Back then, the Captain supplied the island with rum and other luxuries, but because of the increasing tension between the Order and the Guardsmen over land, power, and the use of Alchemy, Deerbolt was sailing back to Land's Edge for the final time.

That's when she met Ash. He'd been sick then, too.

His first honest conversation with Deerbolt had been in the cabin where he now fought to retain his stomach's contents between each lurch and sway. He thought then by the time the now Cerulean Grace reached land, Deerbolt would unload a corpse. She'd been kind enough to give him a hearty meal and a tankard of ale to drown his sorrows. And drown he did.

When Ash woke, the island was no longer in view and the ship was under siege.

Another, larger vessel—seemingly from Dragonborn and intent on exterminating everyone on board—was close to their stern, firing a cannon. Ash heard an occasional BOOM! followed by an enormous SPLASH!

Another miss, he thought, *thank the Gods.*

He shot out of bed and dressed in a hurry. Deerbolt's voice could be heard through the walls as she barked orders at her terrified crew. Ash bounded out of the door to help because it was the least he could do. He was armed and going to die soon, anyway. How could he not help when their perusers were likely chasing him? Despite the curse giving Ash a life expectancy of a few weeks, there were some during Ash's banishment from Dragonborn who wanted his head—immediate blood to assure the future of the flame. They didn't believe allowing him to live and leave the island to succumb to a slower, more painful death would protect it from future sabotage.

Back in the present with his blood boiling, Ash sat up in bed.

They were right about me, he thought. *Here I am, just as they predicted, returning with thoughts of committing that very crime. But it's their doing. By protecting the flame, they have actually endangered it.*

Ash closed his eyes and slammed his face down, pressing it against Deerbolt's pillow. He remembered how she'd granted him passage all those years ago, though they knew nothing about one another. He suspected she saw the desperation in his eyes, felt the pounding of adrenaline in his blood, heard each struggling breath. At first, he doubted she'd agree to carry a liability, not that he'd have blamed her. Besides the obvious bounty on his head, Ash *looked* like a criminal because the facilities on the island were few.

Of his brothers, Ash was the most defiant and ill-tempered. As an Elemental, he was more closely supervised and kept in line. He fell victim to the worst posts and duties as punishment for his practical jokes and attitude, which involved longer shifts and less time for leisure, personal upkeep, and hygiene. In short, Ash knew he smelled and looked unruly.

Overlooking his past, Deerbolt rescued him with no questions asked. Not so much saving him from death, because even now as he wriggled uncomfortably in her bed he was still a dying man, but from being stranded in a place where he had only enemies, and where he might never have known a woman's touch.

It took several days, a haircut, and a few hot baths for Deerbolt to appreciate Ash's true nature and handsome features; to see a man capable of being convivial despite his years of abstinence and poverty. They dined together, danced together, drank together. Ultimately, it was his mindset following their first and his only intimate night in the bed where he lay now that clouded his judgement.

He evoked memories of her bravery.

Once on deck, Ash more easily summoned fistfuls of Salamander magic when he saw Deerbolt's frightened face. He stole fuel from the dawn's torches and directed his rage at their enemies. She and her men were about to lose everything, including their lives, all because they saved his. Ash launched an inferno of blistering heat at the enemy ship, widening his incantations to rain hot ash and molten debris on the opposing crew, torching everything with a pulse. He lost himself to his hatred and resentment. When the ships were parallel, he swung across from the Grace's mast to theirs on a thick rope to finish what Dragonborn's Guardsmen had started.

Whatever he did, no matter who he killed, he *had* to protect Deerbolt. Even if that meant he died trying, leaving her to defend the Cerulean Grace without him. But the curse took its toll sooner than he'd expected. He'd slayed at least twenty men when he grew weary, and during a struggle with the opposing Captain, Ash was thrown overboard between the ships, crashing head first into the Tradeway.

At first, he thought he was drowning. It felt that way; his lungs were burning, starved of oxygen. Beneath the water, his vision was a blur of bubbles and thrashing, and he couldn't tell in which direction he should swim to find the surface. Sinking, he finally submitted to a shameful, pointless death, allowing the water to gush down his throat.

Don't fight it, he told himself, *it'll prolong the inevitable. It's better this way.*

Suddenly, the surrounding water froze, trapping Ash in a smooth, hardened sphere in which he could walk and breathe again. Coughing and spluttering, he found he could safely witness the battle through the thickness of a crystallised wall. Men flailed until the water consumed them and ink-red trails followed each limp body as they sank beneath his sanctuary. Thin arrows pierced the water around them, leaving foamy trails. Some penetrated corpses but none pierced the ice. Cannonballs plunged in after them, leaving spray and white trails in their wake. Bits of wood and cargo floated amongst the fish; Ash wanted to reach out and touch a shoal to confirm he was still alive.

Is this real?

The rest happened automatically as if through a deeply rooted primal instinct he didn't know he had within.

He smashed the ice by pounding the wall with his fists and kicking his feet. He rode a broad, inverted whirlpool to the surface. And all the while, Ash used his palms to create a variety of accidental, previously unused incantations, forming a path to freedom. He carried with him the weight of the ocean and drowned the opposition in seawater from a wave high above their mainsail, praying the Tradeway would wash away their evil and with it, his curse.

His judgement clouded, Ash didn't care if he lived or died, only that they spared Deerbolt's life and livelihood. His manic onslaught was short-lived and his strength could take no more. All at once the water fell, cascading gently over Deerbolt and her men and washing Ash, now unconscious, back across the then-named Equos's deck.

When he woke, they were at Land's Edge. Deerbolt wanted to know how he'd summoned this second Undine element so easily. Wasn't he a Salamander? Were Dragonborn's accusations of his Tetrad inheritance true?

Ash denied everything. He feigned memory loss and blamed the curse, then as soon as Deerbolt left her cabin, he fled with his secret at the earliest opportunity, leaving her to defend the Equos alone. Soon after, she re-named the ship the Cerulean Grace to avoid detection.

With the memory of the betrayal fresh in his mind, Ash dragged himself out of bed, embarrassed and flushed by his longing for the Captain's company all these years later. Fresh air and a change of scenery would do his headache and seasickness some good, he decided, so he stumbled up the stairs to the poop deck where Reverie and Kite were being entertained by Deerbolt's playful crew. Surrounded by plenty to eat and drink, the couple laughed and joked, forgetting the perilous journey ahead and the growing number of enemies they'd collected so far. Though he'd needed solitude, Ash's stomach gurgled and his taste buds tingled at the thought of an ice-cold tankard of ale. He reached the top step and basked in the refreshing salty sea air. It ruffled his hair.

Well-rested and as relaxed as he was ever going to be, Ash was convinced he could uphold his confident demeanour in Deerbolt's clique of boisterous adventurers. But he hadn't prepared his libido to face her beauty again. Despite Deerbolt's petite yet athletic figure and her stern resting expression, Ash was drawn to the Captain's gold-flecked hazel eyes and the way her long, silken plait swayed in the breeze, reflecting the spooky silvery glow of the moon.

Their gaze met. Ash made his way towards her.

The crew sat in haphazard circles, drinking and singing with glee. He was careful not to trip over anyone's boots as he shuffled around the mizzenmast to perch beside Deerbolt. Ash opened his mouth to speak but paused to watch her unravel her plait between delicate fingers.

"You're welcome," she said, fumbling.

Ash entwined his own fingers behind his back and swayed gently on his toes and heels. Still flushed, he turned his gaze and lifted his chin as if to sniff the mouth-watering scent of meat cooking nearby.

"For what?"

"For your free passage."

"I haven't thanked you yet," Ash said.

Of course, he was grateful; she'd risked everything to save his life... again, all on the unreliable prophecy of an old Oracle. But until he'd gathered the courage to talk business with the beautiful Captain, he couldn't get emotional over past debts.

The corner of her thin lips upturned, highlighting the cute little dimples Ash always adored. They brightened her face, lightening his first impressions of her.

"Soon you will," she replied. "How are you?"

"Better. Thanks."

Deerbolt winked. "Sooner rather than later, then."

"*That* was just good manners," he replied.

Ash jumped at the unspoken invitation to sit beside her. Close enough to smell her perfume and the lavender oil in her hair, and memorised by how well she owned her group through posture alone, he didn't see her reciprocate the inhalation. But Deerbolt was blushing at the musky scent of his borrowed cologne and she, too, turned her head to avoid being caught. Ash the Elemental was not really her type. She often faked her fearless masculinity to growl orders and earning the respect of a strapping male crew, but Deerbolt wasn't easily attracted to muscles, scars and missing teeth, even if such an appearance *did* suggest strength and authority to most. She didn't want nor need a reckless, over-protective husband to dominate her life on the Tradeway. Deerbolt could control the Grace and its sailors on her own. She much preferred intellectual men with whom she could share a civilised conversation beneath the stars; someone to discuss politics, Alchemy, and literature with, and someone with whom she could make love, who had a soft touch, and that she could trust with her heart. Or, if necessary, her life.

While Ash's physique was a step above most of the men she'd courted since her last trip to Dragonborn, she was willing to overlook what it suggested about him because of his passion for the divinity of magic and personal integrity. When he'd demonstrated gratitude for his safe passage on the Grace originally, he'd shown what she meant to him and the depths of his intelligence. He saved her life, thinking at the time he was attacking his own brothers. She respected his ethics.

Deerbolt hadn't agreed with Ash's banishment, anyway. She knew half the story—*his* half. She never believed Dragonborn's accusations of deceit and violence. When Ash did speak of the island, it was discreetly and with poise. Back then, his job gave Ash immense pride. Not until she'd witnessed his second Elemental skill—the power of an Undine—had Deerbolt questioned his intentions as a Tetrad.

Does he really know nothing of his second ability, or is he hiding something?

Tonight, Ash's dark brown eyes were muddy and ill-defined in the poor light. Deerbolt still felt him carefully examining her, though. She wondered if she explored his soul in return, would she find it tarnished or pristine, heavily burdened or carefree? And in his heart, would he mirror her lust and longing for their past relationship—for their love?

"Kite and Reverie are a great couple," she said to break the awkward silence. "They'll be good parents."

Ash blinked repeatedly, waking from his trance. "Aye, if a little damaged. Too innocent for all this."

"Aye," she said. "Aren't we all?"

"Some more than others."

"And it's your responsibility to protect them, to protect us."

His brow raised. "Are you asking me or telling me?"

"Both." Deerbolt smiled and swilled the final sips of ale around her tankard anticlockwise. "Though I can take care of myself."

"Of that, I have no doubt."

"It's nice having you around again, Scoundrel, though you never did give me a chance to thank you for saving my crew, or to tell you it was actually pirates you saved us from, not Guardsmen."

Ash sighed with relief. She gestured at the men in her circle.

"Many are still with me because of you. Loyal and hard-working. That little *accident* of yours brought us together. Though, we both know what happened *wasn't* accidental."

After a moment of thought, Ash shook his head and smirked, settling his gaze on his boots.

"This is an interesting development, anyway."

"What is?"

"*You* thanking *me*."

Deerbolt elbowed him playfully in the ribs. "On *their* behalf. What you did for the Grace was astonishing, and I still cannot believe it."

"I didn't disappear because of you," he said, taking her by surprise.

She paused, then said, "I know."

"And I regret leaving without saying goodbye. I was afraid if they caught us together—caught you harbouring a fugitive—the Order would issue the death penalty. It was safer for the both of us if we parted ways. I didn't tell you more because —"

"You wanted me to have plausible deniability. It was a long time ago, Ash. I'm over it." Deerbolt met his gaze. "I still appreciate the risk you took. I think about it all the time."

"We got lucky." Ash wrung his hands together, then held them out to warm them on the firepit. "I couldn't do it again if I wanted to."

"You're sure?"

Ash cleared his throat. "Never happened before that. Hasn't happened since. I attributed it to my body's early reaction to the curse. I've outlived it, somehow—who knows *what* I can still do because I didn't mean to kill Lehana Hazel, but I did. I wanted to keep her away from Kite and Reverie." Ash added, "Deerbolt, you can't tell anyone what you saw me do ten years ago."

"You can trust me," she whispered.

"And your men?"

"Your secret is safe here. But, I have to ask you something."

"You want to know how I'm still breathing ten years past my expiration date?" He shrugged. "If you figure it out before I die, let me know."

"Whatever the reason, I'm pleased. We owe you our lives."

Ash blinked slowly and smiled. "You gave me sanctuary. Twice. I'm owed nothing. What you and Sarronious are doing for Kite and Reverie is very brave." Ash swallowed hard. "What I'm trying to say is *thank you* for taking such a risk... again."

Deerbolt beamed and nodded at Sarronious from across the deck as he appeared on the top step to attract her attention. She handed Ash her tankard, refilled it for him, then set off walking towards the tradesman.

"Duty calls?" he said.

Deerbolt smirked as she peered back at him. "Aye, and now I have that *thank you* I was waiting for, there's no reason for me to stay and chat, is there?”

Ash watched her disappear through the firepit's smoke, and into the night.

CHAPTER FIVE

SLAVE TO THE UNDINE

Chapter Five: Slave to the Undine

It was Sarronious's narrow eyes and straight lips that caused Deerbolt to leave Ash's side and follow the tradesman to the Cerulean Grace's wooden figurehead. Their mascot was a painted blue depiction of the female Goddess of the Senses, with her long golden hair, rotund bosom and dark, watchful eyes. Deerbolt and Sarronious often shared confidential words here where the Captain felt safe beside the Goddess's guiding gaze upon the Tradeway. Here they could tell their secrets and know they'd be kept.

She knew that perturbed expression. Something important was on her friend's mind. The pair said nothing to one another until they were alone beneath the foresail at the opposite end of the ship, where Sarronious grabbed Deerbolt by the shoulders and turned her away from Ash's watchful eye.

“Don't look back,” he said, “because you're in danger, Captain.”

Startled, Deerbolt allowed his strength to ground and comfort her. Against his white shirt and the flickering glow of a nearby lantern, Sarronious's skin turned bronze and shimmered, illuminating the intricate tattoos decorating his chest and arms. She was safe with him even though the restraint was forceful; he posed no threat. Her parents were long dead, leaving her without siblings or any other living relatives. Sarronious became her only family; he cared deeply for her welfare and happiness as a surrogate brother.

"Ash the Elemental," he continued, glancing across the ship. Her crew were busy elsewhere. He exhaled with relief. "He's going to extinguish the Dragonborn flame, isn't he?"

Deerbolt's brow furrowed. "He's not interested in the flame, Sarronious."

"I think he's dangerous and unpredictable—he *could*, he's capable. He's reckless with his life."

"He's a drunken, angry fool, but he'd never do anything to put me in danger."

"He refused my invitation to join us on deck and said he'd rather be alone."

Deerbolt unclasped herself and tidied her shirt. "Ash is a sworn Guardsman; they accused him before and they were wrong. He's not strong enough anymore, Sarronious, and he's not a Tetrad."

"He had a tone," Sarronious said.

"A *tone*?"

"Aye, Captain."

Deerbolt rolled her eyes. "He's always had a bad attitude. Should I make him walk the plank?"

"Captain, we have cause to suspect him of plotting to commit treason and if he does, he'll drag us all to the gallows with him. Reverie's baby, according to the song, is a way to bring down the Order. If Ash *is* a Tetrad, he will rid the Land of magic through revenge on the Guard and with it, his curse. He can live."

Deerbolt cut him off and dragged him aside. "He's too weak. We have nothing to fear."

Sarronious sighed and folded his arms. "Your love is blinding you. Ten years is a long time, Captain. Ash the Elemental is not the man he once was if you indeed truly knew him then. Did he ever reveal the exact accusations against him?"

Deerbolt raised her hand to halt his objections. She leaned against a wooden rail and peered over the edge, staring into the oil-coloured Tradeway as she considered her friend's observations.

"You didn't know him, Sarronious. He was a good man. You and I have been together for eight years."

"Nine, Captain," he corrected. "I joined you the year after your final trip to Dragonborn; the year your parents died."

"Aye, nine. Long enough to have trust between us. People change, and how dangerous is he, really*?* Ash is a Salamander Elemental but any threats he makes right now are futile. As we speak, his magic withers. Though he has outlived his life expectancy, it's clear his strength is fading. Ash is incapable of executing the most basic of fire incantations correctly." Deerbolt sighed and shook her head. "Other than his *tone*, whatever you think he's plotting, Sarronious, I'm sure there's another explanation."

"Perhaps you're right," he said, relaxing his stance, "but you *will* be careful?"

Deerbolt slapped his shoulder and winked. "Aren't I always? If it'll make you feel better, I'll speak to him; he can keep some facts from me, but I'll see right through any facade."

"Thank you, Captain."

"It's too late now. We'll worry about it in the morning when the drink has worn off."

"And you won't mind if *I* keep a close eye on him?"

Deerbolt nodded. "Ash is a mystery, but I believe in him. I have to."

"Aye, Captain," he said, then wished her goodnight and retired to his hammock.

Deerbolt woke early with a pounding head and heavy limbs. The evening's conversation was still fresh in her mind, niggling at her composure and her trust in Ash the Elemental, even after his expression of thanks and obligation to their journey.

She walked the length of the Grace, sipping her weakly brewed tea. Occasionally, she covered it with her palm when the slap of the bow against the unsettled ocean threw back a cooling spray. She didn't mind the shower. It kept her alert to ponder the implications of confronting Ash; accusing him of plotting to commit treason after she promised to keep his secrets was surely in poor taste.

The Grace was now far enough out in the Tradeway's wide channel to see the First Watchtower's spire through a spyglass, dominating the hillside at the edge of Open Country several miles on their left. From this distance, it looked like the spike of a Dragon's tail. In reality, from land, it was an impenetrable fortress, engrossing the coastline to protect it from overseas threats. Its strategic location also allowed a clear line of sight to the Northern Trading Post and parts of the nearby abandoned, nameless island in the east.

Firstly, the Cerulean Grace would stop temporarily at the Watchtower, perhaps overnight, for the crew and their guests to disembark, unload supplies for the fortress, trade with locals or travellers and, of course, restock on consumables.

Most thought it to be abandoned, but Deerbolt knew otherwise. She was anxious for the day to go smoothly and without incident. Though the fortress could protect Kite and Reverie indefinitely from the Order, her ship was going to be vulnerable in the small harbour there. Without it, she and her crew would be homeless and lost to the Land, not to mention unable to assist their friends any further.

"Something on your mind?"

Deerbolt startled, spilling her tea down her shirt. It sloshed onto the recently mopped deck, forming a dark brown stain. Ash chortled and set the cup on the side of the ship for her as she dabbed her chest and stomach, dampening the corset beneath.

"As a matter of fact," she grumbled.

The ship lurched forward, tipping the teacup over the edge and knocking Ash off balance. Deerbolt sighed at his pathetic sea legs and shoved him aside, heading for her cabin to find a clean shirt and pour another drink.

Struggling to stand, Ash stumbled after her.

"Want to talk?"

"About how you lost my favourite cup?"

Deerbolt rocketed down the stairs from the quarterdeck to her cabin and threw open the door, leaving Ash stranded at the top, calling her name. When she emerged a few minutes later in clean clothing, she grabbed Ash by the forearm and guided him, forcefully, to the ship's stern.

"I don't want to talk about this, Ash, but I fear it can no longer be avoided."

Ash scowled and braced himself against a flagpole displaying the Grace's trading flag. The brightly coloured yellow material, embroidered with three diagonal parallel lines in black, symbolised the cargo's status. When travelling the Tradeway, Deerbolt only ever flew the 'cargo removed' identifier to avoid being a target for Open Country pirates looking to steal food and jewels. Whether the flag was true or false, she deemed it irrelevant. A 'carrying cargo' status, in her opinion, was more trouble than it was worth and acted as an invitation to criminals with faster ships.

"I think there's a storm brewing. We should talk inside," Ash suggested.

He cringed as angry waves thrashed and crashed against the Cerulean Grace's rickety body. Deerbolt's crew seemed relaxed, however, and while the skies were dull, it wasn't yet raining.

Deerbolt shook her head and hummed. "A storm indeed."

Ash straightened his back so as not to lose face, but remained close to the flagpole. Deerbolt clutched her second cup of tea as though the heat and scent were the only thing grounding her temper.

"What's going on, Deerbolt?"

She sighed. "Why are you *really* here?"

"I told you, other than to guide the couple, I don't know. My curse has been unpredictable."

"That's not what I meant." Deerbolt sipped her beverage and closed her eyes. "Why are you aboard my ship? When you reach Dragonborn, what are your intentions?"

"I told you that, too, last night. I'm keeping Kite and Reverie safe." He knotted his fingers.

"So they can get the help *they* need, or to fulfil *your* prophecy?"

Ash groaned and shrugged. "I think they are the same. The Cartomancer—I mean, the Oracle—said I had to help them get to Dragonborn because the fate of magic depended on it." Then, realising her suggestion, he rolled his eyes. "I'm *not* a Tetrad, Deerbolt! What happened to me all those years ago was a freak accident, and what they accused me of wasn't true, either. How can I prove it?"

He lowered his head and swallowed hard, fighting both seasickness and butterflies as the ship bounced over a towering swell. It dipped hard at a sharp angle and without warning, throwing Ash against the side with enough force to trigger his stomach. When he'd finished throwing up, he blinked to get his bearings and slid down the pole to rest.

"Does this have something to do with your conversation with Sarronious?" he asked, wiping his mouth on his sleeve. "I saw you talking. He seemed upset."

"Aye." She offered him a helping hand, which he declined. "After all this time, you still can't handle a few choppy waves?"

"Some things never change," he said. He peered up, inhaling deeply through each dip and sway. "Is he worried about me, or about *us*?"

"I'm sorry?"

"I see the way he looks at you," Ash said, grinning.

Deerbolt blinked and turned away. "Sarronious and I have never—"

"Perhaps he wishes to adjust the boundaries of your relationship. He's your First Mate, though you tell others he is a marketplace tradesman hitching a ride home."

"His role is unofficial. He just needed a job, but had no experience. I did him a favour, and we became friends. That was nine years ago."

Deerbolt gave his legs a firm kick with the side of her boot. Ash scowled and tucked his knees in as she paced back and forth.

"Stop changing the subject. I just want to know... are you going to betray us?"

Ash shivered beneath the sails as they dripped sea water down the back of his collar, dampening his doublet and trousers. He figured the stress was causing the curse to ignite the remaining adrenaline in his system, simultaneously blurring his vision and kick-starting a painful jitter in his fingers, so he took a few deep breaths. Suddenly, he no longer felt sick, but faint and confused, and his legs throbbed where the Captain's boot had been. Needles prickled his limbs, too, weakening his grasp on the flagpole and intensifying the sensation in his fingers to violent quaking.

"I will not betray you." He gasped.

Deerbolt crouched and wrapped Ash's arm around her neck, hauling him up in one swift motion. They shuffled together, zig-zagging with the sway of the ship to the top of the stairs where she called for two of her deckhands to abandon their duties and aid Ash to a bench on the quarterdeck. Deerbolt thrust Ash's head down between his legs and told him to breathe in through his nose and out through his mouth. If he was having a panic attack, from guilt or the curse, someone needed to stay with him. If he did something stupid or took a nasty turn, Deerbolt would blame herself. She instructed the men to box him in and keep him still, then waved Sarronious over from his stock-taking duties.

He hurried across the wet deck and skidded to a halt at Ash's feet. “Is it the curse?”

Deerbolt smiled indifferently. “Now is not the time, Sarronious.”

“You questioned him, then?”

Hearing this, Ash's head snapped up. His eyes were unfocused, causing him to crash sideways into one deckhand who, infuriated by the inconvenience, shoved him back. Deerbolt kneeled at Ash's side, relieving the deckhand, and gripped Ash's shoulders to steady him.

“No threat,” Ash repeated, scowling. “Not now. Not ever.”

“Can you explain the fireball?” Sarronious asked. “I saw you light another one. Why, when you're so weak?”

“Practising,” he mumbled, rubbing his eyes with his knuckles. Deerbolt was unsure if he'd wiped away tears or sea water. “No use... without power. Cannot... protect... you.”

“That's what you think, that you're no use to us without your powers?” Deerbolt repeated.

Ash nodded. She sat him upright, resting his back against the mainsail's post. She gestured he take some deep breaths with the motion of her hands.

“Lighting unnecessary fireballs won't help your condition. Save your energy for Dragonborn.”

Sarronious shook his head. “He's still hiding something.”

Sheepish, Ash brushed through his hair with shaky fingers, using the ocean's spray to slick it back. Opening up his face, it allowed Deerbolt to examine his waxy complexion and the dark circles outlining his usually bright eyes. He wasn't sleeping well and most of what he'd consumed recently had been rejected by his body, too. At this rate, Ash wasn't even going to make it to the First Watchtower.

Sarronious placed a comforting hand on the Elemental's shoulder, taking him by surprise. He stiffened, fearful for what might come next.

The tradesman said, “I know you're suffering in many ways. We can help you with them all *if* you tell the truth.”

Ash nodded, so Sarronious gave him a consoling pat.

He cleared his throat. “Aye—”

The ship was thrown sideways, cutting Ash short and tipping him off his seat. He smacked into both Deerbolt and Sarronious and they rolled in unison across the deck, clattering against crew members and loosened items. Deerbolt scrambled to her feet and sprinted up onto the poop deck to survey the damage.

Did we hit something?

Sarronious hauled Ash up by his collar, throwing him forward.

“I want a damage report!”

Ash fumbled along the edge as it lurched back the other way. The mess slid in the opposite direction, wiping out more of Deerbolt's crew—some of it scattering overboard, lost to the waves. Less than a mile behind them towards Blackheart Dock was another merchant-looking ship. It was twice the Grace's size and build and ignoring Deerbolt's trade flag.

It fired its cannons. Once. Twice. They missed, but gained speed. With each near hit, the splashes and waves that followed dramatically rocked the Cerulean Grace, almost flooding and capsizing her. Ash struggled to the poop deck as fast as his legs and stomach would allow.

“Deerbolt, we're under attack!”

Her eyes widened. She snapped her head, flicking her soaked hair across her face.

"We can't outrun them. Take Reverie and Kite to my cabin and keep them safe."

"It's the Order, they found us! They must have figured out who killed Lehana Hazel," Sarronious cried as he studied the ship through a spyglass.

"You're in no condition to fight, Ash." She pointed to the crew's quarters where Kite and Reverie were currently hiding. "Go, we have little time!"

Ash staggered, dodging falling items and crashing waves. The couple were sitting on the floor with their backs to an over-packed chest, anchoring their bodies to its weight. He stumbled and fell beside them, scrambling for an upright position.

"What's happening?"

"We're under attack," he told Reverie. "They've figured it out; they know the Grace is harbouring murderers."

Kite asked, grasping and squeezing his wife's hand, "How could they know?" Before Ash could answer, he added, "If the Grace sinks, so does our baby. Do something; I *know* you can!"

"I'm just a Salamander, damn it!" Ash roared.

CHAPTER SIX
LORD OF THE SEAS

Chapter Six: Lord of the Seas

Ash clawed at his face. Indecision ripped through him. Sharp flashbacks flickered across his field of vision, where he saw Deerbolt's terror and her crew dying one-by-one as they fought past foes who vastly outnumbered the Grace; a meaner, faster and more brutal enemy than Deerbolt, despite her courage and tenacity, could defeat. Ash had once killed their attackers accidentally—he'd been thrown overboard and surrendered to the ocean, offering the Tradeway his life for Deerbolt's safe passage. Against the odds he rose, reborn as a temporary water Elemental—an Undine—and lived to keep that secret for the next ten years. Since that day, Ash had not summoned Undine magic once, fearful it would replace what little Salamander skills he still owned and relied heavily upon.

"Man the cannons!" Deerbolt screeched. "Secure the cargo!"

"Captain, if she catches us—"

"Astrals rely on proximity, Sarronious," she replied. "Let's focus on staying ahead of them."

Through the sound of howling wind, crashing waves and distant thunder, Ash could hear Deerbolt bravely barking orders, preparing her crew for the war they were going to lose. Her long hair whipped and slapped her skin and her piercing eyes glimmered in her reflection in every flying droplet. From the pit of his stomach, Ash summoned gallantry and scrambled to his feet, leaving Kite and Reverie clinging to the only chest still secured.

"Come back! Where are you going?" Reverie cried.

Ash set off in a diagonal sprint, using the chaos as an obstacle course whenever he was thrown aside with the Grace's sway.

Sarronious ran after him, unable to keep to a straight line. He dodged Deerbolt's crew and sliding barrels.

"Ash, wait! What are you *doing*?"

Deerbolt scanned the deck for the unhinged Elemental, catching her most loyal friend's warnings when the wind changed direction. Her eyes found Ash charging at the ship's mascot, where he ripped off his doublet, then set to work on the buttons down his floaty white shirt.

"ASH, NO!"

Under his breath, he recited the Oracle's lyrics and closed his eyes. He blocked all other thoughts and focused only on moving forward, on stripping anything restrictive from his person, including his gloves, and kicking off his boots. The song became his mantra. His Salamander brand burned deeper into his skin.

Deerbolt pushed through her crew and vaulted over a cannon mid-fire. She emerged like a phoenix through the smoke and the Tradeway's spray, wincing in the heat of the explosion as the iron ball left the chamber and sailed towards the enemy ship.

They were gaining on the Grace too easily. She landed with an UMPH! flat on both feet and set off at full speed to catch him. His plan was simple.

He discarded everything at the base of the mast, threw away his longsword and sheathed dagger, and then launched into the air using a kneeling deckhand as an unsuspecting step. Where he was going, he wouldn't be needing possessions.

"NO, ASH! DON'T!" Deerbolt bellowed.

It was too late.

Ash outstretched his arms as he flew above the Tradeway's inky surface. He dived in head-first like a pencil. The water smacked his cheeks and forced its way up his nose, in his ears, and down his throat. Deerbolt threw her body against the ship's wooden rail, unable to slow her speed, and called his name until her voice was hoarse. Bubbles rose to the surface, but she couldn't see anything else.

Beneath, it was calming and peaceful. The battle raged on above as Ash centred his body and tread water, using his arms as fins to manoeuvre in the depths. Against his bare chest, the Tradeway felt cool and certain, allowing Ash to dig within his soul to stir his hidden Undine. His lungs burned—a familiar sensation he feared all those years ago and misunderstood as drowning. Now, he relished where it could take him, raising him above the basic Salamander existence into the leagues of the Tetrad.

With his last breath, Ash opened his eyes. Waves exploded outward from where he was floating, sending cyclones of freezing cobalt into the air and across the rolling waves, sucking more and more of the Tradeway's weight up and over the mast of the Cerulean Grace like a rainbow, pummelling the bandits on their tail. Ash kicked his feet and wound his wrists in smooth, careful movements as the Grace sailed past. A platform of water touched his bare feet, gently carrying him to freedom, casting him high enough to manipulate this new, exciting weapon from the safety of the bow.

The God of the Senses overlooked their enemy's impending doom.

From head to toe, Ash was sodden but glowing; the brewing storm ragged what remained of his clothing—some ripped and fell away—but his balance never faltered. Using what remained of his confidence, he clenched his fists, pulled his arms outward and above his head in a wide arch. As he dropped both arms to his side and allowed his chin to fall slack against his collarbones, a giant wave crushed the ship in its mouth, washing it out to sea and tumbling it in tight spirals.

From the relative safety of the ship, Deerbolt's expression glazed. Ash's response astonished her. Whatever pre-programmed Elemental magic that had previously laid dormant within him had detonated, and she was both thankful for and terrified of it.

"S-Sarronious," Deerbolt managed in a whimper, "bring m-me a rope. We need to pull A-Ash out of the water. Quickly!"

She didn't see him go or return with the rope, only that a lasso had been tied and handed to her, which she pitched over the side. It hooked over Ash's arm and slid it over his head and waist before he fainted and careened from the Alchemic platform into the water below. The rest of his incantations failed too, like the Tradeway's seascape had been expertly wiped clean of any evidence.

If there were Undines on board that ship, their magic hadn't measured up to Ash's anarchy. He'd demolished any living beings, Alchemical and Human.

Using the ship as a brace, Deerbolt and Sarronious hauled Ash out of the water and onto the deck. The Captain pressed her ear worriedly against his chest and listened for a pulse.

"He's not breathing! Sarronious, call the Slyph deckhand. Ash needs air."

"He never boarded, Captain."

Deerbolt slammed her fist onto the deck. "I'll do it myself!"

She parted his lips to breathe life-saving air into his waterlogged lungs. Then she pressed firmly upon his ribcage to restart his heart. Ash convulsed, coughed, and spat up a fountain of water.

Deerbolt squealed with delight and wrapped her arms around him.

"You scared me half to death, you scoundrel!"

Ash gasped. "I'm... sorry," he managed. "Did... it... work?"

"Aye, the ship was destroyed. Don't you remember?"

Sarronious slapped him hard on the back, forcing the remaining water out through Ash's nose and mouth. Deerbolt grabbed an arm and dragged him to rest against a discarded and damaged wooden crate so he could regain some sense of where he was.

Frantically, Ash shook his head. "Kite... Reverie...?"

Sarronious lifted his chin. "Aye, they're fine, they're safe."

"You did it, Ash!" Deerbolt said, cupping his face in delight. "You saved us all... again!"

A searing pain on Ash's hand caused him to flinch and hiss, craning his body back. Deerbolt moved aside; he flicked his wrist relentlessly to shake off the terrible stinging sensation, then cried out in agony as it worsened. Deerbolt and Sarronious pinned him down and called for one deckhand to examine his skin, pale and wrinkled by the water. It was possible this was a new symptom of his curse, or a sea critter had pinched or nibbled Ash as he swam in the Tradeway. Below deck, they carried antidotes and medical supplies for stings and poisons, but neither was applicable once Deerbolt saw Ash's updated Elemental marking. In the centre of his existing single circular brand was a second ring with a faint vertical line adjoining the two. His Alchemic identifier had morphed from that of a Salamander Elemental to a Salamander-Undine hybrid—a never-before-seen symbol. He now bore two rings (one for each of his skills, the first of which represented his fire incantations) plus the line of the standard Undine brand.

Ash passed out again and had to be carried by three of the larger male deckhands to Deerbolt's bed. Reverie offered to watch over him whilst Deerbolt and Sarronious co-ordinated the repairs and clean-up of the Cerulean Grace; she placed a tankard of water and some bread beside him on a low table, and covered him with the blanket he wore the day before.

Ash drifted soundly and dreamlessly into a deep slumber. Meanwhile, the ship continued up the Tradeway towards the

First Watchtower, passing the unnamed abandoned island on their right and many other, but thankfully distant, vessels.

When Ash awoke thirty-six hours later, starving and desperate for a soothing beverage, the First Watchtower loomed above the ship's mast, leering from land as if questioning their arrival and the business they had in the north. On their left, behind a wall of trees and shrubbery (acting as the tower's only defence inland), Open Country's barren, drought-riddled landscape loomed for miles. Between the dry nothingness and the Northern Trading Post, only bandits, outlaws, thieves and risk-taking travellers rode. Reverie and Kite knew the territory well from their travels in the west between their home in Broad Wells and Blackheart Dock. Reverie kept an eye on the treeline at all times; the young couple knew better than most to stay clear of the crime-infested desert. Days before their arrival at the marketplace, they'd lost jewels and their only horse to thieves. They were forced to walk the rest of the way with only the clothes on their back and their basic provisions in tow. Muggers had not considered her pregnancy when they held her at knife-point.

As Deerbolt and her crew docked and stampeded down the wooden ramp into the harbour, the sky finally cleared. Not a single ship nor cloud accompanied them. The Order were no longer following by sea. They were completely alone to rest and recuperate.

Deerbolt couldn't have been happier to see Ash appear on the poop deck. He stood at the top of the ramp, staring at its steep decline. He swallowed hard.

I'm going to end up in the water again.

Sarronious jogged to his aid. "You're not strong enough yet. Let me help you."

They linked arms and staggered side-by-side along the rickety wooden ramp to solid ground. Ash was careful to pick his feet up over the imperfections. He exhaled with relief and sighed aloud when his toes crinkled and caressed long blades of basil-green grass.

"Feels good," Sarronious said.

"Aye," Ash replied, though it hadn't been a question.

"*Where* are your boots?" Deerbolt asked in Ash's peripheral vision.

He turned slowly as not to lose his balance and shrugged. "At the bottom of the Tradeway, I imagine."

She offered him a tankard of water and a handful of juicy, purple grapes. "Thought you might be hungry."

Ash stole the tankard and glugged the icy liquid down in a few wide mouthfuls, then crammed every grape from the branch after it. He wiped the dribbles on the back of his hand and halted, scowling at the new, itchy brand he'd been sporting for almost three days.

He groaned. "That's not good."

"We should talk."

Ash rolled his eyes. "I wonder what about?"

Deerbolt led him barefoot across a bank to a large hexagonal-shaped rock. Other than the looming structure of the fortress, little else caught Ash's eye. She warned him to watch his step, avoiding the prickly weeds and stones poking through the dirt. Ash moaned when he lowered his weight to sit. His muscles ached. He felt twice, if not three times, his age and weight. His skin was tender to the touch, but he was no longer queasy or shivering.

From their spot on the hill, they had a 180-degree

panoramic view of the harbour and the First Watchtower's grounds, offering peace of mind and reassurance they could rest safely.

A midday sun beat down on Ash's head and shoulders and he stretched as far as he could without pain, basking in the warmth and serenity it offered. Living in Open Country had tanned him, and he hoped to maintain a healthy appearance for as long as possible.

"Your brand changes everything," Deerbolt stated firmly.

"It doesn't have to," he was quick to add. "Nobody else needs to know."

"My entire crew saw you summon a second Elemental ability, Ash. The secret is out."

"Your crew already know I'm... different. I'm talking about the watchmen." He gestured at the fortress and swallowed hard. "Would they have me killed?"

"They won't ask me for identification papers. They know me, and they're hiding secrets of their own. But, what if there were any Astral survivors?"

"There weren't." Ash was confident. "I was going to tell you everything before the storm, I swear. When we were on deck, and you—"

"It's enough that you saved us; you don't owe me any explanations." Deerbolt smiled and took his hand in hers. Her delicate fingers caressed his calloused, working ones, soothing him as she whispered. "Thank you."

"No," he began, "thank *you.* I suspected I could be more than a Salamander ten years ago on the crossing from Dragonborn when something unearthed in me. I thought you were in danger then; it took seeing that to conjure those forgotten skills this time. If not for you, we'd be at the bottom of the Tradeway right now."

"We didn't sink. We're here. You protected Reverie and Kite as you promised." She patted him. "We're alive."

"I protected *you.*" Ash sighed and changed the subject. "Where are the happy couple?"

"Kite is hunting in the trees with his bow. Reverie is watching him like a hawk. Not a scratch on either," she reassured. "Aren't you glad?"

Ash ran his tongue along his top teeth. "Sure. You'll be leaving me here, then?"

Deerbolt snorted and shook her head, then burst into laughter. Her grip tightened until Ash's eyes brightened and widened again.

"Whatever gave you that idea? You're coming with us—you're my insurance. Nobody can sink the Grace with *you* aboard."

Ash met her gaze. "Is that all I am to you?"

"We're with you, Ash," Deerbolt replied. "Whatever you decide to do with your newfound Elemental abilities, we're on your side. If your intentions were to harm us, you'd have done it by now. Even Sarronious thinks—"

"Abilities?"

"Sure!" She beamed. "Where there's a second one, there's got to be another two... right? You're a Tetrad!"

"I suppose I am."

Ash shuffled across the rock until their thighs touched and wrapped his arm around the Captain's waist. He brushed through her long, silken hair with the other, guiding her face inches from his own. Seeing her again had been enough for him to fall back in love with this strong-willed, beautiful Velocal.

Hearing her belief in him confirmed his love was true and most likely, reciprocated. The clouds parted, showering them in a haze.

They breathed in unison.

Sarronious's booming voice broke the silence.

Deerbolt jerked her head away, releasing Ash's grip as if pretending to examine his injuries.

"All is well?"

"Aye, and Raven has agreed to your request," he said.

Deerbolt straightened her clothing as she stood, leading

Sarronious away from the rock. She tucked loose locks of hair behind her ear, glanced once over her right shoulder and offered half a smile, then followed the tradesman downhill to the base of the fortress where the First Watchtower's guardians awaited.

Sarronious's narrowed his eyes as he followed her gaze, then touched the Captain's shoulder.

"Were you *two*...?" he trailed.

Deerbolt frowned and shook him off. "I'll take it from here, Sarronious. You are dismissed."

CHAPTER SEVEN

THE FIRST WATCHTOWER

Chapter Seven: The First Watchtower

Ash staggered downhill to the First Watchtower's base. A giant timber drawbridge stretched across a moat cut into the earth approximately thirty-feet deep. Along the bridge stood armoured watchmen. The sight of their Maximilian-style armour sent shivers down Ash's spine; memories of his Dragonborn Guardsmen days flooded his mind, and he was suddenly transported back in time to the last duty he held at the island's port before his brothers had banished him. The structure of the bridge, the two gate towers and the portcullis were uncanny; its sharp, unforgiving metal, the weight of the drawbridge lowering to bar their enemies' entry, and the short courtyard stroll between barbican-topped walls. As upon the Isle of Dragonborn, every wall sported hundreds of arrow loops, especially the outer shell of their village.

The First Watchtower was a pristine work of art. Watchmen on the wall walk patrolled its inner, harmonious acres. It encircled where Ash now laid eyes upon the barracks and the stables. He'd been in many a tavern since returning from Open

Country but men always reported the watchtowers had long since been abandoned; mere crumbling relics, haunted by the ghosts of their former occupants. They obviously spread rumours to stay off the Order's radar.

Ash stood with his feet together, careening at the colossal, square-based keep. He gasped, for he could not see the tatty flag on the spire—golden yellow with an embroidered numeral I on both sides—fluttering through the clouds that hid it, nor the top five or six storeys at least. He became dizzy if he stared too intensely or for too long, narrowing his eyes to count the floors and the watchmen's helms glinting in the light.

"It's something, isn't it?" Deerbolt said, taking him by surprise.

"You are everywhere and nowhere," Ash told her, unable to look away from the fortified structure he hoped he wouldn't have to climb. "How did your meeting go?"

"As well as I'd hoped."

He nodded. "Are those for me?"

Deerbolt offered a stack of clean linens and sparkling armour, then plonked a pair of boots at his feet. Everything looked new.

"Aye," she said, "though I'll keep a hold of them for now. You should change on the ship."

From behind her back, she pulled a halberd mounted to an iron bar instead of the expected eight-foot-long wooden pole. It was sharp and deadly—perfectly shaped and sized to wield in close combat.

"How about that?" Ash gulped. He was useless with anything other than his longsword and dagger. "An illegal weapon to go with an illegal Elemental."

"We should be prepared for anything. I'm loading the ship with whatever we are offered."

Sarronious had retrieved Ash's weapons after they were abandoned, sprawled on the deck of the Cerulean Grace. He placed them in Deerbolt's chambers for safekeeping, which she relayed to Ash. Here in this fortified dream, Ash prayed to the Gods he wouldn't need any of them. Though, looking around, he was sure to find *something* to defend his party at short notice, anyway. Like that halberd.

"That one is a gift for my new, official First Mate," she said, gesturing with her left shoulder where the mound of tradesman lingered. "He's earned the position."

"Is that why he is acting as your bodyguard? After everything I've done for you, your crew and your ship recently, I expect him to hate me less."

Deerbolt sniggered and lowered the halberd. "Sarronious doesn't hate anyone, and he agrees you're on our side now. Hard not to after witnessing those heroics."

"And you know this *how*?"

"I ordered him to." She shrugged. The two of them burst into laughter. "Come with me, I want you to meet someone. I think he can help you."

"I'm beyond help, Deerbolt."

"Most here thought the same about themselves at one point."

"That why they spread rumours this place is abandoned?"

"Aye," she said, "and so the Order's resistance have a safe place to plan a way to overthrow their power."

With a tug on his arm, Ash's legs followed before his head could question who the stranger was. Sarronious wasn't far behind, keeping a few hundred yards away but always within rescuing distance.

In the years they were apart, Ash expected Deerbolt to have laid with other men, fought countless battles, but also, potentially, produced an heir. Sarronious was awkward and feeling jealous, yet loyal and fearless nevertheless. He wondered if Deerbolt had ever considered offering herself to him, yielding to her desire for family; she wanted a son to raise according to the old customs, those her father and grandfathers before him, dating back to the Dragon era of Alchemy, practised. Remaining in her employment allowed

Sarronious to become the alternative she *could* turn to for comfort and release, perhaps, though it was obvious now that she never had.

Deerbolt pushed through two thick, brown wooden doors. Carved into their smooth surface was a history of the First Watchtower's many celebrated armies of the past and their triumphs.

"You'll find them in many of the shared spaces here," Deerbolt said. "They're very old."

At some point, there were sworn Guardsmen defending this tower. Fire-breathing, scaled Dragons decorated both doors, but if the watchmen were no longer sworn to the Isle of Dragonborn then who, Ash questioned, did they fight for now besides themselves?

The doors revealed an empty, echoey room save for wooden pillars, benches and scuffed tables. It was the castle's great hall where the men filled their stomachs and laughed through their strife. Few dined or lifted their heads as Deerbolt led him to the far side and through a velvety-red curtain. It opened into a smaller, mustier nook lined with bookshelves. Tapestries and charcoal artwork decorated the bare walls and a single partial stained-glass window overlooked the lawns between the kitchens and, further afield, the latrines.

"Ash the Elemental, I'd like you to meet Raven of the First Watchtower. Raven, this is the Alchemist I was telling you about."

She winked, leaving Ash and the cloaked, stout man alone to breathe the same stale air. Ash extended a hand in greeting and cleared his throat to further introduce himself. Raven went about his business, flicking through leather-bound books and loose-leaf pages which consumed a small desk and most of the floor space around it. Ash frowned. He was about to back up through the curtain again when the man parted his thumbs and smallest fingers on both hands, clumping the remainder of his fingers together, then flicked them swiftly in

Ash's direction before he could register the incantation. A gust of air lifted him by the armpits and carried him backwards to a rickety wooden rocking chair. Over every stone paving slab, Ash's boots dragged and bounced, sending shock waves up his legs and turning his stomach to jelly.

The wind lazily deposited him and gave the chair a nudge, kick-starting its smooth rocking motion.

"I am Raven the Slyph," said the man before Ash could ask, "born of the hamlet Raven out by Serpent's Sea and the Second Watchtower, at which I lived for thirty-seven years."

Ash raised a single eyebrow. "Your name is Raven, and you lived in Raven?"

The man turned then and lowered the hood of his cloak. He was shorter than Ash by a foot and balding, but greying by the ears and, Ash noted, in his once blue eyes. Ash's narrowed as he studied the man's drawn facial features and wondered if his quaking fingers affected his study at all.

"Aye, I struggle a little," Raven added, beating Ash to his own words above the creaking of the chair. "Captain Deerbolt and I keep no secrets. Upon her arrival, she told me immediately of the handsome scoundrel, Ash and his... *skills*."

Ash wrung his hands together. "She said I was handsome?"

Raven snapped his fingers and swished his right arm from the elbow; he pointed first to the bookcase, then to Ash's lap. A dusty thick encyclopaedia slid out of place. Without warning, it thrust itself against Ash's chest with a THUNK! and stole the wind from his lungs.

"Umph!" Ash coughed and wafted at the choking particles. "Maybe a warning next time you throw a leather-bound block of parchment at me?"

The cover was engraved with four Elemental symbols. At centre right there was an ornate-looking lock intended for an antique key. The lock was metal and heavy, rusting in the nooks. Ash ran his fingers across it, then turned the whole thing over to inspect it.

The book's pages were yellowing at the edges. Handwritten

in curly calligraphy along the spine was a faded title, detailing what appeared to be a Tetrad reference system, whereby each worn section of the book had been indexed for Salamanders, Undines, Slyphs and Gnomes.

"Is *this* what I think it is?"

"Aye," Raven replied. "The pages of this book sublimely detail the fluid bodily motions, hand gestures and facial expressions best-suited to summon and control each of the four elements with ease."

Ash pictured scholars studying the pages and replicating the incantations, though he imagined mostly Elementals mastering a single element. Tetrads were uncommon and feared this far north.

"Keep it. Look after it," Raven ordered, then dug deep in his pockets to retrieve the matching key. It hung on a faded black ribbon.

"Did Deerbolt ask you to give this to me? I'm not even sure I *am* a T—"

The man blinked hastily and hushed Ash. "Don't say that word here. Take care of this. It's... special."

The unceremonious Slyph turned to organise the rest of his books in the makeshift library, running his fingertips confidently across the various textures and smiling. This man did not need steady hands to appreciate the craftsmanship behind each leather-bound edition, and he said nothing further to Ash after the warning. The chair continued to rock and Ash scowled, utterly taken aback by the curt advice and random, unexpected gift. Cradling the book in one arm, resting it on his hip, he then stood to protest.

Raven the Slyph barely moved, but Ash suddenly flew through the curtain and down the centre of the great hall, squealing and gripping the giant book with both fists as it pulled him along.

Deerbolt stuck out her boot and tripped him as he approached the final bench, catching the book mid-air when he accidentally let go and launched it over her head. The

Elemental ploughed head-first through the open doorway, through two incoming watchmen on their way to eat, and onto the lawn outside.

When she emerged, laughing hysterically, Ash was sprawled on his back. His eyes were wide and terror-stricken.

"I *hate* that guy."

Deerbolt stepped over Ash's torso. "He's the reason I'm a Velocal," she said and winked. "*I* think he's great."

Ash asked Captain Deerbolt, "How do you know Raven?" as they stared out at the starry sky.

The ocean was calm tonight. If not for the gently crashing waves against the shoreline and the sloshing of the Cerulean Grace's hull in the harbour, the water would lay utterly still like polished onyx—hard enough and safe enough to dance upon, shining as the moonlight tickled the surface. Occasionally, if they steadied their breathing and closed their eyes, a graceful cooing drifted inland—the soothing sounds of water serpents, mutated from Dragons, and the sea's natural, untouched state became their lover's soundtrack. From their hexagonal rock outside the First Watchtower's defences, Ash and Deerbolt's evening stroll came to a peaceful end away from the great hall's drunken singing and the torches on every wall.

"I should change my clothes on the Grace." Ash continued when she offered no reply. "Won't you tell me where you got them, at least?"

"A friend of a friend owed me a favour. He's the tailor here. I've known him for years." She smiled at a distant memory, then continued. "Before you and I met, I traded with the Second Watchtower in the west. Business dried there, as did our welcome when the Order purchased most of the fortresses, including the Second Watchtower."

"The Second Watchtower fell?" Ash asked, astounded the Guardsmen there would allow it to happen. "I didn't know."

"It's been down, oh, maybe twelve years now."

She sighed and tilted her head to the sky, where Ash spotted shooting stars and constellations. Her eyes lowered, saddened by the shift in the Grace's luck and, therefore, her crew's routine.

"They forced us to trade further south. First, in Serenity. It was *so* humid. Work was tough and exhausting, and some of my men travelled inland to the Southern Trading Post. I sent our youngest and most able through the mountains to the Weeping Hills for respite and to re-stock, but some of them found women or alternative employment. We moved east then, where Blessed opened their purses; the higher tax rates and trouble had yet to creep so far through the mountains. The Order was living mostly in Raven, the Phoenix Marshes and the Gravelands too of course, destroying hope and joy and the earth. Few realised they held such power, but their egos were growing."

"Did you not consider retiring ashore?"

"Well, property along the east coast was appearing in Astral names, and it worried me. They hate other Alchemists, but some hate Humans more!"

"You're a Velocal, though. They still have a use for you," Ash interjected. "Not us Elementals, however."

"No," she said, shaking her head. "The Grace is where I belong."

"I remember how bad it was," Ash added. "Some of the Guard was pulling extra shifts to protect Dragonborn's coastline, in case the Order got any ideas about invading the island. Open Country saw its fair share of rejects from the west, and traders often brought word of squabbles for land and jewels both inland and at sea. They never tried anything, luckily."

Deerbolt was pleased to hear it. "The Grace picked up replacement deckhands somehow for those we'd lost in Serenity, and we pushed up to Blackheart Dock. The first journey lasted several months because we were unsure of ourselves and the territory. It took us maybe five months to realise we had an *unlikely* stowaway."

"That's how you met Raven."

"Aye," she replied, smiling. "And five months is a long time to evade capture when you're eating someone's food! He did well to blend in. Such a frightened Elemental he was. Because the Order didn't want him; they couldn't use him."

"Because of his shaking, I'll bet."

"It has worsened but believe me, that did *not* make him any less useful or capable. Today, his incantations are still accurate, I promise. When I heard Raven's story, I was sickened. An Astral in Raven had chased him out, threatening to suck the life out of him if he returned. They wanted only strong, healthy Elementals working there, so I offered Raven a position on the Cerulean Grace as our cook. Sure, we could have used him to speed up the ship, forcing our sails to work harder, but I wanted to protect him."

"You did the right thing."

"I hope so. He stayed with us a while longer, officially, until we docked here at the First Watchtower before our final voyage to Dragonborn. That's where I met you." Deerbolt grinned. "Since, whenever we come back either to visit or to trade, he and I are able to catch up and he teaches me about Alchemy, promoting my well-earned title as a Velocal. Naturally, he knows all about the mysterious Elemental I once loved, and now about the young friends of his I am harbouring."

Ash chewed his bottom lip and wrung his hands together. The temperature was dropping, and soon they would need to make their way to the Grace, or back to the Keep.

"You must trust Raven to risk our lives."

"Aye, because he's more trustworthy than even I! Raven is a kind, loyal and loving soul. Sometimes he is a little rough around the edges and for that, we forgive him. He's managed the Keep's library for a long time. He knows the books word-for-word. The one he gave you will be a goldmine of information if you read it cover-to-cover."

Ash chortled. "Well, I tried the key."

"Oh?"

Ash scowled, then said, "Doesn't fit."

She grinned. "I'm sure it does. Give it a wiggle."

"Hmm. Raven's intimidation attempts were *not* wasted on me in the five minutes we 'spoke'. I think he cares for you too, and it's clear he is an intelligent—if arrogant—man. If he's playing games..."

Deerbolt winked. "I'll be sure to tell him you have been sufficiently warned."

She crossed her knees and leaned forward, picking imaginary dirt from beneath her nails as she painfully remembered what it was like for Raven in the early days, before Astrals governed the Land and controlled not only what her ship could carry and when, but how many of the jewels she earned she could legally retain.

Before moving on from Raven, her men were starving. They were depressed and lonely, working on ships like the Grace because the Astrals that governed them limited their options. For a Captain, Deerbolt was lenient and kind, allowing leave and paying fair wages, despite this pushing her deeper into diabolical poverty. Some turned her down at first because she was a woman before they saw with their own eyes that bad luck followed only the superstitious.

"Elementals were rewarded and celebrated before the Order became a cult," she said. "Now, I support the resistance whenever I can."

Listening intently, Ash understood why the Gravelands and the Phoenix Marshlands were now out of bounds. The Grace hadn't returned in many years and Deerbolt could only imagine the effects of the Order's narcissism on the local, honest tradesmen. It was all Astral territory now, where the richest and most influential members of the Order ruled, taxed, enslaved and murdered in the name of Gods no Human or Alchemist had seen in *thousands* of years. And after driving most working-class Elementals north to villages such as Liberty, which sat at the base of a mountain range where fresh, crystal water flowed from the snowy caps, crops in the west all went untended by the Gnomes and Undines and died. Elementals and Humans fled in fear, finding safer, more affordable homes in the east, because in the eyes of an Astral of the Order, they were inferior.

The Gravelands shrivelled, useful only to the Slyphs to power their windmills. The further north Elementals travelled across the Land, the colder but calmer it was, even in the Open Country nearest to Land's Edge.

Ash was pleased Deerbolt had never considered returning west—not for jewels, at least. As far as he knew, she had no family or friends living there either.

"When the marketplace Oracle read your Tarot cards, he gave you two options."

Ash sucked the top of his mouth, then shrugged. "As *the Chariot*, yes. But, *the Hanged Man* blocked my present."

"Did he tell you *the Chariot*'s meaning?" Deerbolt asked him. "Cartomancy is one of the first things Raven taught me to understand."

"In short, it's whether I live or die." Ash added, "To stay in Blackheart Dock and accept my fate—death by curse—choosing the white horse depicted in the image. Or, to follow the black horse—you and the Grace—and sail across the sea to Dragonborn to help an innocent woman heal an archer's sight. To beg for forgiveness and perhaps win a reversal of the curse I'm sure they believe has killed me already."

He paused and looked across the fields where wildflowers and weeds intermingled, blowing in the breeze. Their stems entwined, their petals and seeds scattered, and Ash watched the natural freedom of it all with envy.

He shivered and tapped his head. "I am consciously aware the greatest chance of victory lies on this journey, with the black horse."

"You think they will kill you on sight now that you're a Tetrad? Won't they lend an ear to your plight first and give a dying man a fair trial?"

"If the Guard help me, it will be after I offer myself to them and beg for mercy... if I have the stomach for it. But, there's *the Hanged Man*," he grumbled and picked at the blades of grass between his bare feet in deep thought.

"You're still punishing yourself."

"Aye. I was once above kneeling to avoid death. Sacrificing pride and surrendering dignity is worth more now, though. I have more to lose than I did a week ago. I've always been a Tetrad, and someone saw in me what I never could. I can't hang around any more."

They sat together in silence for a few minutes, listening to the distant echoes of music and joyful singing within the fortress's walls. A warm glow emanated from the barracks, causing them both to shiver in response to the breeze's nip.

Deerbolt's breathing steadied as she relaxed into their personal conversation. It took Ash a while to trust her enough when they first met, and to open up about his troubles. She'd expected nothing less from him this time. His vulnerability called to the nurturing side of Deerbolt, stamping down the independent, scrappy fighter she usually portrayed.

"What did you do to raise their suspicion, Ash? You never told me."

He didn't respond at first, but the cogs of his brain ticked carefully, plotting the best explanation and manner in which to deliver the tale. Her gentle nudge was enough to coax Ash's honesty. If anyone was to slay the man he once was with judgement or even violence, he'd rather it come from Deerbolt anyway, he thought.

"There is a lot you don't know about the Guard," he started, "and a lot I can't tell you as the secrets in my past are not wholly mine to divulge. I swore an oath."

"Technically not. Your duty to that place is over."

"But not to myself," he said.

She smiled invitingly. "Tell me what you are able."

Ash shifted his weight. "There was an Oracle on the island; he would reach out to the dead as a Sciomancer. He knew things about us before even *we* were aware. Spirits would whisper to him about the Dragonborn Guardsmen to keep us honest and true to our calling, to stop us hiding anything that might risk the flame, but he relied on Psychometry to confirm Lingerverse rumours. Some souls are trouble-makers, others peaceful, and it was his job to tell them apart and report to our seniors. So, naturally, the men evaded his touch."

"Did you?"

"Aye! When we saw him walking in the caverns, we'd turn and head in the opposite direction to avoid brushing his shoulder or catching his gaze. And the Guard were all good men, loyal to the cause, but imperfect."

Deerbolt scowled, thinking the worst. "How so?"

"One man imported erotic sketches and hid them in his hammock—we were abstinent and it soothed his loneliness. One man learnt of a bush inland that, when rolled into a cigarette and smoked or singed in a bowl and inhaled, it acted as a hallucinogenic drug, which soothed pain from an old injury. Weak as he was, he would not share the temptation with anyone else."

"He wanted to protect you?"

Ash nodded. "I asked him myself once, but he said he could put no one at risk by giving them directions. We protected our harmless indulgences from the man hired to sniff them out and stifle them. Each of us was flawed but harming no one."

Deerbolt relaxed, knowing the Guard was not filled with criminals and vagabonds, choosing a life on the island to escape their pasts on the Land.

Ash sighed, then continued. "Before the banishment, the Dragonborn Oracle experienced something... *unexpected.* You're a Velocal, so you'll know those practising Sciomancy risk bringing forth evil from the Lingerverse when they invite such whispers."

"Of course. Opening *any* channel of communication with the Lingerverse poses risks."

"Something evil began to pound on his defences relentlessly. The Oracle was enraged. He described the mental torture as the constant hammering of fists on a fragile window between the Land and the Lingerverse. Any Astral would have smashed that window and sucked the spirit's energy, killing the threat immediately. But, an Oracle is limited, and is not so gifted."

Deerbolt blinked once to show she understood how painful that must be—perhaps she had witnessed this first-hand or read about it somewhere, but she did not interrupt his story.

"This went on for several days. We tried herbal remedies to sooth his symptoms and calm his nerves. Nothing worked. Slowly, the Oracle was being driven mad."

Ash swallowed hard and took a deep, cleansing breath before he continued. Deerbolt listened with bated breath; he was about to reveal why the Dragonborn Guard had banished him.

"The night before we met, I was on watch. Another Guardsman manned his post a couple hundred metres down the wall, and both of us were freezing, being so high up—the wind from the Tradeway drilled through your skin, attacked your bones. His firepit dwindled and being a Salamander, I left my post to help him replenish it. We talked for a few minutes as we warmed our hands, then I returned to find the Oracle sitting on the wall with his legs dangling above the crashing waves and a sharp rock formation beneath. I must have gasped, because he turned and our eyes locked. Without thinking, I reached to coax him back. I promised him taking his own life was *not* a solution—what he was experiencing needed further investigation, and might apply to the protection of the flame. The spirits obviously chose him because of his location and proximity to it."

"Let me guess, he took your hand."

"He only held me for seconds, but it felt like a lifetime. He read everything—my childhood, joining the Guard, my conversations with the other men (thus revealing the secrets *they* had entrusted me with) and the limitations of my Elemental magic. The mind is a miraculous, intricate web, and he was lost within mine. I couldn't shake his presence; he knew everything about me—things I didn't know about myself! But through our touch, I realised his insanity was not his own. Driving him was something... *else*. Greater in size, magnitude and power."

Deerbolt squeezed his hand as a single tear fell, splashing upon the hexagonal rock between them.

"Did you recognise who the power belonged to?"

Ash sighed deeply. "It was a God."

CHAPTER EIGHT
THE GOD OF UNIVERSAL ENERGY

Chapter Eight: The God of Universal Energy

Through the byzantine maze of thoughts and memories hiding within Ash's mind, the Oracle pulled a manifest of his powers and skills in reverse order.

Ash's subconscious opened too easily, revealing minor details at first. What he'd eaten that day, and those he'd conversed with. Then his probing sank into the steps Ash had taken in basic training; a jab and slash of a dagger; a calculated swish of his sword; the bruises to his knuckles from thrown or blocked punches; his complex, planned, and meticulous incantations to master his Salamander magic.

Those memories were raw because they were the most recent, but a deeper plunge took the Oracle along Ash's timeline and into his past.

He watched as Ash used his Elemental magic to assist in his father's workshop in the Witching Woods where Ash was born. He believed a job would be waiting for him when he came of age—the blacksmith was a family-owned business inherited from his grandfather and many grandfathers before. But when sickness took his parents, Ash realised that was not to be. Instead, he dedicated his life to protecting the Isle of Dragonborn, and he left Witching to travel north, then barter for a crossing.

The Oracle untangled Ash's painful adolescence and early adulthood, how he'd joined the Guard and developed his Alchemy, then jumped further forward to more pressing concerns.

Ash was not only worried the Oracle was risking his sanity, winding psychic fingers around his brainwaves, but he also braced for the pain of a severed connection; he couldn't rummage for much longer, and it was well known when an Oracle was through with research like this, you felt it.

The Oracle saw something nestled in the farthest reaches of Ash's mind that was about to change his life forever, and there was *nothing* he could do, except kill the Oracle, to prevent it.

Ash protected his mind well usually. He learnt how to build solid boundaries around his most private hopes and fears in the first few months of joining the Guard, but his mother and father taught him the first steps in Witching. It was important for an Elemental's resilience, and part of a Guardsman's strength training; not only to prepare the body for an attack, but to prepare the mind to match an Oracle's willpower, or to withstand torture and protect the island's secrets. But the tactics of the island's Oracle caught them off-guard. While some Seers like the nameless marketplace Oracle had no use for another's thoughts, like Cartomancers, Chiromancers, and Hydromancers (who were interested only in using their specific skill to enhance another's well-being, or line their pockets), others held grave intent. They used Sciomancy and Psychometry to be nosey and interfere. Your knowledge was their knowledge.

Unless the Oracle dived too deep, most victims sensed no broken boundaries; it was, on the surface, a sneaky act. With the right spirit guide to whisper secrets and lies to the delicate senses an Oracle used, like a passing breeze, they could be in and out of your head within milliseconds. On this occasion, it wasn't truly the Oracle who rammed against Ash's walls until they crumbled to dust. Guarding his mind was pointless and exhausting. Something, or someone, was controlling the Oracle's spirit guide. So, it was also controlling the Oracle.

Ash explained this to Captain Deerbolt, and shuddered at the memory of encountering the God of Universal Energy.

Against his siblings, he was the middle child. Of the imprisoned Gods, he struggled the most against his father's wishes and posed the greatest threat. He wanted to escape, and Ash told Deerbolt he came close to succeeding that day.

"The impact was fierce and terrifying all at once," Ash told her as he trembled. "I felt his anger. I felt his pain. I felt... his *fear*. He didn't want to be imprisoned; he hated the weakness it created in him. In the true Astral sense, he was using the Oracle's spirit guide to observe the Land, and manipulating the Oracle's actions to impose his will."

"But how can that be?" Deerbolt gasped. "To speak to the Oracle, the God of Universal Energy would have to be in the *Lingerverse*."

Ash shrugged and shook his head. "I don't know. But through his touch, it was obvious there wasn't much of the Oracle remaining when he and I clashed. His energy had been sucked dry, and his soul had withered—most likely, he was mere minutes from being banished to the Lingerverse himself and replaced by a vile, dishonest, *insane* God."

Deerbolt gasped. "So, the God had been controlling the Oracle far longer than he'd been complaining of any discomfort."

"He must have been fighting the influence for months. He couldn't take it. Rather than risk the God of Universal Energy's complete control, he chose to plummet to his death."

Deerbolt fingered her chin in thought. "Why wouldn't he tell someone about it; report it to a Guardsman? He'd been compromised."

"Look what they did to me!" Ash snorted and shook his head frantically. "They risk nothing. If the Oracle told somebody the God of Universal Energy was braying on his door from the Lingerverse, he'd have incited a panic. Guardsmen would have killed him or locked him away. The egg and its flame would have been moved instantly, away from prying eyes. The entire island might have been closed off! If they didn't interrogate and torture him first, they would certainly have executed him."

"Even if he came clean? Even if it wasn't what he thought after all?"

Ash scowled. "I wouldn't risk it. Would you?"

"And what would it have meant for the Isle of Dragonborn to be controlled by the God of Universal Energy, exactly?" Deerbolt asked, unsure she wanted an answer, but curious.

"A God masquerading as a man," Ash confirmed. "Someone who not only wanted the final egg, and the flame destroyed to return to the old ways, but who could lead the Order to complete their domination of the Land. He wants his Alchemy back, and for Dragons to be extinct."

"With the Oracle's powers intact also?"

"Who knows!"

Deerbolt groaned, "Think of the suffering."

"Think of the wars!" Ash added.

"The Oracle killed himself, then?"

"When the Oracle severed our connection, it sent us both careening in opposite directions, like a bolt of lightning had struck the stone between us. It gave me a splitting headache. I couldn't stand at first but thankfully, neither could he. I was able to intercept my brother on my hands and knees. He came to our aid, and I warned him the Oracle was not who he claimed to be. But the God abandoned him then to embarrass and belittle my claims, and the Oracle blinked and trembled and cried. He stumbled safely down from the wall with my brother as his escort, exhausted but obviously thrilled to have his head space back. And when our leaders asked the Oracle what happened, well, you know the rest."

"He exposed you as a Tetrad?"

"What remained of the Oracle's consciousness must also have seen what manifested within me before I knew myself, and he shared that information with the men who governed the Guard to defer their suspicions about his own nature. I was beaten, cursed, and driven out of my home. I'd never used any other Elemental incantations, despite being told I was capable."

"Didn't you know *anything* about being an Undine, or a Gnome, or a Slyph?"

"Only what I'd been told," Ash replied. "Where would I even start? I'd had no other training, and been shown only Salamander Alchemy from day one. My parents never said I was anything but a Salamander." Ash saw the solemn expression on Deerbolt's face as she listened intently. "What's the matter, don't you believe me?"

"Actually, I'm relieved. I thought you were going to tell me you'd thrown the Oracle to his death," Deerbolt said, taking a deep breath first as if to brace herself for Ash's response. "That would have been..."

"Just," he finished for her. "I should have! It would better explain why *Justice* was in my reading. But I didn't, I swear."

"I'm glad."

Ash wasn't. "They called me a murderer before I'd ever taken a life, and when somebody brands you with such a title for so long and with such force, you believe it yourself."

Deerbolt cleared her throat and said, "I'm sorry that happened to you, Ash."

"So am I," he replied.

He leant over to tuck a stray lock of Deerbolt's hair behind her ear. He paused and took in the sight of her for as long as he could get away with, then continued.

"I'm sorry I killed so many of my brothers during my escape. Some of them were good men and I tried to reason with them first, I really did. But I needed to get out of there—I was innocent. I'm sorry I couldn't learn more about the God of Universal Energy's plans before the Oracle severed our connection, too. Not that they'd have believed me anyway. I'm mostly sorry I wasn't strong enough to keep the Oracle from invading my head." He paused, then finally whispered, "I'm sorry for a lot of things, and I can't change any of them."

Deerbolt took Ash's hand in hers and gently squeezed until he'd blinked through his welling tears. He swallowed his emotions, wiped his nose on the back of his other hand, and blew out a huge breath.

"It's in the past." He forced a smile.

"How can we be sure?"

Ash frowned. "What do you mean?"

"Well, if *that* God could penetrate *that* Oracle's consciousness, how can we be sure he won't try again or hasn't already done so? How can we be sure the God of Universal Energy hasn't escaped his father's imprisonment in Akasha and is still hiding in the Lingerverse, *waiting*?"

Ash thought about it, then agreed they couldn't be sure—until his ugly intentions reared again, there was no way to know.

"I can only assume the God of Universal Energy would select another influential Oracle or perhaps an Astral. Anyone able to use Sciomancy to contact the Lingerverse," he advised.

"A God would want to *see* through an Oracle's power," said Deerbolt, "not only experience the Land through an Astral's connection. It is the Astral who drains the spirit's energy and not the other way," she reminded him, and she was right.

Astrals didn't need to search the Lingerverse for too long or too deeply to find a lost soul to draw forth. When they did cast out their net and capture a spirit, it wasn't always a someone. Occasionally, they trapped a some*thing*. If the Astral wasn't wary, or if they were too slow to release that spirit, its energy could overload their mortal soul and literally implode them.

An Astral's Alchemy *was* powerful, but it could *not* do battle with a God and win.

"We cannot trust any Oracle we encounter living on or near

the Isle of Dragonborn," Deerbolt decided.

Ash released Deerbolt's hand as he stood abruptly and paced the hill. He snapped his fingers and pointed at the glowing fortress by the sea, where a library filled with endless Alchemical knowledge awaited them.

"Raven can tell us how any of this was possible, surely?" Ash suggested, and in several huge strides, set off to ask Deerbolt's mentor about how an imprisoned God could inhabit and control an Oracle and their power. He shoved his hand down the front of his shirt and fingered the ornate key that Raven had given him to unlock the Tetrad book of secrets now in his possession.

"Where are you going, Ash?"

"I can't take Kite and Reverie to Dragonborn if there's a chance the Oracle is possessed again. I need to know what the God of Universal Energy wants and how he's doing this from Akasha."

"And you think Raven will know?" Deerbolt set off after him and grabbed him by the back of his collar, dragging him to a halt. "He's an old man, Ash, and he hasn't left the First Watchtower in years. He could only tell us what the books say."

"He met a lot of Alchemists in the west and the Order mistreated him," Ash explained. "There's more to that guy than he lets on. You know it, too. Maybe he overheard plans, but didn't realise at the time what they meant. He had that book and key in his possession, after all."

"I seriously doubt every Astral is conspiring to help the God of Universal Energy re-take control of the Land, Ash." Deerbolt rolled her eyes. "You cannot tar an entire race of Alchemists with such a radical assumption."

Ash raised his brow. "Not all Astrals are of the Order, Deerbolt," he agreed. "But those who are?"

He snorted, dropped the key to allow it to blow away from his chest in the breeze, and forcefully tapped two fingers against his palm with each point he was about to make.

"Astrals of the Order buy the largest properties and trade points along the coastlines. Then, Astrals of the Order begin taxing and mistreating Alchemists deemed less than themselves, enslaving and murdering, using the Land to convert their cult into an empire. Astrals of the Order have also been trying to extinguish the Dragonborn flame since its creation. We agree on that? They are *determined* to remain in all government and royal positions."

"I agree because this isn't news," Deerbolt told him. "Everyone either fears Astrals of the Order, or they work for them."

"Or both."

He was on to something. Ash snagged his collar free and stormed off downhill, chewing his fingernails in deep thought. He stuffed the key back down his shirt before the wind could blow the ribbon off his neck.

Why would the Order want to bring back the God of Universal Energy's influence, he thought, if, upon his arrival, Astrals would lose their powers entirely when the flame went out and the egg was destroyed?

He put this question to Deerbolt.

"Astrals don't believe they *will* lose their magic. They believe their Alchemy is all that will remain."

"Fools," Ash grumbled.

Of the Gods, Universal Energy was the meanest, the angriest, and the most spiteful. He would immediately re-take Alchemy from the Land to provoke his father, the God of Magic, who banished his children. Universal Energy was the reason Humans were jealous, fought over land, livestock, jewels, and even other Humans.

Perhaps he would seek revenge on his sister, the God of the Senses, for surrendering the Gods' influence to their father in the first place.

It didn't matter—any action would birth a war against the God of Magic himself, and the Land would crumble beneath their rage.

Astrals would lose their gifts.

The Land would turn against them.

Genocide: *that's* where they were heading.

Ash insisted they speak to Raven and dragged Deerbolt along behind him as he half-walked and half-ran across the bridge, beneath the gate and its towers, and over the courtyard to the Keep's doors. Within the fortress boundaries, several small campfires were alight and encompassed by men supping ale, crooning, or performing for their brothers.

"Ash, it's the middle of the night!"

He ignored her, intending to wake Raven and escort him to the library to begin their research. He had questions. A lot of them. And these questions needed immediate answers.

Ash recoiled and held open both arms as he paced the only space in the library that was not stacked four feet high with dusty old books.

"What do you expect *me* to do about it?"

Deerbolt rolled her eyes. She waved off his shock; Raven wasn't known for his subtlety or patience, but he was one of the most honest people she'd ever met.

"Ash, I think what Raven is trying to say is..."

Raven cut her off. He handed Ash another unrelated volume, bound in red leather, which Ash glared at quizzically,

"He wants to know if you have Tetrad knowledge."

"Don't use that word here!"

"And don't call me that," Ash snapped.

He slammed the book down on Raven's desk, sending a cloud of dust up into the air. All three of them coughed, but Raven continued working.

"Ash is looking for some advice, Raven, that's all. You've met many people in your years and crossed paths with the Order more times than I'd care to. *Surely*, you can—"

"I can't," he said, interrupting her again, "and you know why, Captain Deerbolt. I suggest you take this man back to the Cerulean Grace and lock him in your quarters until he has read and understood the entire book I gave him. It *locks* for a reason!"

"I know, you said this is the key. Only, I tried, and it doesn't fit."

"*Yet*. It doesn't fit *yet*. The book is an Elemental incantation guide that will—"

It was Ash's turn to jump in. "To train me to use all four of my Elemental powers, but I can't get it open!"

"What do you mean the key doesn't fit *yet*?"

Raven stopped abruptly and glared at Deerbolt, meeting her gaze. He flicked his wrist to pull back the curtain, releasing some of the dust in the air, then he took a deep breath.

Never had the men at the First Watchtower met a Tetrad, nor any other Alchemist in Raven's circle. Already, he thought Ash was cowardly—not at all the behaviour he'd expected of one so influential and capable beneath his thin skin. From what Deerbolt told him, this scoundrel was a traitor and a thief amongst other things, but because Raven loved the Captain as the daughter he never had, he hadn't expressed his concerns about their affair. Deerbolt so obviously still adored Ash the Elemental. Until Ash proved himself worthy of her and mastered his other Elemental skills, Raven wouldn't be issuing his blessing. That key would do the job for him, if Ash lived to use it. Besides, Tetrads were *rare*. Not only in the north but across the Land overall. Thousands of years ago when the Dragons ruled, there were many Tetrads and all with varying levels of skill. Usually, it took a Salamander parent carrying the Alchemy for a Tetrad to be born, and so Raven assumed either Ash's mother or father possessed the gift and, despite how difficult it must have been, managed to hide it. Perhaps they didn't know they could manipulate other elements. But, either way, Raven made it clear to Ash he'd likely been lied to. If not by his parents, then certainly a grandparent. So *rare* were Tetrads, Raven pondered, that if a Dragonborn Guardsman found out about his abilities, he'd be strung up immediately to protect the flame without a trial. Those by his side may suffer the same fate, so Deerbolt's life was at risk. Wasting time taking Ash to Dragonborn would prove too risky for the Guard; they'd either shoot him with an arrow, hang him, or cut him down where he stood.

The Order would be quick to capture and imprison him, though, then transport him to the island themselves. They'd use him to extinguish the flame to further their cult's cause and he'd most likely spend the rest of his days in a dungeon somewhere beneath the Gravelands until they needed him again. If they could find a suitable female Elemental, Raven knew of a few rich Astrals who would pay Ash well to produce Tetrad offspring, too. If he refused? Ash could still produce Tetrad children with or without his fingers, toes, his sight, or his tongue. In his weakened state, it wouldn't take much to convince him to perform as directed.

"The key is the key," he said without explanation, then continued about his business, shuffling books around with one hand and using the other to rearrange them from shelf to shelf with basic Slyph incantations.

Deerbolt cast Ash a sideways glance. "Raven, be reasonable."

Ash fired back, finding his bark and his bite at the sight of Deerbolt's frustration. "I've only known I could officially do this a few days. Just because some ridiculously heavy, stupidly intricate key doesn't fit into its lock, is that *my* fault?"

"You knew back then about your abilities, Ash the

Elemental," Raven countered. "You are in denial."

"An Oracle told me I was a—"

"Don't say the T-word."

"I wasn't going to." Ash rolled his eyes, then argued, "I didn't show symptoms. How was *I* to know it was the truth?"

Ash lost his temper then and wiped a whole stack of organised books off the window ledge with his arms. He swayed and leant back against the stone wall for support.

"Deerbolt tells me you've been a wonderful mentor to her, like a father," Ash said through laboured breaths. He pinched the bridge of his nose and sighed. He was starting to feel unwell again. "She entrusted you with this secret so you'd help us, or at least point us in the direction of someone who can. Why can't you do that?"

"Because," Raven began quietly, concerned their argument was drawing too much attention to the library, "other than the book and key I gave you, young man, there are *no remaining records* of such Elementals in existence. Let me say that again... there are NO REMAINING RECORDS. Aghh, you're not going to listen," he grumbled and waved Ash aside. "The Order burned anything and everything they could find in the west, and whatever made it east is either lost or owned by Dragonborn to protect the flame. Deerbolt is correct—I have travelled and met many Alchemists. None, I'm afraid, were like you. What you and Captain Deerbolt now hide," he said, gesturing at the key beneath Ash's shirt, "is the extent of my offering. Now, may I suggest you leave, *silently*, and make haste for Land's Edge before anybody here gets the wrong idea and informs the Order of your whereabouts?"

"Can you at least tell me where the book and key came from?" Ash begged. "Where did you find them? Were they given to you?"

"I acquired them. Now GO!"

Ash couldn't bear feeling useless and ignorant any longer. He thanked Raven for nothing before storming through the curtain and back through the main hall.

When he'd gone and was out of earshot, Raven gently squeezed Deerbolt's shoulder.

"Are you *sure* you want to go through with this?"

CHAPTER NINE
UNLOCKED

Chapter Nine: Unlocked

The key is the key, that's what Raven said before Ash had bailed. But, it made little sense, at least not to Ash and Deerbolt. He was over Raven's cryptic nonsense and in two minds about whether to throw the key into the dock. Before he did, Ash knew he really should try one last time to get it to unlock, but with the internal mechanism rusty and old, and the key's guardian equally as ancient and rough around the edges, he wasn't sure he'd have much luck.

Ash left the Keep and made haste for the drawbridge, counting his footsteps steadily in the soothing evening air. With only a few fires lit and torches on the wall, the sky overhead was clear and crisp, shining brilliantly with stars so large and so twinkly, he wanted to reach up and grab one.

He'd almost made it to the bridge when a man on the wall gave the signal to lift the walkway, barring anyone from entry or exit. Ash scowled and side-stepped to avoid two more men scurrying past and up an inner stone stairwell, which led to the main patrol above the entrance. Behind him, he could hear more men gathering their armour and weapons, shouting warnings and orders.

“What's going on?” he asked one of them, grabbing him by

the sleeve as he sprinted by.

"It's the Order," the man replied, fixing his helmet and then bending to tie the laces on his boots. "There's a ship bearing their flag heading this way."

"Not to trade?"

"They're not supposed to know we exist!" the man snorted and set off running again, leaving Ash alone in the courtyard, panicking.

Of course. He'd promised Deerbolt there were no survivors of the ship they'd defeated in the Tradeway, and they were well out of view for any others to see where they'd docked and follow. But if someone here was disloyal and leaked they'd arrived after murdering a whole crew and sinking an Order vessel, no doubt those in power would seek revenge.

"Not good," he whispered.

He turned on his heel and ran back through the Keep's open doors to the library. Deerbolt was already on her way out, and her eyes widened with fear when she saw Ash's stricken expression.

"The Order," he began, panting, "they know we're here. The guards have locked down the fortress."

Deerbolt drew her longsword from its place on her belt and led him outside. The wall was now lined two bodies deep with armed Guardsmen, all with arrows, crossbows or swords. They were covered head-to-toe in thick armour, which clanged when they changed positions. Ash thought the sound was reassuring, though he still didn't feel completely safe.

"We did this," he said, "and the Order will destroy this place searching for us. Men are about to die."

Deerbolt turned to him and narrowed her eyes. "Not if we can help it."

"The Order has greater numbers and weapons."

"They don't have *you*." Deerbolt raised one eyebrow and grinned. "They don't have a Tetrad on their side."

Ash groaned and tried to walk away. He knew it wouldn't be long before someone tried to use his so-called powers before he was ready.

"This is insane. *I* can't fight them off, Deerbolt."

"Sure you can! You just took down one of their ships," she encouraged, "and you weren't even trying then. You said it just happened, right?" When he didn't turn back, Deerbolt raised her voice. "If they get in here, we are all dead. You know that." She paused. "Could you live with yourself?"

Ash halted abruptly. His jaw tightened.

I have your attention, Ash the Elemental.

"I must not have killed them all. They wouldn't be here if I did!"

"Nonsense. This is not your doing. Raven's book contains everything you need to defeat them again now—*ten thousand* of them if you wanted."

"It won't open, and the book is out *there*," Ash said, pointing at the wall, where the Grace was currently docked on the other side. "They raised the drawbridge and they were smart to. But don't think for one minute a moat and a wooden bridge will prevent them from getting in. We should search for a way out—a way to escape so Kite and Reverie are far, *far* away from here by the time they do."

Without warning, Deerbolt took his borrowed longsword and pulled it behind her back when he reached to reclaim it.

"What are you doing? Go to the barracks and get Kite and Reverie. We have to go. Now."

"No, *you* have to get that book open, or what else are you going to fight with?"

Ash sighed. "I have a dagger in my boot and Salamander magic... sort of." He clenched his knuckles and then grabbed fistfuls of his mousey hair. "They are not going to let me out of here, and if they do, they are not going to let me back in."

"Let me handle the Guardsmen," she said and clapped with delight. "If I can get you that book, will you at least *try* to take Raven's advice?"

Ash nodded, but as soon as Deerbolt had gone to speak to the guards on the wall, the pit of his stomach dropped and he doubled over, taking deep, soothing breaths.

He could do this. He had to do this.

If he didn't, he would die. Deerbolt would die.

Deerbolt will die. Kite and Reverie will die. Their baby, too.

Deerbolt called his name from the base of the wall. He had no idea what she'd said to convince them, but the guards were lowering the drawbridge.

"Run, I only got you a few minutes."

Ash set off in a frantic sprint for the Cerulean Grace. She slapped his back, leaving a sweaty handprint on the leather of his doublet.

Heading uphill were the Grace's deckhands, with Sarronious at the rear urging them to move faster. He waved a lit torch back and forth as a guide in the pitch black, and a man at the front responded by waving his. Deerbolt's crew would be of better use in the fortress where, Sarronious thought, he could also better protect her from the Order. If they wanted to harm her, they'd have to get through him first.

They would, eventually.

But he wasn't going down without a fight. He'd take as many of them with him to the Lingerverse as he could.

Astrals described the Lingerverse as a black, white and grey wasteland, populated by spirits and other ethereal beings trapped between their life on the Land and death in Akasha, with unfinished business, regrets or tormented by mistakes made in their physical form. Unbound by the laws of the Land, the Lingerverse was an Alchemical arena where some spirits battled for the Gods' attention, hoping to be favoured and transported from their haunting of limbo to a freeing afterlife. Other spirits, and most the Astrals encountered, were lingering and lost there for eternity, with few to remember them on the Land and even fewer to look upon them without prejudice in Akasha.

Though Ash had never seen the Lingerverse, travellers across Open Country and even the Dragonborn Guardsmen told stories and spread rumours. It was known to be a dark, lonely place, and souls imprisoned there were at risk of being controlled by Astrals and, if not released back into the Lingerverse in time, destroyed—completely removed from existence and forgotten. He liked to imagine it was actually a calm and gently colourful place, where souls could temporarily rest before moving on; a pause between worlds, reducing the impact of the drastic change from life to death. Perhaps Astrals only saw the Lingerverse in darkness because of their ill intent. If Ash could peer through the pane himself, he imagined being able to then report differently to his fellow Alchemists.

Every Alchemical group believed something unique, from every branch of Seer to an Oracle, Astrals, Velocals, and Elementals like Ash, no matter their preference of earth, air, fire or water. If they followed the old ways, they believed in the Gods and their imprisonment thousands of years ago. If they followed the new ways, they still believed in the Gods, but they had twisted beliefs about their place and purpose on the Land, and the vast opposite to others of their kind. Such Alchemists were cults of their own, including the Order, and how their views and morals were selfish compared to Astrals living separately to their organisation.

Sarronious wasn't afraid of death; he followed the old ways of Alchemy and always had. He, like Ash, had been brought up inland but to a Human family, and they'd taught him how to be generous, kind and hard-working away from most Alchemists who'd wish to do them harm. In his mind, the Lingerverse was the natural step between life and death, and if it meant protecting Deerbolt from whatever fate she feared, he would happily go there.

“Where are you running off to?” he called as Ash dashed past.

“The gate is open for a few more minutes. Run!”

His feet thundered heavily on the gravel pathway. The weight of his boots, plus the steep decline of the hill, forced Ash into a speed he wasn't entirely comfortable with. Unlike the marketplace's trading hill, lined with stalls and littered with people going about their daily affairs, there was nothing for Ash to grab hold of to slow him, and nothing to prevent him ploughing off the dock into the water, either.

Sarronious shouted, “HOLD THE GATE!”

The Cerulean Grace came into view as he neared the bottom. Ash was feeling dizzy and his vision was blurring through sweat and exhaustion. The enemy ship wasn't far off shore now, and he could see the burning torches flickering, hear the voices of angry Astrals, and feel the energy of the souls they sucked from the Lingerverse waiting to be directed into violence.

Ash put the brakes on his legs and locked them, skidding to a one-legged stop at the base of the Grace's wooden rope ladder, which he then clambered up clumsily. The book Raven gave him was hidden in Deerbolt's quarters. He knew exactly where to find it without rummaging or making a mess, but had no idea where she'd stored his weapons. But because of his speed, he knocked over a stack of books and forgot to close the lid of the chest, leaving Deerbolt's personal possessions on view. If the Order boarded and raided her things, there was little of any worth there, anyway.

Ash set off up the hill with the book tucked under his arm, using the other to propel himself forward in a scooping incantation, hoping to activate his hidden Slyph. For a minute, he felt lighter somehow, as though his cupped fingers were a paddle against the air. It lifted him, doubling his speed.

He couldn't see in the darkness. Could Raven be helping him from within the fortress grounds, or from the wall?

“Hurry, Ash!” Deerbolt cried from the gate.

An impatient, worried Guardsman was already giving the order to lift the drawbridge again. Ash picked up the pace, using the last of his energy despite now feeling light-headed and sick. He hoped there was time to rest before the Order reached the First Watchtower's waters, or he wouldn't have the energy to perform any incantations, never mind those he wasn't familiar with.

The bridge was already several feet off the ground, leaving an increasingly large gap between safety and the depths of the moat. Murky, algae-covered water that stank of fish and sewage sloshed, ready to meet Ash's enervated body. He squeezed his eyes closed and leaped up, feeling a gust of supportive wind beneath his buttocks and thighs as his free hand clasped the bridge.

Deerbolt vaulted up the other side, fighting the angle to grasp hold of Ash's arm and pull him over. When they locked eyes, Ash handed her the book, which she slid down the ramp first, then yanked him with all her might. The Guardsmen didn't pause for them, either.

“Jump!” called Ash.

In unison, Ash and Deerbolt let go of the bridge's edge and plummeted to the gate's stone base. Deerbolt landed on his chest, stealing the air from his lungs, but there wasn't time to recover.

“OUT OF THE WAY!” someone screamed, then hauled Deerbolt off Ash from horseback, throwing her to a stance.

She offered Ash a hand and pulled him up, then grabbed the book and led him up to the wall where Guardsmen were preparing for a battle. Seeing a Salamander, one bowman lit another torch on Ash's left and instructed him to stand beside it to fuel his powers. Unable to speak, still catching his breath, Ash nodded in thanks, but doubted he'd be able to muster the energy to perform any incantations.

“Here,” Deerbolt said and slammed the book on the wall. “Where's your key?”

Ash slid the key up his bare chest by tugging the ribbon and fumbled to fit it into the lock. He twisted and pushed, then hammered the end with his fist but nothing worked.

Deerbolt watched with eager eyes.

Ash had failed to take the first basic step to save the First Watchtower from the Order's fury. The distant boom of a cannon shook the fortress's foundations, and the men on the wall ducked together, blind to the cannonball's path.

"INCOMING!" someone screamed.

The shot impacted the latrine wall, collapsing the outbuilding. Two horses reared, throwing off their riders, and bolted behind the Keep.

A second boom sounded, and the men ducked again. This time, the cannonball hit the side of the Keep, and part of the spire crumbled. Ash heard wailing as a guard was crushed beneath the rubble.

"Do something, Ash!" Deerbolt cried.

She flung her body off the wall, landing in a crouched position, to run to the man's aid.

Ash watched the unfolding scene in horror. The Order's ship had already destroyed an outbuilding and part of the fortress's largest structure. People were dying before his eyes, and yet he was out of ideas.

He inhaled sharply, then stuck the palm of his hand through the torch's base to light a small fireball. He played with it a moment, nurtured it through steady breathing and a clear head, then grew the size and density. The ship was now in range but when he pitched it, he missed.

Try again, he urged his power. *Try harder.*

Ash stuck both hands into the flame and smacked his hands together. To onlookers, it looked like he was clapping for a job well done, but Ash was testing how sturdy the fire was against his skin; how well would his Elemental power connect the heat to his palms, and how well could he roll them into grand, robust fireballs?

He arched his hands in a pirouette formation, then threw them forward, tensing his chest as he launched both at the same time towards the enemy ship.

"It's a hit!" the bowman called through cupped hands, pointing at the ship's sail as it burned, forcing men to jump overboard.

With a renewed sense of worth and ability, Ash formed several more and fired them two at a time, gaining confidence and accuracy with each shot. Seeing his progress, the bowman lit a second torch and fixed it to his right, meaning Ash could now open and close his arms like the beating wings of a butterfly to light and fire, light and fire, light and fire.

Ash tired. It wasn't long before his power reversed, and the curse crept up his spine with each attempt, stealing back his energy. Deerbolt could see Ash's shoulders slumping. His fireballs were smaller and dull; rather than their searing electric blue colour, they were now pale yellow and flickering.

Using the wall to support him, Ash leaned forward to re-focus, propping his upper body against his elbows at either side of the book.

The worn leather mocked him. *Worn like your powers.* The stiff lock taunted him. *Stiff like your joints.* But, the weight of the parchment grounded him through its solidity.

He craned his neck and scowled. He stretched every limb to increase his flexibility and jumped up and down to increase his stamina and warm his muscles.

Deerbolt called his name from the courtyard, pointing to his chest.

"ASH, *LOOK*!"

Rather than hanging limply on the ribbon, the key was floating directly in front of him. It glowed, catching the attention of the bowman and the other guards on the wall. For a few seconds, all was silent and everyone stopped to witness Ash's amazing Alchemy.

"How is he doing that?"

"Who is that guy?"

"Where did he come from?"

"He must be a Slyph."

"I thought he was a Salamander?"

"Tetrad."

"A Tetrad?"

"We're saved!"

Ash drowned their voices out and fingered the key until it landed, effortlessly, in the palm of his hand. He stole another flame from the torch and spread it across the leather, then inserted the key into the lock once more as the cover seared. With a click, the lock popped open.

The precious information within was his.

CHAPTER TEN
WE SAIL AT DAWN

Chapter Ten: We Sail At Dawn

As if the book sensed Ash's intentions and requirements, the pages flicked open themselves, offering him a myriad of incantation options to boost his Salamander magic, explore his Undine abilities, and toy with his Slyph powers. Gnome capabilities were still completely alien, and because the ship had not yet docked, control of the earth would be of no use to him yet until the Order's crew were on the ground.

The book guided Ash, training him slowly. It started with the very basics; movements Ash hadn't used since he was a boy, playing with fire in Witcher on his parents' property. He didn't need to read the words—touching the pages one at a time instructed him the way a spirit guide instructed an Oracle, or Tarot cards guided a Cartomancer. Pencil and ink drawings depicting the motions covered every page, read from top to bottom, then left to right, in uneven columns.

Easy and quick incantations allowed Ash to reconnect with the little Salamander strength he still had lurking inside, luring it out in manageable pieces through wrist flicks, finger wriggles, head cricks and shoulder shimmies. Tensing his abs increased concentration. Relaxing facial muscles eased fluidity.

He'd forgotten what such childish Elemental games were capable of when rolled off the back of one another, interconnected for rapid bursts and attacks. Ash could not only form marble-sized fireballs with a wrist flick followed by an open-and-close palm—capable of penetrating a ship's hull in the blink of an eye—but the book also re-taught him to use his own body heat and that of people nearby to increase reach and sustain his ammunition for longer. All he needed was friction or, like a Psychomancer, physical contact. Those nights in Open Country Ash spent freezing and alone, he now regretted. They were unnecessary; in his memories was the knowledge to have made those days and snowy evenings bearable, had he only wound them back far enough to his childhood.

Ash's attack was effective. There were men in the water and fires burning all over the ship's deck, sails, and even its mascot. But the cannon was still firing, wiping out buildings in the fortress's compound and injuring its Guardsmen. Another building fell. Another man was crushed.

Fuming, Ash swished a hand over the pages to find something more complex that would push the ship back out to sea and out of range without tempting his curse. In response, it offered him a three-step incantation involving a wind-up motion from his knees, through his hips, his upper chest and his head. Almost like a worm, Ash would arch his body first, drawing with him damp from the air, then on the exhale, he would rock forward onto the balls of his feet and push with as much force as he could muster.

Wind. Collect. Push.

This would lift and force the water away, carrying the ship and its crew from the First Watchtower and back into the Tradeway to give them time to evacuate.

Nobody else needs to suffer or die.

Ash rubbed his hands together, eager to practise. He dived straight in, following the steps. In a fluid motion, he performed the incantation, sucking the water up in a huge tidal wave and throwing it back out to sea. The water roared as the wave crashed in upon itself, draining the dock of every drop. Without water, the Cerulean Grace lay semi-capsized on the seabed, but Ash knew when the water returned, she'd be afloat again. Surrounding it, fish flopped and flapped. They gasped for breath, and Ash panicked with them.

"WATCH OUT!" Deerbolt shrieked.

Ash hadn't accounted for the friction caused by his quick, excitable hand-warming exercise. Inadvertently, he'd added a fourth step to his incantation, expanding the severity of the wave and the rate at which it would return. Careening towards the fortress, almost twice the height of the tallest, thickest wall and half-way up the Keep's remaining structure, was a tsunami.

When he turned to warn her to get Kite and Reverie to safety, she was already gone. Deerbolt headed straight for the barracks, screaming their names, until Reverie appeared first, followed by her husband. Deerbolt took Reverie by the hand and led them both towards the Keep; if they could manage to climb to the top in time, they'd have a chance at staying dry, or at least, not being dragged under with the current and carried out to sea.

Ash watched as they went inside, then turned to face the gigantic wall of water now only a mile offshore. He swallowed hard. The book wasn't offering any strategies for reversing this error—that's exactly what it was, an innocent mistake. His intentions were pure, he just wasn't skilled enough yet as an Undine to know creating friction affected water, too. The speed of his gesture rather than the heat had obviously ramped up the force of the wave.

And what goes up, must come down.

Deerbolt, Kite, and Reverie were out of sight, but the top of Sarronious's head could be seen as he charged up the winding stone staircase inside the Keep when he passed through a portion of its exterior that was now missing, thanks to a cannonball. Guardsmen bailed off the wall, risking broken bones and bruises to escape the tidal wave.

It crashed over the Cerulean Grace, lifting her hull up and over the docks and forcing her uphill, straight for where Ash was standing above the gate. The force at which it propelled Deerbolt's whole world was unforgiving. Ash could only close his eyes and wait to die, keeping tight hold of the book in front of him, praying to the Gods for a miracle. Maybe when they recovered his body—if they ever did—they could prise it from his fingers and return it safely to Raven's library.

He hoped the old man was hiding somewhere secure, too, but had no doubt the water would find its way inside and destroy his paper. Ash didn't know what to do, and he didn't want to cause so many deaths and so much destruction, not when he was their only possible saviour.

"What should I do?" he asked the book as he pulled it to his chest. "Help me! PLEASE!"

Suddenly, the humongous wall of water smacked against the fortress's wall, throwing men off the top and into the now-flooded courtyard. Ash dived down behind in time to miss the force of the initial contact, sitting within a small, temporarily protected space as the circular grounds filled like a soup bowl. Behind him, the Cerulean Grace was mere meters away. Before Ash could make his next decision, it was on him, ploughing straight through the wall. It collapsed a large, thick part of the front defences and wiped him off his perch backwards.

"I can't swim!"

"Help me!"

"Somebody, please!"

Ash heard men calling from all directions. He witnessed some disappear beneath the water and not resurface, as others swam to save their horse or a fellow Guardsman. From above, Reverie's tiny voice could be heard trying to direct him to a rooftop not yet submerged or destroyed by the weight of Deerbolt's ship. Still trying to save his book, Ash kicked his feet frantically and shimmied his shoulders to propel himself forward.

Salt stung his eyes and his lungs burned as he puffed and gasped to the rooftop. He called for a few men to follow him to safety. Others swam behind in a chain of survivors.

But the water was getting higher and faster.

He *had* to do something. Quickly.

Ash lodged the book on the rooftop and used it to anchor his body weight to that spot, then he hauled himself up. Water sloshed across the area, making the angled roof of the barracks slippery. He wasn't too far from the Grace now, which was lodged between the main gate and the stables on his left. Most of the water was getting in because of it and through the metal grid blocking the main entrance, too.

Ash wiped his eyes on his sleeve and narrowed them, searching for Raven's familiar face in one of the higher windows. He spotted Deerbolt ushering Kite and Reverie higher, then again in the window above. They clamped eyes. But, there was no sign of the old man. He was so sure there was another Alchemical presence supporting him in the water, but how, when Raven was a Slyph?

She gestured using a pushing motion that Ash needed to remove the Cerulean Grace from its imprisonment and pointed it out to sea. This would allow them to sail again, but would also let out the water collected in the fortress grounds. He nodded, but there would be no point shouting back and forth—the chaos was too loud, Ash could barely hear himself think.

He struggled to his feet, sliding a few metres before his boots got a sturdy grip, then opened the book again and held it aloft, trying to keep the final few pages dry. They were already soggy and stuck together, but still readable and, once dried, he imagined they'd be crinkled but useful—*if* he could keep it from floating away completely!

Remembering not to create any friction this time, Ash re-performed his incantation and directed his attention at the Grace's mascot, the God of the Senses. He urged her to reverse, thrusting the current beneath the hull to gently manoeuvrer her back downhill to the docks, or close enough. Keeping one hand flat to balance the book open, he used the other to guide his power. It was a little clumsy at first, but Ash got used to the way the water moved and reacted to his orders, and he was able to do the job of two hands with only his left. The Grace creaked and rocked as the Elemental Alchemy tickled it, then spread around the hull and through the gap in the wall. He fought with the motion for a few minutes, then felt something give. Unplugged, the Grace backed out and turned gently, then floated on a swollen river of water back to the dock. Ash and the men beside him gaped as the water exited through the damaged wall as a smooth waterfall. Debris and three bodies floated past.

Overall, casualties seemed to have been at a minimum.

"Thank you," said the bowman who'd helped him earlier, and he slapped Ash on the back.

He scowled. "Don't thank me, thank the Gods."

"You were trying to help us," the man said.

He grunted. "Look where that got us."

Ash appreciated what the bowman was trying to do, but it didn't make him feel any better about messing up the Undine incantation. If he'd argued less with Raven and spent more time studying, this would never have happened.

The bowman waited until the water had drained, then helped the others down from the barracks' roof. Ash handed him the book first and immediately felt naked without it, then, feet first, he lowered himself to solid ground. The grass was still waterlogged and squishy, but Ash's mistake hadn't caused any more damage to the buildings. That had mostly been the Order's doing. They now had a huge hole in the fortress wall they didn't have before, and three fewer Guardsmen to protect what remained of the First Watchtower if the Order tried another attack.

"Captain Deerbolt is going to be furious with me," Ash told the bowman. "It's not the first time I've damaged her ship and

I'm sure it won't be the last."

"If you hadn't acted, the Cerulean Grace would have been completely pillaged and destroyed, and we'd all be dead. We got off lightly."

"She won't see it that way."

The bowman grinned. He shook Ash's hand firmly, then set off towards the Keep where Kite, Reverie, Sarronious and Captain Deerbolt were waiting for him. Ash wasn't in a hurry to rejoin them; their expressions were of disappointment, fear, and exhaustion. Deerbolt probably regarded him as a foolish idiot by now, and might refuse to take him any further, if the Cerulean Grace was still in a fit state to sail.

She beckoned him over. He responded, dragging his boots through several inches of mud and sludge, bits of seaweed and a few dead fish.

"Are you alright?" she asked.

Ash nodded, then turned to Kite and Reverie. "Are you?"

"Swell," Kite grumbled, "but I'd rather that be the extent of this journey's *excitement*... for now."

"Me too," Ash replied and slapped Kite hard on the shoulder. "I'm sorry about that."

Reverie smiled. "It's alright. We're alive, aren't we? You did your best."

"My best wasn't good enough," he said. "Is Raven safe, too?"

Deerbolt nodded and moved aside to allow Sarronious to get back to work. He pushed through, knocking into Ash purposefully to express his disdain, then barked orders at a bunch of her deckhands to return to the Grace and check for damage.

"I deserved that."

"He'll cool off," Deerbolt told him. "What's important is we're all still in one piece, and we can set sail at dawn."

"So soon? What about the First Watchtower?" Reverie asked, surprised she didn't want to stay and help them rebuild.

"We're needed elsewhere," she told her, "and the Guard

may not want us here when they bury their dead."

"I see," Reverie whispered, then led Kite back to the barracks. "We should gather our things."

When they had gone, Ash turned to Deerbolt and sighed. "Alright, tell me the truth. We're in deep trouble, aren't we?"

Deerbolt shrugged. "I think we would be worse off had you not intervened, personally."

"You're not serious?"

"Deathly."

"But I killed three people, knocked down a thousand and something-year-old wall, and almost destroyed your livelihood." Ash rubbed his head with his knuckles. "I can't be their new favourite Elemental."

"Without you, the Order would have killed thirty, maybe more. They'd have blown more of this fortress to smithereens and the Grace would have been pillaged, burned, and sunk. You and I would be dead, if not captured and imprisoned for slavery or worse. The Guardsmen here are smart—they know you saved them," she finished, her mouth pressed into a thin line.

"Doesn't make me feel any better," Ash said.

Out of the corner of his eye to his right, Ash saw the bodies of the three drowned Guardsmen being wrapped in cloth and laid out for mourning.

In the tradition of the watchtowers, their bodies would remain close to the location of death, so those fighting alongside would have a chance to pay their respects. This period usually only lasted a day or two, before they were ceremonially cremated on a large wooden pyre. A Salamander Elemental often helped with that stage, but the First Watchtower hadn't had a Guardsman with the ability for many years now. They also hadn't had a death in half as many, so it hadn't mattered much that the flame came from a firepit or a torch rather than one of their brothers.

Now Ash was here, he considered offering his services because it was the least he could do. But, after Deerbolt's earlier remarks, he wasn't sure their killer would be welcome at the funeral, let alone the one to send them to Akasha or wherever their souls were destined to go.

"I'll gather my remaining crew and have them bring supplies to the Grace for our voyage to the Northern Trading Post."

"What about Raven?" he asked.

Deerbolt scowled. "What about him?"

"Is he coming with us? The library—"

"Don't worry about the library. Raven keeps his most precious editions locked away."

Ash was relieved. His shoulders relaxed. "Will you be sad to leave him behind again? Why not bring him with us? He's knowledgeable, he could help to train me."

"No, Raven is too set in his ways and he's happy here," she whispered, then winked. "He's been through enough, anyway. Raven and I will see each other again. I'm sure."

Ash lowered his head, hoping that was true.

Deerbolt inhaled sharply, grinned, then said, "No more moping around here. Hop to it, *Scoundrel*, we have work to do, and we sail at dawn."

She gave his backside a firm pat, jolting him from his depression. Ash's brow lifted and he sucked his lips, wide-eyed and wondering if that gesture was intended as anything but a motivator.

Ash watched her leave and re-adjusted his grip on the book, then checked the key was still safely around his neck. The ribbon was sodden and stuck to his skin, but the key dangled in place, glowing whenever Ash thought about using his powers, or of times he already had. It was as if he and the key were made for one another, and that ancient bit of metal could read his thoughts. The key was the key to his Tetrad inheritance, it seemed.

The key is the key, Ash remembered Raven saying, and only when he truly embraced who and what he was, knowing it could protect those he loved and make a real difference, did its abilities ignite.

Trying not to make eye contact with passing Guardsmen, Ash removed himself from the fortress grounds and headed downhill to the Cerulean Grace. He left behind the damage he'd caused and the lives he'd taken, but held his head high as he thought about the evil he had prevented, and would continue to if he could perfect a few more incantations. He hadn't tried to use his Gnome powers yet. He wasn't sure, but he may have tapped into his Slyph powers when he pushed the Grace back out to sea. Either that, or Raven had been assisting from somewhere high and dry.

I didn't get to say goodbye, he realised, peering back over his shoulder at the devastation. But it didn't matter—he and Raven had already exhausted the extent of their relationship. The old man had given him everything he needed to keep Deerbolt safe from this point forth, and for that, he would be forever grateful.

I never was that great at saying goodbye, anyway.

CHAPTER ELEVEN
A CARTOMANCER'S CURSE

O
THE FOOL.

XI
JUSTICE.

XX
JUDGEMENT.

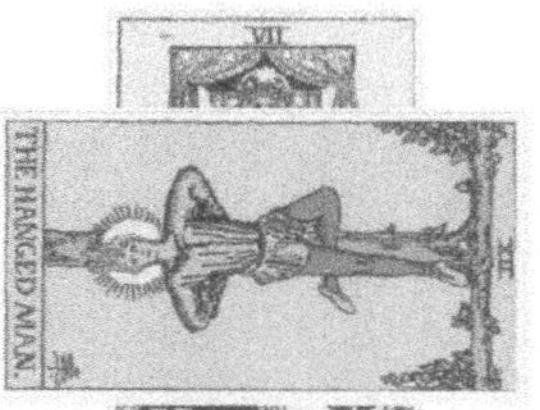
VII
THE HANGED MAN.
XII
THE CHARIOT.

VI
THE LOVERS.

XIII
DEATH.

I
THE MAGICIAN.

IX
THE HERMIT.

XVI
THE TOWER.

XV
THE DEVIL.

Chapter Eleven: A Cartomancer's Curse

Ash boarded the Cerulean Grace and braced himself. Would he face a broken mast, more holes in the deck, a damaged mascot or worse, a hole in the ship's hull? A breach would mean they'd take on water, and she couldn't sail to the Northern Trading Post if they'd sink or capsize. Deerbolt wouldn't risk it.

He was surprised to find the ship in one piece, except for the odd bump and scrape to the wooden panelling and a rip in one of the lower masts. Items were strewn everywhere, barrels had spilt and everything was soaking wet, but otherwise, the Grace was ready and able to sail at dawn.

Sarronious halted Ash as he hopped up on deck, de-tangling his foot from the last rung of the wooden rope ladder and groaning.

Could this day get any worse?

"I need to speak with you."

Ash barged past him, cuddling the damp book to his chest. "Not now." He sighed.

"I *said*—"

“I heard what you said,” Ash snapped, storming towards Deerbolt's cabin, between two deckhands busy tidying the poop deck. He dodged boxes and chests on his way there, all of which should have been secured with the rest of the cargo.

“We need to talk.”

“Aye, she's expecting me, Sarronious.” Ash grumbled.

“No, you and *I* need to talk.”

“About what?”

Ash didn't bother to turn around. He continued walking to make it absolutely clear to Sarronious he didn't have the time nor patience for his games. He knew the smitten First Mate would do everything in his power to have Ash banished from the voyage after the stunt he pulled, though it was accidental. Then, he'd be in with a chance at wooing the Captain, who he so obviously loved.

“About what you did back there.”

“It was dumb, and I'm sorry. Deerbolt is over it. So should you be.”

“I'm not trying to berate you,” Sarronious finally said, and Ash stopped abruptly.

Wait, he *wasn't*? This gigantic, over-protective sailor wasn't about to hold him responsible for damaging the First Watchtower's defences and ruining their lives?

“I wanted to thank you,” he said, a little sheepishly.

He didn't want the other men on board to hear him give in to this reckless Elemental—Sarronious was all about asserting dominance and power over them.

“You saved our lives.” He swallowed hard, then corrected himself. “You saved *her* life. Takes a brave man to reveal he's a Tetrad—something that could get him killed or make him a target, for selfless reasons. I wanted you to know we all appreciate it.”

Ash didn't know what to say, so he opted not to say anything. He nodded and half-smiled.

“For what it's worth, I don't think what you did was dumb, Ash. I think it was incredible, and something none of us have ever seen, nor will ever see again. Tetrads are—"

"We're rare."

We, Ash thought. He owned it.

He grinned. "I'm not in full control of the other elements yet, but I'm learning." Ash adjusted his grip on the book and tapped the cover. "A gift from Raven."

"Is that how you were able to form the tsunami?"

"Hmm," Ash responded, then shuddered at the memory of its enormous weight heading straight for everything he knew and its intent on destroying his new life, however brief it had been.

Ash set off walking, but Sarronious stopped him again.

"Is the girl alright?"

"You mean Reverie?" Ash asked.

"Aye."

"Safe and well. She and her husband should already be onboard, or heading this way soon. They are still our priority, don't worry."

"And your powers?"

Ash frowned. "What about them?"

"Can we expect any further... accidents?"

Ash screwed up his nose and shrugged. "Let's see, shall we?"

"Aye." Sarronious grinned, then headed off to assist with the clean-up, leaving Ash alone with his thoughts, and a huge smile on his face.

He sat for a while in Deerbolt's cabin, trying to prepare what he was going to say to her when she arrived. Before leaving the First Watchtower, she wanted to find Raven and say goodbye, and somehow find a Gnome to help rebuild the defences of the external wall. There weren't any Elementals in the Guard there as far as she was aware, but if she could get word to one of the nearby hamlets or even far enough inland to Liberty, she could send for help.

Though the thirty-foot moat was now overflowing with seawater, if the Order returned to find and kill them, the

Guardsmen would have a harder time defending the fortress without a way to keep out the Astrals. In an army formation, Astrals could suck the energy from a battlefield in seconds by conjuring a spirit from the Lingerverse to do their bidding. To their enemies, it would create a lifeless vacuum, ripping the air from their lungs and strangling them to feed that spirit.

Feeding a spirit did nothing to affect their death, however. Once a soul had died, there was no way to bring them back to life no matter how much energy they consumed when an Astral opened that window. What it did was quite the opposite and self-defeating. An Astral conjured a Lingerverse spirit by weakening the barrier between the Land and Akasha, allowing them to reach in and pull a soul at random. The soul's energy in the Lingerverse existed on another plain, and so whilst it had no effect on the soul's capabilities there, it gave an Astral a boost in strength and confidence here. Using that energy meant the soul would be weaker, so they needed to feed on the energy of another living thing through proximity. Doing that boosted the soul's energy, which boosted the Astral's energy, which then drained that soul again.

Sadly, no matter what that soul did to survive the Astral's enslavement, they would always be weaker when they were finally released, if ever. By choosing not to release a soul, the Astral was dooming them to break down and disappear completely from existence.

No more Land. No more Lingerverse. No more Akasha.

Nothingness.

It was a barbaric act. Unfortunately, some Astrals didn't care about the consequences of using the same soul for too long. They allowed them to expire before moving on to another. But, the most skilled Astrals—those who tended to either work higher in the Order's government or refuse to join the Order completely—knew it was safer and easier, even, to soul-hop from one spirit to another.

The Lingerverse's plain ran parallel to the Land's, but it was not visible to anyone unless they were able to use Sciomancy to peer through the barrier between worlds and listen in on the rumours and memories those souls held. Some took secrets to their grave, but those secrets were easily accessible to Sciomancers. When an Astral soul-hopped, they could move around normally and conjure spirits to aid their business as they did so, then leave them behind and rapidly claim another. This form of Alchemy prevented those souls from tiring or vaporising, whilst still fuelling the Astral's energy and benefiting from the spirit's influence all the same.

Ash hoped Deerbolt had been successful. He didn't want to be on the fortress's end of an attack from so many angry Astrals of the Order.

He wasn't alone for more than an hour before Deerbolt returned to her quarters.

He smiled. “Had an interesting talk with Sarron—”

Without greeting Ash, she let down her hair and took off her boots, which were caked up the soles and laces in mud and seaweed. Ash wasn't able to finish his sentence before Deerbolt was on him, her lips pressed tightly to his and her arms wrapped around his neck. He pulled her to him and felt her chest relax against his.

She kicked back with a bare foot and slammed the cabin door closed.

The sun seemed to rise in a blink, and the light burned Ash's eyes when he stepped out of the cabin at midday. The Cerulean Grace was well on her way to the

Northern Trading Post, and the crew were excited to replenish their supplies of ale and bread, fruit and weaponry. Some of their items had been washed overboard during the tidal wave, and some had been destroyed by water in other ways.

He missed turning over and seeing Deerbolt's peaceful sleeping face beside him. Her long black hair was plaited again which meant she was already deep in giving orders and commanding her crew. The Grace was picking up speed; she wasn't wasting any time putting distance between them and the Order's ship. So far, they hadn't seen its sails on the horizon.

"Good morning." Ash beamed.

Deerbolt handed him a cup of tea and blushed. "Sleep well?"

Ash lowered his eyes and grinned. "Did you?"

They stared at one another for a few minutes in silence—a private, cheeky conversation ongoing through their body language—before Deerbolt gestured at a young woman Ash hadn't met.

"This is Brogan."

Ash shook the woman's hand. She had a firm grip, and was taller than him, though she wore heeled boots. A long, ochre coat graced her thin body, and wavy blonde-brown hair covered the collar and decorated her shoulders beneath a hood.

"She's a Cartomancer."

Surprised, Ash tore his hand away. "Uhm..."

"Don't worry," Brogan said, taking no offence. "I'm not an Oracle. Touch does nothing to aid my gift. Shall we?"

Ash glared at Deerbolt through dark, narrow eyes. "Shall we what?"

"I'm going to finish your reading, Ash the Elemental."

"Finish it? You and I have never done business, Brogan," he reminded her, glaring at Deerbolt.

"Cartomancy is both a blessing and a curse. I am ready and willing to give this a try if you are."

"Give *what* a try?"

Deerbolt chuckled. "She's going to read the rest of the Oracle's predictions for you, Ash. I've already warned her you can be a handful."

Ash's lips down-turned. "You can do that?"

"Your fortune is your fortune no matter who reads it," she explained, winking. "Hate the message, not the messenger."

"I borrowed Brogan from her travels to the First Watchtower. She was there to see Raven," Deerbolt said.

"Oh, you know Raven?"

Brogan nodded. "Aye; he's an *interesting* guy."

"Understatement."

She laughed. "Raven and I go way back. I once had a few questions about Elemental magic, and Raven was my first choice. Your Captain has permitted me passage to Land's Edge lots of times. I hitched a ride at the last minute to get away from the chaos. I hope that's okay?"

"It is if your cards can tell me I'm not a dead man."

Deerbolt put an arm around the Seer and the two women giggled over something Ash wasn't yet privy to. He wasn't sure he liked or trusted this stranger, despite Deerbolt promising she was a friend, and of Raven's, too.

"I decided not to stay at the Watchtower when I saw what you'd done to it," Brogan started, then continued through Ash's protests, "and then I saw Deerbolt coming through the gate and asked if I could come."

"I thought she could be helpful," Deerbolt said, then kissed Ash on the cheek and went straight back to work. "Be nice, Ash."

"I'm always nice."

Brogan gestured for him to head back to Deerbolt's cabin, where she could lay her Tarot cloth and the cards atop the bedspread. He told her about the four cards the marketplace Oracle pulled before he'd set sail at Blackheart Dock, but he needn't have bothered; Brogan had already removed them from her deck and laid them all in the correct places. To the side, she'd placed *the Fool*. It identified Ash overall—as he had acted so far. Then, in the centre, she placed *the Hanged Man*, crossed with *the Chariot*. His current situation, and that which blocked his path now. To their left, to represent his past, she selected *Justice*.

The next card to pull would go above the others, and represented what Ash was conscious of. Brogan fanned the cards and allowed him to select his own. They worked better when they could identify their user.

"*Judgement*," she said. "Do I need to explain?"

Judgement was a beautiful Tarot card, depicting *the Fool* releasing their inner spirit. In this Seer's deck, *the Fool* was a woman, but it varied depending on the Cartomancer and the artist who'd designed the cards for them. If they inherited a deck from a relative, which happened occasionally, Seers would normally enlist someone to make them a pack from scratch. A deck needed to belong to the Seer to truly read their fortune, and the fortunes of those seeking the Seer's help. Second-hand decks were useful, but not connected to the Seer enough to give a deeply personal reading. So, they were often vague.

Judgement here was an emerald green colour, with a woman who looked like Reverie releasing all the negative things she thought about herself.

Ash had seen this card crop up before, though he hadn't pulled it in a long time. It made sense, though.

The card (when upright rather than pulled upside down), represented an awakening of some sort. It symbolised rebirth and revival, self-awareness, and the outcome of a personal evaluation. Ash had been doing a lot of thinking recently, and he'd accepted his new life as a Tetrad; something that, until now, existed in his subconscious. It was up to him to find and follow this new purpose, and to do it without lying to himself that he was anything but a powerful and rare Elemental.

"I'm familiar with the card."

"Then we can move on."

Brogan didn't waste time. She fanned the cards out again without shuffling them, and gave Ash time to carefully pick his eighth Tarot card. In this position, whatever he chose next would represent Ash's future.

Ash pulled *Death*.

Usually, this card was a terrifying sight, depicting a skeleton in black robes with a sickle coming to take the individual to their afterlife. Most people would worry about *Death* being in their future. But not Ash. Because he already knew.

“You do not seem surprised.”

“I'm not,” Ash told her. “I'm cursed and deteriorating every day. These new powers I'm using are useful to others, but they are draining what little energy I have. It's why I need to learn the basics so I can still help before my time is up, without it happening prematurely.”

“I see,” she said, then took a deep breath before offering Ash a much kinder explanation of this card.

In her deck, it was a pretty pink-red shade, and the cloaked figure was not a skeleton but what appeared to be a beautiful night sky, with stars and potential. The card almost breathed, which Ash found unusual for something that represented an end.

“I am sure you will be pleased to hear this card does not always mean you are destined to die.”

Ash was ecstatic to learn the card in this position actually merely represented the end of something, of letting go and moving on. It symbolised a transition, that's all.

“Death is a beginning, wrapped cosily within an ending,” Brogan explained. “It's a beautiful, peaceful card, and one that tells me something troubling is about to cease, and a transformation is going to occur. This transformation must be linked to you because these cards are yours, but it may not mean the death is your own.”

“And death doesn't necessarily mean...” Ash pulled his index finger across his neck to suggest a beheading and made a CRKKK noise.

She chuckled behind her palm and shook her head.

"That's a load off."

She held up a finger of warning. "But, it does not always mean survival, either. *Death* can, sometimes, simply mean death, and the start of a period of mourning for our loved ones."

He thought about Deerbolt, and how she might feel if the curse won and he was forced to leave her forever. His chest tightened.

"Pull another," she said, offering him the deck again. "This card will tell me what has settled in your unconscious mind, what has always been present, but not necessarily useful... until now."

Ash closed his eyes this time, still thinking about his night in Deerbolt's bed, which had been destined to happen, and he wanted it to happen again and again so badly, he couldn't clear the image of her soft skin from his mind.

Not so surprisingly, Ash pulled *the Lovers* card next. Brogan's deck displayed two bare people entwined by their hair, one baring a bow and arrow tattoo and the other grinning. It looked like such a romantic card.

"What does the arrow symbolise?" Ash asked, tapping the tattoo on the man's forearm.

"You are struck with emotion!" Brogan began, "And, you have been thinking a lot about choices and commitment, but until recently pushed related decisions to the back of your mind, believing you could do nothing to influence the outcome. In the upright position here, *the Lovers* is a card that symbolises love and duality. It is unconditional. Trusting. Affectionate. Whomever this card relates to in your life, you empower one another in a beautiful, complimentary way."

"Deerbolt and I have a strong working relationship," He cleared his throat. "Can we move on?"

"Aye."

Brogan beamed; it was nice to see a client so happy with

the outcome of a reading, particularly when *the Lovers* appeared in that position. More often than not, people were desperately in love and not quite willing to admit it to themselves. When they did, it was stunning and special to be a part of—to prompt.

The following four cards were more about Ash as a person, and began with the way he saw himself, followed by the way others saw him.

Internal vs external.

Some Cartomancers placed them in a line running from bottom to top on the right of the others, and some placed them in a square. It seemed Brogan was one of those Seers.

Ash pulled these two cards together as they were so similar. Effectively, two sides to the story. The card to identify how he saw himself was *the Hermit*, and the card to identify how others saw him right now was *the Magician.*

“As I expected,” Ash commented when he saw the lonely girl sitting on the mountaintop, with only her own soul's glow for company.

The Hermit was a lonely card, and reflected Ash's search for wisdom, likely linked to the Tetrad book he now possessed. Brogan's version was aqua with a golden character on a steep hill, with only one rocky staircase leading to her perch.

“You are withdrawing, retreating within yourself,” she told Ash. “I think unintentionally you are doing the opposite; your gift is blossoming, and your circle of friends widening. Your inner lantern illuminates your mistakes, and these you focus on too strongly. Mistakes are supposed to be made, because that is how we develop and mature.”

Ash grunted. “I killed three people.”

She argued, “And saved countless others. Do not let the quiet consume you, so you dwell endlessly on your wrongdoings, Ash. Introspection will only achieve so much.”

“And others seeing me as a magician... is a joke?”

She paused, then replied, “What do you see here?”

Brogan graced her hands across the spread. Ash followed them but said nothing, holding a blank expression.

"These cards are *all* major arcana."

"Is that bad?"

"Rare."

He began chewing his nails. "Don't your other clients pull major arcana cards?"

She sighed. "Not without minor arcana cards intermingling. The cup, sword, pentacle and wand cards are all more common because there are more of them; one has more chance of pulling some, if not all, minors."

"But your skill is not based on luck," he said flatly.

"Exactly. Your fortune is your fortune. If it requires major cards, there is nothing I can do to intervene. I have never done a reading like this before. Not in thirty years."

"You're how old?"

She smiled but said nothing. She didn't need to. Most Seers began practising at six or seven years old, so she was thirty-six or thirty-seven years old according to his calculations. She looked mid-twenties, though.

"*The Magician* is a card I've pulled before."

"It is a creative, manifestation card."

Ash added, "And a powerful Alchemical one."

"They are all powerful and Alchemical. *The Magician* slightly more so. This card represents *the Fool* turning into a key."

"A key?"

She nodded. "To all magic, aye. You can create the life you so desire. You alone. You have the skill. You have the power. Others now know you are a Tetrad. They understand what you are capable of. You hold their adoration and fear."

The card was brightly coloured, covered in symbols and lights. In it, a hooded man controlled four streams of starlight, which Ash thought corresponded to his Elemental abilities: earth, air, fire and water. On the man's arm was also a spiritual symbol. Ash had heard rumours that there were, in fact, five elements and not four, as recognised by the God of the Land: earth, air, fire, water and *spirit*.

CHAPTER TWELVE

THE TOWER

Chapter Twelve: The Tower

Hopes and fears were dominant in Ash's mind, more so the fear of death than the hope of a future. He wasn't at all stunned to see *the Devil* in this position, with its open palm, beckoning him to take the character's hand and be led astray. This card was Ash's *shadow self*, the term a Cartomancer used to recognise Ash's dark side.

What had he repressed? How did he indulge? What was he manically addicted to?

"*The Devil* comes when you are at your lowest," Brogan went on to explain. "He offers you many gifts, temptations and promises. Sometimes, we cannot resist him. But *you*, Ash the Elemental, must see through these niceties. You hope for a future though you believe you face only death; this curse you speak of masks the truth, and so you are allowing *the Devil* to lead you blindly, praying that by accepting your fate, you can numb your pain. We both know that is futile."

The cabin seemed suddenly darker. The candles didn't quite offer the same comfort and warmth they had a few cards ago, when he'd pulled *the Lovers*. The melted wax at their base was ominous, and spilt over to form cream icicles.

"There are parts of your past that cause you great shame.

You loathe who you once were and fear that man exists within you still, perhaps only in part. But you are learning to identify what scares you, and you are challenging these debilitating beliefs."

"So, I should confront my *shadow self*?"

"Aye, because in doing so it will lose its hold on you."

Would Ash feel free and alive if he was to release his past mistakes, and not allow the way they made him feel, or how they affected his present actions, to control him?

He grinned. It was an illuminating idea.

"Are you ready for your final card, Ash?"

He sat back and gestured she ought to draw this for him. If the pattern so far had taught him anything, it was to expect a major arcana card, something life-changing and eye-opening. This last spot on the cloth was where his reading concluded. The outcome.

Brogan wasted no time. She flipped the top card, and Ash faced the misunderstood image of *the Tower.*

The Tower, in Brogan's deck, was a grassy hill, alive and pretty in oranges and greens. Animals pranced, but they seemed scared, because a bolt of lightning had struck the peak, and rocks were crumbling. Were they happy to be living in the safest part at the foot of the hill, or were they actually fleeing? Ash pondered the implications of this card. So often, it was assumed your life would come crumbling down around you, when in fact, *the Tower* was a new beginnings card. It could point to a crisis, but most likely, it symbolised a sudden change—destruction must occur to purify something else.

This was how Brogan explained the card to Ash.

Overall, it was a gloomy idea and it created a sense of moodiness in the cabin as Ash came to terms with what aspect of his existence would need to tumble in order to rebuild elsewhere. Not his relationship with Deerbolt, surely? Ash would do anything to keep her happy now; he couldn't—*wouldn't*—lose her to his stupidity again.

"In this position, Ash, I would consider your foundations;

think back to roots and beginnings. Why are you the way you are? Where did this Tetrad ability originate? And though what lies ahead may be chaotic and sporadic, a clear path can be forged through the dust and debris."

He sighed. "Things get worse before they get better."

"In essence, aye." She added, "Mayhem can also hide within your core values and beliefs. If what you have followed and trusted for so long is false or tarnished, this can tear down your infrastructure to make room for a fresh perspective. It may be as simple as assessing your religion."

"I don't actively follow any religion, not since leaving Dragonborn. But, I do trust in the old ways."

Brogan took his hand then, unexpectedly. Ash didn't recoil. He found her touch comforting. Though Ash didn't want to hear much of what she'd said, it was her curse to know and to speak it. Nothing was her fault—only Ash could act upon the messages she delivered.

"Your time as a Guardsman doesn't have to be painful," she whispered. "Trust instead, in *the Tower.* Things happen for a reason, and there is always a reaction to every action. *The Tower* symbolises that reaction."

"I understand."

She patted his hand, then retreated to her deck.

In eleven Tarot cards, Ash had witnessed a visual expression of his life from past to present, conscious to unconscious, and through his emotions. Brogan allowed him a moment more to view the layout, then gathered the cards to shuffle and place them back in her coat pocket.

There were more pleasant cards to pull, for sure. Ash had hoped for *the Page of Wands* (enthusiasm, adventure and exploration), or maybe *the Three of Cups* (friendship and celebration). He'd have settled for a sword card—at least with a sword, he'd expect a conflict, and conflict was... survivable. He could cope well with a disagreement, or a fight. Fights, Ash often won. But swords were air cards, and in the Elemental world, he would have been more likely to pull wands, the fiery and energetic, creative and passionate side of any Tarot deck. Raven, being a Slyph, would have been prone to swords, and with his argumentative nature, Ash could see those being an ideal fit. His, however, were *not*. Ash was not at all creative, and he did not have much willpower, especially since leaving Dragonborn.

On the Grace and at the First Watchtower, Ash used Undine abilities. Water went well with cup cards. Was something like *the Three of Cups* too much to ask?

"You are saddened by your reading," Brogan speculated.

"I'm not sure what I expected, to be honest."

"Wands, pages and numerology-wise, I'd say... rather early. Like aces or fives, at a push?"

Ash gasped. "That's *incredible*. How do you know all this, just by looking at a bunch of illustrations?"

"You're a Salamander," she said, then chortled. "And I've been doing this over thirty years. Give me credit."

"Sorry."

"Here's the thing about wands, Ash, they spark life and they fuel energy. As a Tetrad, you'd have been closer with pentacles, because these five-pointed stars connect us to the material world around us. Oh, and to nature."

Confused by the material part of her definition, Ash asked Brogan to elaborate on how that aligned with *his* truth. She added pentacles were often associated with possessions and property or jewels. Ash was head-to-head with the Order right now, and they wanted nothing more than to absorb the Land's resources. Pentacles were his life at the moment.

"And if I read Raven's cards, they would've been swords mostly, because these are intellect and knowledge-focused. He spends his time reading and imparting all he learns to travellers."

"That's Raven," Ash agreed, smiling.

"Now you're getting it. And our Captain Deerbolt, should I get the chance to read her Tarot cards on this voyage, may pull mostly cups. They are emotive and instinctive. Cups are mysterious, and correlate to water. Deerbolt lives out here on the sea. She has given second chances—given *life*—to so many lost souls. Raven, Kite, Reverie and, of course, yourself. Water is life."

Now, he understood. Cartomancers could use what they knew about you already to better interpret the cards you pulled. A more in-depth explanation would then be offered. If the client and the Seer were strangers, Ash thought, they could offer definitions and examples, but it would be up to the client to bond each image to their circumstances.

The minor arcana numerology cards ranged from ace to ten, and were then followed by a suit of four court cards: the page, the knight, the queen, and the king. In Tarot terms, Ash was semi-familiar with how the numbers represented life experiences, and the court cards were archetypes for family and corresponding roles played. Queens were motherly. Pages were childish. And so on. But suits were, at the centre, elemental.

"More complicated than reading tea leaves," he murmured, much to Brogan's amusement.

"The Oracle offered you a classic spread," she continued, "which can be used without having to ask you questions prior to the reading."

"He didn't," Ash confirmed. "I helped him and in return I think he felt it was his duty to read my cards, to warn me about upcoming *options*."

"And you resisted?"

Ash shrugged. "A little. I'm not sure I believe Tarot is as spiritual as Seers make out."

Brogan nodded and inhaled, winding up to offer Ash insider's information into the world of Tarot. She gestured he lean in, though they were the only Alchemists in the room, and whispered in his ear.

"Tarot itself is not spiritual," she admitted. "Just like tea leaves and palms are not. These are a means to offer personal insight, to guide a client into studying and assessing their life as it stands—their past mistakes and the future, such as ways to correct the evil within them, or to meet their goals. Tarot was not born with the Dragons and their Alchemy, Ash, it was an ancient game Humans played long before, which Seers have adapted as a comfortable and friendly *delivery* system."

"To deliver what?" Ash asked, frowning.

Seers were Alchemists *because* of their abilities to read a person's past, present and future, which was Alchemical and spiritual. How else would the Seer be able to learn so much about their clients? How did they know what you had done and were about to do—to deliver what we have seen? Seeing is within us; our choice of outlet brands us a Cartomancer, a Hydromancer or a Chiromancer." She winked, then added, "So you're right to believe Tarot is not mystical. The cards don't predict what's going to happen to you and those you love. *We* predict this, and we instruct the cards to communicate it so you can understand; it is an Alchemical conversation—a relationship, if you will—between the Seer and their method."

Ash offered a half-grin and reached out to shake Brogan's hand. She had clarified a lot and given him much more to think about. He wished he could get his hands on a deck of his own to better study the illustrations and get a feel for hidden meanings. Receiving a reading *had* helped him, but he and the Seer were always limited by time, or space, or his work. In the past, Ash's readings were sometimes only a few minutes long and in a simpler three-card spread, or a single one.

Of them all, Ash was mostly curious about *the Tower.* In his heart, this no doubt correlated to what Ash would give up when they arrived at the Isle of Dragonborn. His life, perhaps. Any rebuilding to follow would be done by those he'd be leaving behind: Deerbolt, Sarronious, Kite, Reverie and their baby. In his head, this more likely referred to the existence of Alchemy, and that surviving Dragon egg. The Oracle in the marketplace said Ash was at the centre of magic's future, and dying in a rather sad, pathetic, and anti-climactic way at the hands of some angry Guardsman seemed... wasted.

Brogan left Ash to his thoughts. Readings tired her, and his had been quite difficult. She retired to a hammock below deck.

Ash sat for about an hour, feeling the gentle pulse of the ship as it sailed toward the Northern Trading Post, and thought about his next step. He needed to unlock the book again and learn some other incantations. Something that wouldn't drain too much of his energy or worsen the curse's symptoms, and something he'd remember in an emergency to control all four elements, should they be needed. He decided not to waste too much time on Salamander Alchemy, and instead turn to some Undine, Slyph and Gnome actions. After all, he'd had his whole life to know how to manipulate fire!

It seemed quiet on the poop deck, so Ash locked himself away until he heard stirring. The book responded well to Ash's commands, and the pages turned to show everything he needed. All the while, the key dangling around his neck glowed, offering additional light to read by, but also the comfort of knowing a higher source of power was beside him somehow.

He wished he'd asked Raven how the key and book worked in line with his Tetrad Alchemy, and if it would respond the same way to other Tetrads if they existed.

Shouts coaxed Ash from the cabin as they approached the Northern Trading Post. At the front of the ship, a few of the young deckhands were pointing, gathered around a tall thin man with a spyglass, who relayed what he could see to Captain Deerbolt on his right. Ash didn't have to ask what everyone was arguing over, because his Elemental fingers tingled at the sight and smell of burning. Since bonding with that book, Ash's body wanted to respond to the flames he saw licking and tickling the Northern Trading Post's only port.

"What happened?" Ash asked Deerbolt.

She shook her head and tapped her fingers methodically on the ship's side, thinking about how they would manage without the additional rations and what they could do to avoid meeting the same fate. The man with the spyglass advised there weren't any other ships in the water, there wasn't any debris floating, or men swimming ashore. All he could see was burning buildings, smouldering trees and shrubbery, and, when the haze cleared enough, bodies strewn along the roadside. This suggested the attack had come from inland, rather than from the sea.

"The Order is sending us a message," he said.

Deerbolt turned to him. "Message received."

She barged past and rallied her men to ready the cannons. Sensing the urgency in the tone of her booming voice, they scurried out of sight, immediately following instructions.

Kite and Reverie appeared at the base of the stairwell. Ash ushered them out of the mayhem. Reverie's stomach was really popping now, and Deerbolt had given her some looser-fitting shirts belonging to the larger men to provide her with extra comfort and dignity. She brushed her palm across her belly button as Ash explained what the lookout had spotted.

"They found us," Kite said. "I'll fetch my bow."

Reverie stopped him. "Wait, Ash said there was nobody for miles."

"Not that they can see," he added.

She released Kite. Without further prompt, he felt his way back to their cabin to retrieve his bow and arrows, hiding them beneath his cloak.

Ash took this opportunity to brace Reverie for what they were likely to face between the Northern Trading Post and Land's Edge. It was the last northern dock before the Cerulean Grace would set sail for the Isle of Dragonborn, and those waters were perilous. Prior to its destruction, the Northern Trading Post had been a welcoming little village, where travellers from all over could barter, buy and exchange items of use including food, weapons, Alchemical items like Brogan's Tarot cards, gunpowder, ale, and more. There were rarely disagreements there other than over the price of something, because everyone who attended wanted and needed the same thing. Few journeyed all that way to start a fight or for war. Men and women at the Northern Trading Post were reasonable and just wanted to get in, get their stuff and get out again; they were eager to be on the road.

Beneath the village existed only Open Country—another reason those at the Northern Trading Post were happy. Relief and gratitude washed over them. Surviving Open Country's bandits, thieves, murderers and more was an achievement that deserved celebration and reward. Men like Ash lived there and were familiar with Open Country's laws, despite the official lack thereof. If you lived there, it was for a sketchy reason, but you got to recognise familiar faces and, together, developed a code of conduct. There were certain folk you did not mistreat.

Between the Northern Trading Post and Liberty, there wasn't much besides Open Country, and the Land there was flat, dusty and barren. In some places inland, woodland offered a brief, shady respite for travellers. They camped, rested and saw to wounds under the canopy of green. Wildlife took what it wanted, when it wanted, too. Without the constant presence of Humans and Alchemists, larger mammals and birds ruled the landscape and were not afraid to approach for a meal at the traveller's expense. Ash knew not to feed *any* animal he came across in Open Country, no matter its size or how cute its little face seemed. Where there was one hungry beast, there would be another. Teaching them you were the answer to silence their grumbling stomachs was *not* a wise move. Whiskers and button noses did not necessarily mean their owners wouldn't bite or kill.

Reverie accepted Ash's warnings and relayed them to Kite on his return. He'd stashed his weapons in the same way as when Ash first met him. The archer, though blind, had a better chance of keeping Reverie safe through his skills than Ash did at the moment. His Salamander magic was unpredictable, and there was no guarantee he wouldn't create more searing infernos like the one that killed Lehana Hazel in the marketplace. Ash still felt guilty.

The Cerulean Grace crept past the port of the Northern Trading Post like a ghost. Smoothly and silently, Deerbolt steered her north-west around the coastline so they could get a better view of what they all hoped had been caused by a natural disaster or a mishap, rather than an act of war. Thatched rooftops were caved inwards, still alight and burning homes, stores and businesses. Scorched, bare bodies lay strewn along the road, discarded like useless toys. Their clothing has been stolen. Their faces were twisted and frozen in agony, and some lay reaching for those beside them. Reverie turned her head, incapable of watching as entire families lay slaughtered and abandoned by the Order. There was no doubt about who actioned this, and Ash confirmed it when he identified their symbol drawn in the dirt and burned into the crops. This was no accident. This was a vicious message from the Order to Ash the Elemental.

Turn yourself in, or we will continue our tyranny. Their blood is on your hands.

"What do we do now?" Kite asked Ash as he ground his knuckles against the wood. "Should we stop and help them?"

"They are beyond our help," Sarronious interjected. He turned to Ash and shook a finger. "And don't you go thinking this was your fault; I see the cogs in your Elemental brain turning. The Order has done much worse for a lot less. Right, Captain?"

"Aye," she murmured. "There is no evidence to suggest this has anything to do with us. If it does, it says more about the Order than about your nature, Scoundrel."

Ash nodded, but he couldn't help feeling responsible for the village's downfall. If he hadn't killed Lehana Hazel, been seen in the Lawful Hand associating with that singing Oracle, or if he hadn't pushed their attacking vessel back out to deeper waters, Ash was sure they wouldn't be on the Order's radar. Maybe, under those circumstances, they wouldn't be here *at all.*

"Alright. Any ideas?" he asked Deerbolt.

"We're going to have to head straight for the Isle of Dragonborn."

"If we hang around here, we increase our chances of coming under attack," Sarronious said.

"What else is there to do?" she finished and sighed, knowing they didn't have enough food or fresh water aboard the Grace to keep its crew and passengers happy. They'd make it to the Isle, of course, but if they were forced to hide and travel most of the way unseen, many would go hungry.

"I'll have to learn to grow food," Ash said aloud, flexing his fingers.

"What?"

He cleared his throat, realising that conversation had taken place internally, and she had no idea what he was talking about.

"You're concerned we'll starve," he began, "and with a Gnome alongside you, I can grow what the crew needs to survive if I can master the relevant incantations."

"Do you think you can?"

"If there's some dirt onboard, I'll try. Unless they have changed the system, if we dock at the bottom of the Isle closest to the Guard's fortress, we will be near several storage shacks, but we risk getting caught. We can raid whatever is there if necessary, providing it isn't guarded."

"The original plan was to dock on the western side of the island," Deerbolt said, "and make our way inland, then south once we're sure its safe. The traveller's road is how most pilgrims navigate the island, so there'd be less suspicion."

"I don't think Kite and Reverie can make it that far, and if we continue north and the Order are still out here, we're vulnerable. If they see me, they'll be aroused, anyway. I'm a wanted man."

"I agree," said Sarronious.

He whipped an arm in the air to suggest they turn around,

and in the background, Ash heard someone yell 'Aye!'. The Grace turned so harshly in the water Ash lost his balance and stumbled against the side of the ship. His stomach churned and suddenly, he felt light-headed, like the pressure of responsibility against the curse's symptoms was catching up with him.

"Are you alright?" Sarronious asked.

Ash nodded. "Sea sick."

He sat down and took a few deep breaths.

Deerbolt scowled. "That'll be all, Sarronious. We'll follow Ash's plan and pray the Dragonborn Guardsmen don't blow us out of the water before we're able to dock."

When he'd gone back to work, leading Kite and Reverie back to their cabin, Deerbolt handed Ash some water. He hesitated before drinking it, guilty for consuming what little they had left if he was supposed to be able to manipulate the sea. The book offered a method to purify salt water into drinking water. Before he looked into growing food, he would research how to filter it.

"How are you *really*?" Deerbolt asked, crouching in front of Ash and looking him up and down.

He swilled the water around his mouth first, rubbed a little on his dry, cracked lips, then swallowed.

"I can make it."

"Perhaps you should stay with the Grace?"

Ash's eyes widened. "What? No!"

"You're getting weaker every day, Ash. Raven's intentions were kind, but that book is sucking more life from you than you can regain at this rate."

"I'm strengthening my Alchemy. Physically, I know I look dreadful."

Deerbolt tutted. "Worse."

He rolled his eyes. "I'm the most useful and the deadliest weapon you have right now. Let me learn to grow food for your men; it's the least I can do, Deerbolt, before..."

"Don't say it." She covered his mouth with her palm and

lowered her head, biting her lip to prevent crying. "Just... don't say it."

He mumbled, "I'm sorry."

"It's not your fault you're having to learn this from scratch. You didn't know about your Tetrad gifts."

"That's not what I'm sorry for." He touched his forehead to hers.

Deerbolt pulled away. "Well, Brogan told me about your outcome card," she admitted, embarrassed to have pried into Ash's personal reading. When he didn't respond, she added, "I hate to say it, Scoundrel, but I think that book is your *Tower.*"

Ash wrapped his arms around her neck. She fought him, knowing if she gave in to her emotions they would flood her consciousness and bar her from doing her job.

Ash inhaled the scent of lavender oil in her hair and closed his eyes.

She relaxed into him, and in her left ear, he whispered, "Me too."

CHAPTER THIRTEEN
BLESS ALL WHO WATCH

Chapter Thirteen: Bless All Who Watch

The Isle of Dragonborn loomed in the distance, with its high central mountainous range, thick jungle-like plant life and fine, sandy beaches. This tiny off-cut of the mainland was a stunning paradise, where the water was crystal turquoise and the sun beamed down. Ash had experienced his fair share of snowy winters here, but when the weather was brighter, the air entered your lungs twice as easily and the sounds of multicoloured birds filled your heart with inspiration and creativity. Often, Ash would walk to the beach and look out at the water, listening to those birds singing behind him and the waves crashing before him, and believe he was in Akasha. Serenity did not come close to explaining the glow in Ash's soul back then.

Now, he gasped at its beauty, but he no longer thought of the Isle of Dragonborn as his home. Once, he'd been comfortable and relieved to live in this haven. He no longer oozed joy when he thought about those birds or the sand between his toes. He was filled with rage, embarrassment, and a longing for revenge.

Revenge was unwise with vulnerable passengers trusting him to keep them safe and, ultimately, solve their problems. Reverie's baby was almost due—he didn't have long to help the innocent couple get their lives back. They were present only to restore Kite's sight—he wondered if Echelon would lose his vision when Kite's was healed.

Ash already had a few names of people who might help them in mind, if those 'friends' were still on the island and practising Alchemy in the same way. Specifically, he thought of two close friends above any other men in particular; they'd turned the other way when they caught him running for his life that day ten years previous, feigning ignorance to allow his escape. Well wishes weren't part of the deal, though. But, they smiled and nodded, then turned their backs. If he saw these brothers, Crane or Cage, on their travels, he was confident they'd believe his story and be pleased to see him alive. Ash was beginning to feel he may not have many days ahead of him.

They had not seen one another in so long, but Ash would recognise their long white hair anywhere. With not a speck of grey or blonde, they often plaited their matching thick manes, braiding in beads and feathers. In their Dragonborn Guardsmen uniforms and armour, they looked more like *identical* twins. Each believed strongly in the old ways, which is why Ash bonded so well with them during his first days on the island. Between jokes and stories, they found solitude in each other's company, and mourned the death of Ash's sponsor. They were inseparable after that. He hadn't thought about how they were or what they had been doing since they let him pass unscathed.

Ash wished there had been a way to safely keep in touch with them. Sending letters on and off Dragonborn came with challenges. Messages were read, and their messengers were searched. The risks weren't worth the hassle.

Once in the throng of the Guardsmen's village they'd built together, he could look Crane and Cage up. Finding his old quarters would be easy, but he had no doubt they'd have moved position in the Guard by now and be living within the village in their own huts somewhere. They were of Ash's age, so unless there had been any battles or accidents the Land had not heard word of yet (because Dragonborn were notoriously secretive about the island's ongoings), Crane and Cage should still be alive and serving.

The village was initially the Oracle's idea. Thinking back with an outsider's perspective now, he had no doubt it was to keep the Guardsmen together and distracted as he investigated their thoughts and intentions. But, it quickly became their luxury for days off. Together, the Dragonborn Guardsmen gathered the supplies and built the village to meet their needs—a purpose-built sanctuary for tired, off-shift friends to meet and socialise. There was a single tavern, where ale was rationed but served. Each Guardsman was entitled to one tankard of ale per week when Ash lived there, to ensure men were not intoxicated the following day. Ale made men sloppy and lazy, their leaders believed, but they also did not wish to deprive them of certain needs.

Women were a prohibited need, in the sense of intimate relationships. Many women made the pilgrimage to pay their respects to the island and its history, and a few stayed to help occasionally in small ways such as to trade, mend clothing, polish armour and cook alongside the men already working in those roles. They were greeted with open arms once interviewed and 'vetted' by the Oracle's Psychometry to ensure their intentions were not to extinguish the flame or steal the egg, but that's all. And they could never cross certain physical boundaries; there were gates and bridges off-limits to pilgrims for that reason.

Any Guardsman caught having an affair or sneaking off with pilgrims was punished and/or banished.

After a few weeks, most of the women would miss their families and catch the next ship back to the mainland with stories to tell anyway. It wasn't unheard of for whole families to make the journey, either, but the island demanded hard-work and a strength children were unable to understand before their adolescence. So, Dragonborn pilgrims were, mostly, over the age of twelve, and male.

Deerbolt appeared beside Ash as he watched the island draw nearer from the front of the ship. His mind whirred with anticipation, replaying memories whilst simultaneously being terrified of losing the chance to make new ones with the woman he loved. Fearful, he didn't turn to greet her. Tears would flow, and panic would swiftly follow.

"You don't have to come with us, Ash. Kite and Reverie are here safely. You fulfilled your promise."

Ash smiled but didn't turn to look at her. "This is something I have to do, Deerbolt. Something I should have done a long time ago, and it's a chance for me to rectify mistakes. Who knows? They *could* take pity on me and undo my curse."

"Hopefully," she said and sighed, "and if they don't... *then* what will you do?"

Ash had thought little about the possibility of dying on Dragonborn. He'd served the isle for years and it dominated his history over any other experiences. His Guardsmen brothers were by his side much longer than his blood relatives. If he had to die here, it wouldn't be so bad, because he'd been blessed with friends and wonderful adventures, too. He recalled the peaceful graveyard approximately one mile from the village on foot. No matter the weather, the location was harmonious and always high-spirited. Guardsmen did not mourn or grieve over their dead. Of course, they missed their brothers, but life was to be celebrated, and they paid tribute to the time that Guardsman dedicated to protecting the island. By entering the graveyard, you were expressing gratitude and in a small way, relief their watch was over—they faced only eternal rest in Akasha.

"Ash?"

"I'll embrace my fate," he finally answered.

He wrapped an arm around Deerbolt's waist and gave her a

gentle squeeze, fixing his gaze on the island. His fingers quaked and tingled as the curse pumped through his digits. He caressed the soft material of her shirt and looped his thumb down the back of her belt to steady himself.

"Did you ever see the fifth egg, Ash?" she asked. "Rumour is the surface is polished and reflective."

He clicked his tongue. "I thought I saw it, once. The egg and the flame were often moved to prevent theft. Sometimes, if there were thunderstorms or heavy snowfall, we had no other option but to relocate what we protected. After serving around six months, there was a private operation ongoing involving those who led the Guardsmen. Whispers tipped us off they'd be passing through, and I hid to catch a glimpse. It wasn't shiny, if what I saw was real. It was scaled and rough, with serrated edges in earthy colours."

"A decoy?"

"Perhaps," he said.

Her voice was quieter now. "What a *shame* you don't yet have an authentic memory."

Ash scowled and turned to look Deerbolt in the eye. He didn't need to question what she'd meant by that. She shrugged, grinning through a cunning plot. She had ideas about how to give Ash the send-off he deserved. Did she want him to see with his own eyes what he'd devoted so many years to protecting? Did she want him to feel the heat of the Dragonborn flame against his skin at least *once* before his death? To know each day he'd adhered to their rules—going without certain luxuries—had been worth it?

"I'd love to see it, too," she said. "I believe in the old ways, and the times when Dragons ruled the Land. Sounds like a magical, harmonious era without the tyranny of the Order around every corner. When Dragons, and Dragons only, possessed Elemental, Astral and Seeing gifts. Before we murdered them."

"*We* didn't murder anyone," Ash corrected, saddened by the Land's history. "They became extinct because of the God of

Universal Energy's followers. Humans."

"Humans you originated from."

"We," Ash corrected, "because Velocals are *far* from mere mortals, Deerbolt. In the past, Humans of the Order wanted Alchemy for themselves. Power. Greed. Jewels. Slaves to do their bidding. They thought by killing off the Dragons, it would release their Alchemy for the Land to consume and use for their own benefit."

"They were right," she said. "It turned them all into Astrals."

"Their theory of how to release magic was right, aye. And they climbed high socially. But Astrals of the Order are no more powerful than you or I, Deerbolt. Look at Kite and his fantastic aim. A lack of sight hasn't prevented him from being loyal and loving." He added, "Either way, I think those two will make great parents."

"I have no doubt about it."

"Would be nice to grant his wish to see his child," Ash said and beamed. He squeezed Deerbolt's waist a little tighter. "And to restore his Alchemy so he can calm Reverie's pregnancy nerves with his Hydromancy."

"Will your brothers help us?"

"Directly, they won't offer me anything. Those who always believed my innocence won't be seen with me. Punishment here is harsh. But, I have two friends on the island who I know will risk their reputations."

"Are you sure we can rely on them? Trust them?"

"Aye. The way you trusted Raven."

Deerbolt seemed satisfied. "Alright, then let's make finding..."

"Crane and Cage," Ash backfilled.

"Crane and Cage," she continued, pondering how odd their names were, and wondering where they originated, "a priority. Will they source somebody capable of reversing Kite's curse? Or, can they do that themselves?"

"The twins are old souls," he said, "though no more capable

of reversing a curse than you or I. If not for my years off the island, I'd have been able to find more powerful Alchemists myself. But, who knows if they are still living here, serving the Guard? It's better to rely on fresh intelligence than to risk making any mistakes."

"I'd be surprised if they recognise you," she said.

"You did." He grinned, slyly. "Do I look so different?"

Deerbolt rolled her eyes. "Ten years is a long time."

Ash's face contorted. "Oh, they'll *all* know my face. Some of the newer guards may take a minute or two to realise *exactly* who I am, but be assured my wanted poster has been in enough taverns, lodges and villages across the Land—including those on the Isle of Dragonborn—to cause us concern. A few of the older Guardsmen may have died or retired to the mainland. However, I'm confident everyone else will still man their posts like good little sheep."

Deerbolt didn't seem to like this comparison. "What you did there, Ash, meant *so* much more than blindly following orders on faith."

"Are you sure? Like you said, I never witnessed an egg resting above an eternal flame. I never experienced the instant boost in motivation from moving it with my bare hands, or the awe of being in its presence. Supposedly, merely gazing upon the surface of the egg is life-changing no matter who you are; it grounds you in a way no other religion can. Yet, I served, believing in the old ways, and trusting the Dragonborn Guardsmen around me to be honest about what went on there."

"There would be little point to serving there if it didn't exist. Why would men like you be invited to live and work on the island if the egg was a myth? You believe in the Gods, don't you?"

Gruffly, he replied, "Aye."

"Well, you haven't seen one of those, have you?"

"Alright," he said, giving in to her logic. "They're all imprisoned, though, in my defence."

“Not according to the Oracle who had you banished and cursed, they aren't. The God of Universal Energy was in the Lingerverse, not in Akasha.”

“Right,” Ash said, narrowing his eyes.

“I believe in the fifth egg,” she told him. “And I believe in you, Ash the Elemental.” She paused and giggled, then said, “I mean, Ash the *Tetrad*.”

Ash shoved her away playfully. “Raven didn't like us using that word in public places.”

“Raven isn't here.”

“Well, we should get ready,” he said.

“Aye.”

As Deerbolt walked away, she peered back at Ash over her shoulder and whistled the Dragonborn song:

“Bless all who watch o'er the flame,
Where loyal guards are duly sworn,
For here they are re-birthed to new name,
So unto pledge their hearts to Dragonborn.”

CHAPTER FOURTEEN
RUINS

Chapter Fourteen: Ruins

Without having to Ask Brogan, Ash already knew there were three stages to the major arcana's anatomy in a deck of Tarot cards. Irrespective of their design or the Seer wielding them, the twenty-two major arcana cards fell into either the conscious (which included external and outer concerns), the unconscious (which included internal and any moral concerns), or superconscious (which included spiritual and hidden concerns). It was of no surprise to Ash four of his cards fell into the unconscious category, because he had always struggled with his identity. The rest were evenly divided between Ash's conscious and superconscious.

Was he more than the cursed Dragonborn Guardsman the wanted posters made him out to be? More than a scoundrel with a tainted history, criminal record, and a love affair?

Strangely, Ash contemplated how he'd pulled a superconscious card, *Judgement*, in the conscious location of Brogan's spread. And he'd pulled *the Lovers*, a conscious card, in the unconscious place. Defying the structure of the deck this way was not uncommon. Cards fell where they fell. In his opinion, it was almost as if Ash's fortune wasn't entirely sure of itself overall, either; opposites proved Ash was not your average Elemental, and defied the laws of the Land.

Universal forces of the psyche, not to be confused with the God of Universal Energy's influence, covered Ash's hopes and fears, plus his overall outcome. Should he take that as a sign these things were waiting for him on a higher plain?

The Order continued to startle him; their behaviour convinced him Humans should never have meddled. They weren't capable of handling Alchemy's responsibilities and refused to be accountable for their evil. Might he only know the maturity and enlightenment of the Dragons following his death, the way it once was—the way Ash now believed it should be again? To look upon the Land then, perhaps he could understand why there was such unrest. The more Ash experienced the Land's cruelties and witnessed the Order's destructive forces, the more he dared consider committing treason and extinguishing the flame.

Only the Dragon in that fifth egg deserved Alchemy.

Unsure what his next steps needed to be as the Cerulean Grace floated slowly into dock at the south base of Dragonborn, he asked Brogan for one final favour. A single card pulled by the Captain of the ship might solve his internal moral dilemma, and take the choice to act against his values out of his hands.

She'd expressed an interest in finding the egg. Did that mean she wanted him to act selfishly, and to use his Tetrad abilities to extinguish the flame? Or did she want him to deliver Kite and Reverie's unborn child to its presence to test the theory of a new era of Dragons being possible? Either way, Alchemy would leave the Land's inhabitants and return to the beasts qualified to harness it. Surviving the curse could be a pretty bonus.

Ash posed the suggestion to Deerbolt. Her eyes lit up with excitement and devious intent.

"Aye, let's try," she said. "I haven't had my Tarot cards read in an awfully long time. I'd be interested to see where a single card pulled in our hour of need takes us."

Brogan wasn't so sure. She offered Ash warnings and guidance against allowing another person to dictate his thoughts and actions. If Ash's own cards were not enough to mentor him, was he a lost cause?

"Please, Brogan," Deerbolt begged. "As a favour to me. I understand you're exhausted from Ash's reading, but we're curious."

"Curiosity kills," she groaned but reached into her coat pocket for the deck, anyway. "I'm going to regret this, aren't I?"

Ash laughed. "Of course you are."

Brogan led Ash and Deerbolt to the front of the ship, and rolled an empty barrel of ale between them to use as a table. She created a fan with the cards, facing away from the Captain, and offered them to her.

"One card," she instructed.

"One card," Ash repeated under his breath, hopeful this would unite the path he *wanted* to take with the path he must, morally, take.

There were seventy-eight cards for Captain Deerbolt to choose from—twenty-two of those were major arcana cards, several from Ash's reading, and fifty-six were minor arcana cards. And so, she gasped when she pulled *Temperance* in the reverse: *what* were the odds of that?

"My Gods," Brogan whispered.

"What is *Temperance*?" Ash asked.

She and Deerbolt glared at one another, then simultaneously looked at Ash and smiled.

"Good?"

"Depends how you look at it," Brogan said. "In reverse, this card represents being caught in the middle, recklessness, and extreme circumstances or actions."

She tapped the card, depicting a man surrounded by violent light. On his back was an outline of wings, and in either hand *the Sun* and *the Moon*, individual Tarot cards Ash had not pulled before. In reverse, *the Sun* suggested a lack of enthusiasm and over-confidence; Ash thought this to be laziness. An inability to try hard, assuming one already knew the outcome.

Alright, he thought, *I'm guilty of this. Why bother following the law, staying with Deerbolt ten years ago, or searching for one capable of reversing the curse sooner? I'm going to die. What's the point?*

Upright, *the Sun* was a happy, optimistic card. The man wielded Alchemy in vibrant dusty rays and sat casually in the centre of the scene, with a serene expression. Deerbolt was *the Sun* incarnate, he thought. But *the Moon* was not so positive. The man in the picture had a fifty-fifty chance of losing his way and deceiving himself. In reverse, that's what *the Moon* represented. Was Ash lying to himself that ending Alchemy in any way possible answered his prayers? Though it did also ignite imagination if pulled upright, was Ash simply feeding a fantasy?

Temperance was Deerbolt's card, though. Not *the Sun* or *the Moon*, and so they had no way to know if their reference was upright or in reverse. It appeared, more so, the character on the card was resting on *the Sun*, whereas *the Moon* appeared to sit upon him.

"Brogan, I don't understand what this is telling me."

"Captain," she said in a low voice, "*Temperance* acknowledges the concept of Alchemy as a union of all perspectives, exhibiting a greater whole. It is my interpretation of this card as a Seer, Deerbolt's decisions alone will yield few results."

"Whatever I do, I need to do it with you in tow," Deerbolt told Ash. "Individually, we will never achieve equilibrium."

"Diversity is the way forward," Brogan said.

That finally puts to bed any suggestions of me remaining on the Cerulean Grace, he thought.

What Deerbolt's card foretold, was success only through unity. No matter what they did or where they went, remaining together as a team was their only chance. And that chance included Kite and Reverie.

At the base of the Isle of Dragonborn, visible from where the ship had docked during their conversation, were ancient ruins. The Dragonborn Guardsmen called them the Dragon's Circle, where the Alchemical beasts once met to make decisions. Overgrown and crumbling as they were, potentially even unsafe, Ash felt drawn to that location as a place to set up camp and make some decisions of their own. Prior to his expulsion, Ash visited the ruins on his rounds and as part of his watch. Occasionally, Dragonborn posted a guard there to ensure nothing had been stolen by pilgrims wishing to take back a souvenir, and also to prevent trespassing. If they passed through, Ash would need to remember that.

Reverie's pull, naturally, would be towards saving her husband's sight and the safety and prosperous future of her baby. It was the initial reason for their voyage. According to the marketplace Oracle, Ash's responsibilities did not end there. Could she be convinced to seek the location of the fifth egg and its seething flame, with the potential to hand Alchemy back to the final Dragon?

"We have a rare opportunity here," Ash told Deerbolt, who was already nodding in agreement and smacking her lips, anxiously. "The Order don't have to win. If we can persuade Reverie to play, we can completely change the future of Alchemy. By the time we achieve success, it'll be too late for the Guard to intervene."

"You do want to extinguish the flame?"

Ash and Deerbolt startled at Sarronious's sudden presence. Initially, that godforsaken firepit had been the last thing on his mind; he wished only to deliver Kite and Reverie as promised and, as a reward, ask for the curse to be removed. Being a Tetrad seemed an impossibility, and he'd planned to demonstrate how feeble his Elemental powers actually were. A mere Salamander Ash had been born, and not much more he would die.

"Treason was not my intention."

"I believe him," the Captain said, furrowing her brow as she stood to face her First Mate. "If you can't trust Ash, then trust *me*. What Ash is suggesting seems like a treasonous act, but surely allowing the Order to spread their cult across the Land and do to others what they did to the Northern Trading Post would be worse, if we have the power to stop it right now?"

"Do we, though?"

Sarronious folded his arms. He loomed over Ash, still sitting cross-legged by the empty, upturned barrel.

Ash sighed. *He has a point. My power, like my body and the Dragon's Circle, is in ruins.*

"We understand if this is too much of a risk for you," she added, sincerely. "I won't hold it against you if you choose not to be a part of this, but I wholeheartedly believe we can convince that final egg to hatch for Reverie's baby. Imagine the subsequent possibilities, Sarronious!"

"Ask yourself: do you envision a world without Astrals of the Order, sucking innocent Humans, Velocals and Alchemists dry of their wealth and their *lives*?" Ash pleaded.

Unsure, Sarronious began to pace. After a few minutes of consideration, his only soundtrack being the slop of water against the Grace's hull, he inhaled sharply and groaned.

"Fine. I'll follow you, Ash the Elemental. But, I have a condition."

"I would expect nothing less," Ash said, smiling.

Deerbolt grinned. "Let me guess, you want to escort us to keep me safe from harm?"

Sarronious's expression fell flat. For a while he'd held feelings for the Captain. They weren't a secret—many on her crew knew of his longing to protect her, to *marry* her if she'd take his hand. After seeing Deerbolt welcome Ash back, he'd witnessed true love and realised, at last, their union was not to be. Deerbolt loved Sarronious like a brother, not a husband.

Well, this is awkward.

"Actually, I was going to insist you get Reverie and Kite on board with this ludicrous plan first. Then, and *only* then, will I give you both my blessing."

Before Deerbolt could react, Ash announced, "Agreed," and shook his hand.

The giant First Mate stormed off to find the unsuspecting couple and put these options to them. When he was out of earshot, Ash bit his lip and grinned.

Deerbolt slapped his shoulder. "Shh, *Scoundrel*, or I'll have you thrown overboard."

He winked. "You would miss me too much."

Reverie was more for following Ash and Deerbolt than they thought she'd be; Reverie felt safe and comfortable in their company, and they'd grown to be loyal friends of hers. After everything they'd been through so far—Lehana Hazel and Aldwin's attack at Blackheart Dock, the Order's pursuit of them in the Tradeway Approach, the First Watchtower's tidal wave and, finally, how they'd burned the Northern Trading Post to the ground for no other reason than to rattle Ash's nerves and send him a message. All these things only happened to them because she and Kite were in Ash's presence, but when she thought about leaving him now, guilt and sorrow set in.

Through his own pain and suffering, Ash promised to get her and Kite to the Dragonborn Guardsmen to fight to return the sight Echelon stole from him; it was a completely selfless act, and one that, eventually, Reverie thought would kill Ash. Each day and the more he developed his Tetrad powers, the less his body willed itself forward. With his mental and Alchemical development, his physique and energy withered. She'd accidentally stumbled in on him at the First Watchtower changing his sodden shirt following the tsunami, and witnessed the bruising across his torso and shoulders. It didn't seem to take much to harm him, but he never complained.

Helping him to survive the curse and rid the Land of the Order was the least she could do, and when she explained her feelings to Kite, he was hesitant but understood her logic. They owed Ash for getting them this far. When their boots touched the Isle of Dragonborn's southern sandy beach, their minds were made up.

"Are we agreed?"

Kite nodded. "Aye."

"I did not wish to extinguish the flame. But, a chance at rebirthing Dragons to the Land would both save our friend's life and rid us of that awful cult's influence," Reverie said. "It would mean offering our child to the Dragonborn Guardsmen. If the egg responds, our baby would be taken away."

Kite assured her, "We could stay here until the birth, and live alongside them here on the island."

"Eventually, we would miss Broad Wells."

Kite shrugged. "There is nothing to prevent us from visiting. Without taxes on the roads and the fear of slavery or violence, travelling without a guide like Ash will be easier when the Order no longer govern."

Reverie bit her nails. "Our only other choice would be to extinguish the flame without risking the baby."

"That's treason!" Kite gasped. "No, it's what the Order want—we cannot aid their vision to be the last remaining with Alchemy."

"They wouldn't be," Reverie explained. "Ash and I discussed it; they believe by extinguishing the flame it would kill the egg, and thus all Alchemy but theirs would cease to exist. No flame, no magic. No Dragon egg, no future of magic. In its entirety. And a Land without Alchemy? Elementals grow crops and control windmills, but they can also cause horrible natural disasters and storms. Astrals used to redirect their energy for good; they healed, motivated and strengthened us. Now, they interfere with the natural order of life and death. And men like you, Kite, could predict wars and illnesses, helping the people to prepare."

"It may not always be a good thing to know what heartache is to befall those you love, if you are unable to prevent it."

Kite took her hand in his and kissed it gently. "So, whatever you decide, my love, I am with you."

Reverie collared Sarronious as he hauled his pack down the wooden ramp. The Cerulean Grace was docked and anchored in place, and Captain Deerbolt was insistent she would not be sailed again unless it was toward a future free from Astrals of the Order and their authoritarianism.

"Sarronious, we have decided to help Ash by offering our unborn child to the egg."

"Then I'm with you," Sarronious replied.

"Thank you."

"And if the egg does not respond?"

Reverie frowned; she hadn't considered the egg wouldn't accept their offering of an innocent soul as its vessel. They assumed their act of kindness would be enough.

"I don't think I can commit treason," Kite told her.

"Me neither," she said.

"I'll let Ash and the Captain know what you have decided, Reverie. For the record, I don't want to commit treason either, no matter the benefits."

He dumped his pack, then set off back up the ramp. But he paused and checked over his shoulder one last time.

"Are you *sure*? A child is a precious thing; can you live without yours?"

Reverie lowered her gaze. "I would see to it we could remain here. Do you think—"

He interrupted, "There can be no going back."

"We understand," Kite answered, fingering the bow and arrows fixed to his back.

He'd have to use them today, and against men of the Dragonborn Guard. If they were not met with the warm welcome they hoped for, considering what they had to offer, Kite's responsibility lied with Reverie and the baby. He would die for them. Without hesitation. No questions asked.

Ash told him what the men of Dragonborn were taught and how. They were ruthless when necessary, and highly trained with weapons including the longsword, bows, crossbows, knives and even those deemed illegal on the mainland. Kite's aim was true even without his sight—if they granted his wish to see again and reversed Echelon's cruelty before turning against them for any reason, Kite would *definitely* have the edge. With a bow and arrows, Kite was deadly. Ash saw firs hand outside the Lawful Hand Tavern his capabilities. Stunned by his instincts, he'd been impressed. His Alchemy being passive (rather than active like Ash's Salamander incantations), could not be relied upon to save any lives. As a Hydromancer, Kite read tea leaves to predict the future with his Seeing Alchemy. He could predict disagreements, battles and even long-term wars, but for the here and now, it was of little consequence.

"It's the honourable thing to do, Sarronious," he said.

"Honourable does not always differ from stupid."

Kite grinned. "We understand that, too. We're ready."

Sarronious thought for a moment and almost challenged Kite again, but continued on, leaving the couple to enjoy the beach before their party set off through the jungle to the Dragonborn Circle's ruins.

Ash was touched when he heard the news. With Deerbolt by his side, he didn't want to show the emotion their sacrifice welled within him. He was close to tears. Of course, he'd expected Reverie not to agree to treason and in the long run, removing any chance of the return of Dragons was a terrible idea. Ash, like any other honest Alchemist in the Land, longed to set eyes upon their incredible valour and beauty. Being an Elemental used to be thrilling, but as Ash aged, wielding a flamethrower vexed him—he'd lost his edge, anyway.

So locate the egg they would, and offer Reverie's unborn child to it they must. With his hands together, staring at the ship's mascot from the beach, Ash prayed the egg would respond and, in return for their generosity and spirit, restore Kite's vision. Without Alchemy across the Land and in the man who cursed him originally, Ash's troubles would be over automatically, and any chance of the God of Universal Energy gaining traction through another Oracle would be withdrawn, too.

Please let there be no guard on the wall of the ruins, he prayed. *I do not need another Guardsman's blood on my hands.*

Ash tucked the Tetrad book down the back of his pack, then hid the key beneath his shirt, and set off, leading his party of five across the beach and into the jungle. On their side, fighting thanklessly for the future of the Land, were two Humans, a Velocal, an incapacitated Hydromancer and Ash... a Tetrad.

CHAPTER FIFTEEN
ARISE IN FLAMES

Chapter Fifteen: Arise In Flames

Unfortunately, Ash's wish to avoid a confrontation on approach to the ruins was not granted. Manning the ancient wall was two visible Guardsmen, wearing full head-to-toe armour and carrying longswords. Ash didn't recognise either of them, and was absolutely stunned to see one of them wielding Gnome Elemental magic to rebuild sections of the fallen ruins. A deep scowl burrowed into his brow and remained there as Deerbolt crept up behind him and gasped at the sight.

"But, he's an Elemental?"

"Aye," Ash grumbled, now more determined than ever to confront and challenge them.

"They're suddenly trusting Elementals in the Guard?"

"Rarely," Ash whispered, careful to make a mental note of the incantations used by the Gnome for lifting and transporting heavy bricks, soil and plant-life. "What are they doing?"

Deerbolt skulked back to Kite, Reverie and Sarronious to relay what they'd seen. With no one by his side to harm if the incantations went wrong, Ash mimicked the Guardsman's actions, which he noticed were mostly in the upper body, but with a firm stance. The man was using the wet dirt as cement, to rebuild the wall around the Dragon's Circle, creating a surrounding barrier to act like that at the First Watchtower. All it lacked was a deep moat and a huge Keep in the centre.

By mirroring the guard's incantations, Ash was able to shift some rocks and dirt by his feet, but didn't want to draw any attention. With his eyes still firmly fixed on the watchmen, Ash slipped back through the canopy of leaves.

"They are preparing for something," he told Deerbolt.

He gave Kite's bow a tug to subtly inform him he ought to be ready to use it. Kite nodded but said nothing.

"Like what?" Reverie innocently asked. "Surely they are just preserving a piece of their history?"

Sarronious narrowed his eyes when he saw the concern in Ash's. No, this was something more. Re-building the existing ruins was a way to conserve the past, but adding additional structures that high and strong suggested they were preparing to be attacked. Or, they were trying to impress someone.

"Do they still use this area for anything, Ash?" he asked.

"They didn't when I served, but it was patrolled."

"Any ideas what they might be up to?"

Ash had a few concerns. "Aye. Knowing what I know now."

Sarronious and Deerbolt gestured he should share his theories, but Ash was hesitant. Starting a panic now, even if only within their party, wouldn't help their cause. And if word got out, widespread fear that the Dragonborn Guardsmen were not who they claimed to be anymore would be the end of the Land, with or without Alchemy.

"Please," Reverie added in the quiet.

Ash inhaled deeply. His theories were exactly that... theories. There was no evidence to prove any of his suspicions held sustenance. Kite and Reverie needed to trust the Guardsmen if they were to convince the egg to hatch with their unborn baby's presence, and telling them Ash thought the Guard had other, sinister intentions would *not* help his cause.

"The Dragon Circle is supposedly where the flame was initially ignited, and where the past Dragons were born. They met here to discuss Alchemy and the Land's future, but when the Order started killing them off, it fell to ruin," he explained. "If the Guardsmen are employing more Elementals—as you know that's unusual because there's a risk they might be concealing a Tetrad ability—their security is lacking and suggests their focus has shifted from protecting the flame to protecting... something else."

Deerbolt felt for the knife she concealed in her right boot; fingering it comforted her.

"You said *something* and not someone," Kite added.

"Aye," Ash replied. "The return of..."

"The God of Universal Energy," Deerbolt finished, remembering how Ash had come to be banished in the first place, and the Oracle's possession by the God of Universal Energy from the Lingerverse.

Together, they explained this to Kite, Reverie and Sarronious, and waited for their decision to bail and return to the mainland. Ash wouldn't have blamed them for choosing not to go up against one of the most powerful Gods the Land had ever seen, and one of the most influential and cruel. The God of Universal Energy was a warlord, encouraging greed and dishonesty, power over life and death, and a single, rich government. If Dragonborn had become corrupted, or infiltrated by Astrals of the Order, it would make sense to use Elementals to prepare the island for the return of the God they believed would allow them to keep their Alchemy if they served him well.

"Is that possible?" Reverie asked Ash. "Releasing a God from Akasha and reincarnating him somehow?"

Everyone ducked in unison as the Gnome Guard passed by; Ash could hear the crinkle and crunch of leaves and twigs beneath his boots as he stomped along the outer edge of the Dragon's Circle, kicking occasionally to look for pieces of the original monuments. When the Dragons reigned, forming the circle were six large pillars of stone, facing inward. Five of the pillars represented the original Dragon eggs, only one of which still remained under protective custody. Nobody really knew what the sixth stood for, except perhaps to represent Man, and the Land the Dragons safeguarded. There were also theories the six pillars had been erected for the six 'species': Elementals, Velocals, Seers, Humans, Astrals and Dragons. But, many disregarded the idea because Velocals were basically Humans.

Elementals thought they represented the senses their Alchemy covered: earth, air, fire, water, the spirit, and the Tetrad gift, however rare. Dragons were capable only of the spiritual sense, but this still equalled six pillars for six gifts. Astrals, including those of the Order, sometimes wondered if six represented the maximum number of spirits one could conjure from the Lingerverse. Many had tried to call upon multiple souls. Few succeeded.

Finally, Seers held their own beliefs. Could it be there were six Seeing gifts if you counted Shamans as the final ability? Of fortune telling: Cartomancy, Hydromancy and Chiromancy. Of an Oracle's remit: Sciomancy and Psychometry. Soothsayers, those without physical sight but all of the other gifts. Shamans were medicine men working only with herbal remedies, but they were often categorised as Seers.

Humans and Velocals without an Alchemical stake in the pillars thought the most logical explanation was one pillar for each God: the God of Magic and his five children: the Land, the People, Universal Energy, Emotion and the Senses. Without a Dragon to ask, nobody would ever have a direct answer.

The sixth pillar remained a mystery.

After many years without Dragons, the circle was abandoned and crumbled to the ruins they were all familiar with.

When the guard was out of earshot and they were less at

risk of being discovered, Deerbolt continued.

"They would need a vessel to do it. Right, Ash?"

"Aye. Forget innocence sparking a Dragon's curiosity," he told them. "If they've discovered a way to force that egg to hatch, the God of Universal Energy could return to the Land by possessing the beast and tarnishing its soul. Then, it could wield the Dragon's Alchemy for its own benefit."

"Isn't the God of Universal Energy a *he*, not an *it*?"

"Kite," Ash said, sighing, "any creature willing to do *that* much harm to so many people deserves only to be an 'it' in my opinion." He paused and wrung his gloved hands together. "Makes me feel less guilty about killing *it*."

"Do forgive me if I falter," Kite grunted.

"Is that what we should do?" Sarronious asked. "Find the egg and destroy it before the God of Universal Energy can be reborn?"

Ash shrugged. "Honestly, Sarronious, I can't say for sure what is going on over there, but it can't be good. The God of Magic initially sent the Dragons to rule the Land *in place* of the Gods—they were blessed with a piece of the Gods' Alchemy to weaken and imprison them in Akasha, but also to help the Land govern itself."

Ash lowered his voice; the guards were branching out and widening their patrol route. Soon, they'd be forced to move.

"The question is, would the God of Universal Energy be strong enough to survive without the entirety of his Alchemy?"

Deerbolt said, "If reunited with a Dragon egg, I believe so. It is a terrifying thought. But the bigger dilemma is *how* did he escape from Akasha in the first place, and why isn't his father interfering?"

They retreated deeper into the canopy to avoid detection.

"We can't stay here much longer," Kite told Reverie.

Sarronious agreed. "It's not safe for her. They could attack and strike Reverie before seeing she is carrying a child."

"Motherhood won't stop them, not if they deem her a

threat," Ash told him, ashamed he once followed that same ruling.

The Elemental guard Ash had been studying came to a halt, paying close attention to where Ash's party were crouched. With a delicate lifting motion, the Gnome's incantations raised the plants and trees ahead of them from the roots, revealing everything behind and beneath. Dirt rained down as Ash tried to get everyone to move. A clear path was being forged to their hideout.

Reverie's size and shape, plus Kite's blindness, hindered any chance of a quick getaway, and the Gnome called out before he sprinted directly at them.

"Intruders!"

Ash drew his longsword and darted in his path, clashing metal on metal to protect his friends from the swish of the sharp, unforgiving Dragonborn blade. He forced the Guardsman backwards and off balance, then charged at him.

Deerbolt gave Kite a shove in the opposite direction and told them to run; Reverie overtook him and led Kite through the trees, heading the way they came.

"I can help," Kite protested. "Turn back."

"No! I'm not going to lose you," Reverie said.

Sarronious was already head-to-head with the other Guardsman, who didn't seem to possess any Alchemical gifts. He was quick with his sword, though, but not quick enough. Sarronious dodged a clumsy strike and tripped the guard. He hit his head on a flat stone slab and was instantly rendered unconscious. Sarronious checked him for a pulse, then once satisfied he hadn't accidentally killed the man, bound his hands quickly with rope and ran to assist Ash. Deerbolt had beaten him to the fight, so he went back to lift the man into a sitting position and tie him to a tree trunk instead.

Mercilessly, Deerbolt screamed and swung at the Dragonborn Guardsman, giving Ash the chance to fling open the Tetrad grimoire and find an incantation he could use to defeat a Gnome at close range. She held him off well and with short but accurate attacks, moving with fantastic grace and stamina.

"Whenever you're ready, Scoundrel!" she grunted.

"*Working* on it!"

"I could use a break over here!"

Without warning, the Gnome threw his sword with both hands at Deerbolt, and she spun to the left to dodge it just in time, whipping her plaited hair around her face. He lifted the earth beneath her boots and, like a shaken carpet, flicked Deerbolt up and onto her backside. Air puffed from her lungs and she lay winded, but the Guardsman wasn't through with her yet.

"Oh, no you don't!"

Ash yanked the key from his neck and begged the book to show him a way to help her. The pages flew open, drawing the man's attention and distracting him long enough for Deerbolt to roll onto her front, then hoist up onto her grazed knees.

The guard tore a giant block of stone from the base of the wall he had been rebuilding, and performed an incantation so fast Ash couldn't make out his movements. It rocketed over the raised mound of earth and plummeted at Deerbolt. With her back turned, she was blind to the attack. The impact would instantly kill her.

Ash growled and planted his hand on the Tetrad book, allowing the knowledge of the first Gnome page to enter through his fingertips, absorbed by his skin and into his veins. It travelled through him as an electrical blue light similar to that the key projected. But this was an igneous fire, ramping up Ash's rage, and making its way to his heart.

"NO!" he boomed.

Performing a thunderous punch to amp up his energy, he then slammed both fists into the dirt, sending a shock wave across the Dragon's Circle. The earth cracked and broiling magma rumbled beneath. The force felled trees and sent a plume of leaves and muck up in the air, clouding the Guardsman's vision long enough for Sarronious to tackle him.

Ash leapt into the path of the falling stone in time for it to crash into his chest. It catapulted him up and over Deerbolt who was still coughing and gasping for breath, and crushed him against the sixth pillar, ending the incantation. The earth remained cracked, but the hot lava beneath instantly cooled and hardened.

The pillar swayed. Ash followed the slab to the ground, landing heavily on his back, and groaned in agony. Sarronious blinked and blew out a puff of air, relieved.

"ASH!" Deerbolt cried. She set off crawling and picked herself up. "Sarronious! Help!"

Captain Deerbolt's First Mate scooped Ash up and settled him comfortably on a pile of long, luscious green leaves in the centre of the circle. It took Ash several minutes to come round, blinking, staring up at the sunlight beaming through the gaps in the trees overhead. He spluttered and murmured, then reached to wipe a layer of sweat off his forehead.

"How are you not dead, Ash?" Sarronious asked, offering him a canteen of water. "That was... *volcanic*!"

Ash sipped. "Are... the... guards... dead?"

"No, I tied them both up."

He glugged again. "Good. The... book?"

"It's here. Can you sit?" Deerbolt asked.

She tucked her shoulder under Ash's arm and Sarronious aided his right. Together, and slowly, they got Ash to his feet. Deerbolt wasn't sure they could make it, but once upright, they clasped hands and hobbled to the sixth pillar to support their weight. The fog in their heads cleared and their balance returned.

"How did you *do* that?" the Gnome asked; he had ceased to writhe in his restraints, stunned by Ash's Elemental abilities. "I've never seen such... power."

Ash glared at him. "You haven't seen anything yet."

CHAPTER SIXTEEN
BY THY SWORD

Chapter Sixteen: By Thy Sword

Ash dusted down his clothing and secured his longsword, collecting the blade the guard had thrown at Deerbolt and handing it to Reverie.

"Are you both alright?"

Reverie was out of breath from their escape, but the baby seemed to be kicking as usual.

"I could have helped," Kite argued. "Why did—"

"Because somebody has to take care of Reverie," Deerbolt said, interrupting Ash before he could snap at the young Seer. "If we die, you still have a chance. If you die, our entire voyage was for naught. You and Reverie are the most important souls in this party, and your little baby."

Kite's mouth contorted as he thought about her logic. Nobody on the journey was disposable or worth less than any other, but hearing Deerbolt say how vital they were out loud, gave Kite a new sense of worth and responsibility. As they had tried to protect his wife and child, he would fulfil his new role, using the only weapon he had now—his trusty bow and arrows.

He re-adjusted his cloak, bringing the arrows to rest across his chest. A twig snapping in the overgrown ruins startled

Kite, and he gripped his bow tightly, pointing it in the noise's direction.

"Ash, behind you!"

He let off a warning shot, striking a tree trunk.

Between the fourth and fifth pillars, a group of Guardsmen marched through in formation, with their weapons drawn and shields raised. Ash recognised their leader. As the man passed the arrow, he yanked it out of the wood in one swift tug, then snapped it across his knee and tossed it aside. Kite couldn't see the action, but he heard the familiar crack and crunch as the two parts hit branches on the ground.

"Ash the Elemental," the man said.

He held up a closed fist to indicate his Guardsmen should halt and lower their weapons. They followed this silent order immediately. Dressed in thick, metal armour including chain mail and helmets with nose guards, their presence was ominous and territorial.

"Never thought I'd see *you* again," he added.

Ash's fingers found the hilt of his sword, but he resisted drawing it. Until they learnt more about their intentions, there was no use starting a fight Ash knew they wouldn't win. They were outnumbered five to one, easily. And many of those in the Guard were Alchemists. A few of the faces he thought he recognised. They were older now; their features seemed drawn, and the few with long, braided hair had greyed.

"Zarro?"

"Aye," the man said. "Still alive?"

"Unfortunately."

Deerbolt scowled at Ash's response. "No thanks to *you.*"

The man raised an eyebrow and took a few cautious steps forward to examine her. He was an overweight but tall man, with long black hair and piercing green eyes. His nose was crooked from a certain angle, as if it had been broken several times, and he sported a long black beard. He carried himself with poise because being in charge satisfied his power complex. Deerbolt wasn't afraid of any man, let alone a snivelling Dragonborn Guardsmen; from the way he glared into Ash's soul, she knew he was the one who'd caused Ash so much pain and suffering over the years.

"And *you* are?"

"It doesn't matter who she is. Get behind me," he said, "it'll be okay."

"The lady can speak for herself, Ash."

Deerbolt glared at Zarro and cracked her knuckles.

"It's me you want, Zarro, so let these innocent travellers and their Captain go."

"Travellers?"

He peered around Sarronious at Kite, then widened his eyes when he saw Reverie was carrying an unborn child.

"Interesting."

"Not at all," Ash lied. "They're here only because I bartered for passage across the Tradeway to the Northern Trading Post. We were attacked and almost sank. The village is on fire. We don't know who they were. Looters, perhaps."

"So your arrival here was accidental?" Zarro chortled. "I highly doubt that."

"Aye, we had no other choice but to dock here. It is through no fault of theirs they're stuck with me." Ash paused, wrung his hands together and rolled his eyes. "What, you think I *chose* to be here?"

"You are not normally one to accept help, Ash," the man said, examining Kite and his raised bow. "I think you are here for a reason. Seems to me *you* are the one giving orders."

"The Captain does as she pleases," Ash said. "I'm a passenger on the Cerulean Grace. Let us go, and we will return to the ship. Once repaired, we can be on our way."

"I don't think so."

Zarro snapped his fingers. Half of his men seized Ash's friends one by one, stripping them of any armour and weaponry, and searching them through their clothing for anything concealed. The other half marched to the dock to secure Deerbolt's ship.

Once satisfied, everyone was bound and walked through the ruins, out of sight.

"Where are you taking them?"

"I am not in the habit of butchering pregnant women for no reason, Ash," Zarro said.

"Is that supposed to make me feel better?"

"You have my word they will not be harmed."

Ash surrendered his longsword and dagger to an Elemental Guardsman with a Slyph birthmark, but he made it clear by hissing through his teeth and spitting on his boots he wasn't pleased. The guard gave Ash a backhanded slap and dragged him after the others.

"Your word never did mean much," he said, passing Zarro. "We know something inhumane is going on here. Why else would you be rebuilding the Dragon's Circle and employing more Elementals?"

Zarro laughed. "Oh, his body is withering but his mind is still sharp." He waved off Ash's accusations. "Maintaining a piece of our history, that's all."

"And building a new wall to protect this place is for *fun*?"

"I have to keep my men occupied somehow. The Dragonborn Guard has come a long way since your service, Ash. We are no longer prejudice against your kind; we welcome all Alchemists to join if they have the heart and the will to protect our precious flame."

Behind him, the front row of the formation demonstrated a variety of Elemental incantations. One lit a fireball while another blew a pile of leaves up into the air. Then another quaked the ground in a less sinister way than Ash had, which shook dew droplets from the trees overhead, giving the final Elemental the opportunity to collect and pool it in the air. Each grinned knowingly.

Zarro nodded at the Slyph. He pulled a black sack over Ash's head and led him deeper into the jungle. Ash couldn't see anything, but he could smell smoke and cooking meat, and could hear chattering and laughter nearby. It grew louder with each footstep until there were hands on his arms and chest; fingers poked him, hands rummaged in his pockets.

"Out of the way," Zarro grumbled at them.

The ground was easier to walk on here—dirt, rather than grass and leaves, he thought. *They must be walking me through the village.* He considered calling out Crane and Cage's names to see if anyone responded, but decided dragging them into this too soon was unwise. Zarro would want to know what their ties were, and before they could deny knowledge of Ash's plan, by association they'd be strung up alongside him. He couldn't risk the lives of his only remaining friends here. But when he did find them, and he planned to... *soon*, he would warn them the Dragonborn Guard had been infiltrated by the Order, and ask them to betray their comrades. By staying here, they might die, but they could return to the mainland and live in Open Country with Ash if he made it back alive.

The sack was ragged off, ripping some of Ash's hair out at the root. He groaned and blinked, waiting for his eyes to adjust in the candlelight. This room was familiar—it was Zarro's office, where Ash was initially questioned about the Oracle's accusations.

"Why blindfold me?"

Ash didn't see the logic; he could remember the path to and from Zarro's office because he'd walked it so many times. The familiar stone table and hand-carved wooden chair sat in front of a dirty window. Torches hung on either side, but rags now blocked out the natural light, forcing additional lanterns placed strategically around the room to work twice as hard.

"Want me to get that for you?"

Ash gestured at one that was flickering and smiled.

"You intend to do what, exactly?"

"I'm a Salamander," Ash reminded him, confused.

Zarro sniffed and shrugged. "I'm sorry, I thought you may have been offering to snuff it out with water or a gust of air, perhaps."

Ash sat back in his seat; his hands were still bound behind him and the rope dug into his skin, making it difficult to burn his way through. The rope also felt cold and wet. Obviously, Zarro hadn't missed that trick, and he read the confusion and frustration in Ash's expression.

"You *are* a Tetrad, are you not?"

"I am not."

"Now who's the liar?" Zarro sat behind his desk and leaned forward, clasping his hands. "Waste my time all you want; the more we talk, the more your friends will hurt."

Ash lunged at him across the desk, but Zarro was ready for the reckless response. He grabbed Ash by the back of the neck and slammed his head down, pressing his right cheek against the cold stone.

He whispered in his ear, "Let us not play games."

When he released Ash, he asked again. There was now a metallic taste in Ash's mouth; he spat a glob of bloody saliva at Zorro's feet and wiped his chin with his shoulder.

"Aye," Ash uttered.

"Better."

"You won't get away with it."

Zarro cleared his throat and stared, unblinking, at Ash. He sat unmoving, waiting for him to offer further clarification. In his position, he'd got away with many illegal things over the past ten years, and living on an island with a bunch of sheep willing to do as told without asking any questions allowed him to continue the reign.

"Mika won't allow it when he finds out."

Zarro threw his head back and roared with laughter. "I doubt he can do much about it where he is." Ash scowled, so Zarro finished, "Most likely the Lingerverse, because we all know that self-righteous fool has unfinished business."

"*You*, probably." Ash huffed.

Mika had been in charge of his barracks when he served on the island. Though a little older, Ash appreciated his fair and just nature, and his strong belief in the old ways and the Gods.

Mika led with authority but was not above mucking in with the men, or sharing his weekly tankard of ale alongside them.

"I don't believe I have admitted to anything yet," Zarro said, fingering his chin.

"Give me credit. You are a sanctimonious worm and always have been. My theory won't be far off the truth, Zarro. You may as well confess."

"Confess to what?"

Ash sighed. "You are probably going to kill me anyway, even if you decide to let my friends leave unscathed, so what's the harm in catching me up? Maybe I could help you. If you didn't already know, I *am* a dying man. What do I have to lose?"

The flickering lantern gave up, and one corner of the room suddenly fell into darkness. Ash shivered.

"Everything I do is for the good of this island," Zarro told him. "Mika failed to grasp the importance of maintaining a position of power. He wanted to invite pregnant women back here to face the egg and tempt the rebirth of the Dragon era. Imbecile."

"So you murdered him."

Ash saw the beginning of Zarro's monologue as an opportunity to work his wrists free. With warm palms, he used a tiny Elemental incantation to evaporate the water that dampened them. In a few minutes, once Zarro had admitted guilt and his affiliation with the Order, Ash could burn them to ashes and strangle the life out of his old leader once and for all.

"He had a heart attack," Zarro grumbled, almost disappointed he didn't get the chance to take Mika out himself. "Regardless of the cause, Mika died and I took his place, choosing not to backfill my role so there would be nobody there to challenge or overthrow me when I opted to use my head and not my heart."

Zarro stood and began pacing the width of the room. In the light, Ash could only see a dark silhouette moving left and right whenever he came near the window. He focused on Zarro's voice, trying to use the cruelty in every word to fuel his Alchemy.

"Why would you align with that *cult*?"

Zarro stopped walking and pressed his nose against Ash's. He could smell the rancid, rotting meat lodged between his crooked teeth and more ale than he was rationed.

"That *cult* is the only group making any sense these days." He pulled away and continued pacing. "The Dragonborn Guard have a once-in-a-lifetime opportunity to welcome the return of a God. This is history in the making, Ash the Elemental."

"*Tetrad*," he groaned.

Zarro snorted. "Oh, it's true then! We... *I*... will be known for reincarnating the most powerful God of them all, Universal Energy!"

Ash ran his fingers across the rope. It was dry. He chewed his bottom lip as he lit a tiny torch on the end of his index finger, hoping it was enough and Zarro wouldn't smell burning amidst the lanterns and wall-mounted torches.

I need to keep him talking. "So it was you who freed him from Akasha all those years ago? The Oracle *was* possessed, wasn't he?"

Zarro scowled, unsure how Ash knew about the God of Universal Energy's presence in the Lingerverse. It didn't matter much now—Ash had been banished, out of the way for Zarro to manipulate the new Dragonborn Guard, bending them to his will.

"I had nothing to do with his release, but the Oracle's behaviour was a little... irrational."

"Then you knew long before that night on the wall."

"Aye, it was obvious."

"So how did the God break free, I wonder?" he stated.

Zarro bit. "An Astral learnt of us." He shook his head at Ash's stupidity, then continued to ramble. "During training, he accidentally accessed part of the Lingerverse he shouldn't have."

"That's not possible."

"Your Velocal female *friend* will tell you it is. He went too deep," Zarro replied. "He witnessed a presence at the boundary between the Lingerverse and Akasha."

Genuinely intrigued now, Ash forgot to continue burning his way through the rope for a moment. What presence could be powerful enough to move in and out of Akasha by choice, other than the God of Magic himself?

"What kind of 'presence'?" he queried.

Zarro shrugged. "How should I know? The Astral panicked and pulled away before he could figure it out himself."

"Is that Astral still here?"

"He's dead too."

Zarro didn't seem bothered the Astral had potentially stumbled upon the cause of the God of Universal Energy's release, but chose not to find out more. Did Zarro want him to investigate? Was he not punished or forced to return to the Lingerverse before Zarro killed him?

"Was the presence God-like?"

"There are no other Gods," Zarro informed him, as though Ash didn't already know the creation story or follow the old ways.

Ash resumed his escape and amped up the heat to fry the remaining bits of rope. He didn't want to have to yank his hands to rip through and alert Zarro.

"I did have the Oracle check the Astral briefly with Psychometry, but it was of no matter, anyway. Shortly after, his personality and behaviour changed. We knew there was something the Oracle wasn't telling us."

"That's when the God possessed him?"

"Aye," Zarro said.

Ash laughed. "Did you think maybe he possessed him because you had him poke holes in the Astral's consciousness? In doing so, you opened a gateway, Zarro. You're a fool."

He turned his back to Ash and grumbled, "It crossed my

mind."

Which, Ash thought, *means you had no idea and it has only just occurred to you.*

Ash took advantage of Zarro's diverted attention and tore the last of the rope free. He caught it just in time to prevent it from falling at his feet, and shoved the remnants in his pocket.

"Are you going to tell me where you're keeping Deerbolt, Kite, Reverie and Sarronious?"

"Now that *would* be foolish. I'll level with you, Ash the Elemental..."

"*Tetrad!*" Ash corrected, again.

Zarro ignored him. "If we didn't like outsiders invading our island before, we are even less fond of treasonous trespassers now. As you can see, we're working on preparations to welcome home the God of Universal Energy, and Dragonborn needs to prove its dedication and worth. I can't have you running off to share our big secret, can I?"

Ash had to pinch himself before he lunged over the table at him.

"But, you're not an Astral, Zarro. Even if the God does allow the Order to keep their Alchemy and wipe everyone else's, you're still a mere Human. What good is the God's return to you other than fame?"

It was Zarro's turn to correct Ash. "Now I possess your interesting book, I do believe I can call myself a Velocal."

"Not until you know what it contains," Ash snapped.

If Zarro thought by owning an Alchemical grimoire he was instantly wiser to the Elemental power, he was mistaken. Ash, already a Tetrad, didn't yet know all it contained, and he could still feel the key cool against his chest. Thankfully, Zarro's Guardsmen hadn't been so thorough in their search, focusing on his pockets and boots rather than what hung around his neck.

"I'm going to kill you, Zarro, before this day ends."

"I *highly* doubt that. Fame is enough for me, Ash. But a God's gratitude could grant me an endless list of favours.

Alchemy being one of them. I can't allow you to get in my way. Don't fret, I'll let you say goodbye to your girl."

How could Ash have been so stupid? Of course Zarro wanted to be Alchemical. Why would this arrogant, self-involved traitor want anything else? Ash had heard all he could take of Zarro's selfishness. Free of his restraints and feeling the key's blue fire burning within him, Ash's rage boiled. He lunged over the table, using his feet as a battering ram, and booted Zarro in the chest. The Velocal crashed backwards through the glass, wrapped and flailing in the curtains. Shouts followed immediately, and the sound of metal and boots neared.

To escape, he would need to hurry. He grabbed a torch from the wall and exited Zarro's dim quarters, mentally navigating to where he assumed his friends were being held.

The door opened into a narrow stone corridor, with an arched ceiling and torches dotted every few meters to light the windowless space. Ash hurried, praying the torch he carried stayed alight so he could use it to maintain his Salamander Alchemy out in the open. The square courtyard was alive with Guardsmen, and five were bounding up the wooden staircase to find and punish the man responsible for killing their leader. Ash poked his head around the doorway to see Zarro's twisted frame motionless, surrounded by glass. His bones were broken and his neck snapped. Shards poked from his face and blood was pooling beneath his lifeless body.

There was no sorrow or guilt in Ash's soul for murdering Zarro. Cold-blooded as it was, what Zarro had planned for their party was cruel. If he was to die by anyone's sword, it would be Deerbolt's, and through mercy alone. Nobody else had yet earned the right to put him out of his cursed misery.

Ash was without a blade, or any other weapon. He would have to rely on his Alchemy. And he realised, debating whether it was wise to charge at the men and catch them off guard or to hide and grab them as they came around the corner, his body had not been responding to the curse as it had at the marketplace. Before this voyage and before Ash had a purpose, physically he was weaker and sick, but as he stood deliberating his next move, Ash felt a burst of energy he recognised as a mixture of youth, vitality and *control.*

Zarro would have sent Deerbolt and the others to the holding cells across the village. They were made only of wooden slats—obviously, not designed to hold a Salamander or a Gnome—but they were thick and difficult for any other to escape. With his torch, Ash could burn the wood and kick it free to create a hole large enough for his friends to crawl through. But first, he would have to get across the courtyard and through the village without being captured or killed.

CHAPTER SEVENTEEN
ZARRO'S WISH

Chapter Seventeen: Zarro's Wish

By the pace of their boots, Ash expected he had a few seconds left before they were on him. Still in the doorway, he closed his eyes and counted to three, then swung the lit torch, using it as a melee, and wiped the first two guards off their feet and over the side. They landed, breaking a stack of rotten crates, but were otherwise unharmed. The three following skidded to a halt and pinned their bodies to the wall on Ash's left; he knew they were there, but would play their little game of wait and see.

One man tried his luck, and Ash saw the tip of his longsword first. Using the thickest part of his boot, Ash kicked the blade up and away from the man, snatching it mid-air with his dominant hand and pointing it back at him. The two men now on either side pointed theirs back, and for a moment they were frozen, unsure of each other.

"Let me pass," Ash said.

The leader's hands were raised, but the two behind weren't giving in so easily.

"We can't."

"You're under orders."

The man nodded. "Aye. Zarro's orders."

"Zarro is dead." Ash gestured with his head at Zarro's lifeless body. "You've seen it."

"You killed him."

Ash took one step forward, and the three facing him took two back. Seeing the confrontation, the men now in the courtyard stood and glared up at their conversation, waiting to either join the fight or run for reinforcements.

Ash swallowed hard and said, "Aye, I killed him. He deserved it. Dragonborn Guardsmen are sworn to protect the innocent and the flame. Zarro has imprisoned my friends. One is blind, and the other pregnant. She's here to offer her child to the fifth egg. Did he tell you *that*?"

The men stole quick glances at one another, relaxing their stances. Ash had found a trigger, and he planned to put pressure on until common sense fired.

"From your blank expressions, I guess not." He sighed. "I'm not here to cause any of you harm. We travelled from the mainland by my friend's ship, the Cerulean Grace. Many of you know it as the Equos; she once transported your luxuries to and from the mainland."

The lead man, still without a weapon, nodded.

"Aye," he said. "The Captain brought me here when I pledged my service."

Ash's eyes brightened. "You'll know of Deerbolt, then?" He almost lowered his weapon, too.

The man hesitated, then grinned. "Aye, a beauty."

Ash let the compliment go. "She's here in your holding cells with her deckhand, a Human named Sarronious. We were transporting Kite and Reverie to the Isle of Dragonborn for your help. A Shaman cursed Kite, stealing his sight and with it, his gift of Hydromancy. His wife is heavily pregnant and they were hoping for a cure so he can see the baby, and help to care for it."

"We know nothing of this," one of the other men said. "Zarro ordered us to imprison them and to ensure the Elemental in their company never sees the light of day again."

"He mentioned he was planning to execute me?"

"Why would he do that?" the other man asked, stalled by the news.

He was under the impression Ash would be imprisoned, not killed.

Ash exhaled and lowered his blade first, but he did not back down. As best he could without dropping the torch, he whipped the flame into a fireball. Focusing his Salamander Alchemy on the key beneath his shirt, Ash channelled its energy. Blue rays shone through the cloth, causing the three Guardsmen to gasp and retreat a few paces further. Ash didn't waver or panic, proving there was nothing for the men to be afraid of. Then, with a double blink, the fireball went out suddenly.

"We are familiar with Salamander Alchemy," the leader said, wondering where Ash was going with this demonstration.

One corner of Ash's lips upturned. Across the courtyard, a five-foot tornado turned, picking up dirt, twigs and pieces of the destroyed crates as it did so. Ash pushed and pulled the air with his Slyph breath. Astonished, the men dropped their weapons and they clattered against the wooden decking.

The tornado made its way up the stairs behind them, forcing each man to squeeze against the wall again. Ash reduced its speed and impact when it reached them, as only to ruffle their hair and take their breath away, then he let it drop its contents between them. Using one of the Gnome incantations he'd memorised, he grew a few shoots atop the dirt, then wiped the sweat from his forehead and showered them with the water. His movements were jerky and awkward, because he wasn't used to manipulating any other element but his own. It seemed to do the trick and the shoots grew a few inches. They did not flower.

"I'm not here to extinguish your flame, either," Ash told them. "I promised an Oracle on the mainland I would help Kite and Reverie to find a solution to their misfortune, and act as their guide."

The lead Guardsman narrowed his eyes. "I... I think I recognise you." He turned to his friends. "He's that Tetrad they chased off the island a few years ago."

"Ten," Ash grumbled, "and wrongly so."

"Not if you're a Tetrad," one man argued, scowling.

"I didn't know I could do this then."

"You're probably the only Tetrad to exist right now."

He shrugged. "Probably."

At hearing the word 'Tetrad' the men on the ground set off running to spread the news that a rare Elemental had made it into their midst. Any minute now, Ash would be overwhelmed with attention and once again need to fight his way free.

"Please, I need your help," Ash pleaded. "Before his death, Zarro confessed something terrible to me. You have no reason to believe me but you *need* to. If Zarro's wishes are allowed to come true, you are all in danger. The island... the Land, will be soon consumed by the God of Universal Energy's rage."

None of the men so far had bothered to reach for their weapons again. They were interested in Ash and intrigued by his mystical abilities—something nobody had seen for hundreds of years, though Humans held no doubt Tetrads still existed in secrecy.

"I don't have time to explain everything, but if you can take me safely to brothers Crane and Cage, they can vouch for me."

He paused and decided he would make more of an impact without a direct connection to fire, so he extinguished the torch completely and threw down the stalk.

"Do they still serve here?"

The men looked between one another, then nodded. Across the courtyard, men were appearing and gathering, but not all had weapons. Stunned by the sight of Zarro's corpse and Ash's presence outside his quarters, some men were enraged and arguing amongst themselves that Ash was not to be trusted, but others watched carefully how the three men he faced assessed his behaviour, and how likely his story was to be true. There weren't as many men serving as Ash imagined.

"That *glow...*"

Ash remembered the key and pulled it from his shirt by the ribbon. It was still blue and pulsing now, waiting for Ash to give it an order or pull its light within him.

"It feeds your gift?"

"I don't know. It was given to me by a Velocal on the mainland and it opens a book that helps me to control my powers."

From the base of the staircase, a man shouted, "We have it. It's locked in the cells with the other prisoners. Zarro said it must be kept hidden."

"Aye," Ash said, "but there is no use separating it from them. Nobody but I can open or use its instructions. This key is the only way to gain access. Without the guidance, I'll make mistakes, and I'm trying to be a better Elemental. Free Captain Deerbolt; you know she is honest, because she follows the old ways. I'm begging you, and I never beg. Please give the book back and release my friends. They are here only to ask for your help and to offer something in return."

"We have no need for jewels," the man yelled.

Ash called back, "Nor shall you get any! Kite and Reverie are poor, and I'm a dying man. Why else would we travel so far and rely on the kind nature of strangers? They asked an Oracle at Blackheart Dock to reverse Kite's terrible curse. He refused. Another advised I could persuade *you*."

"Zarro makes the decisions around here," said the leader.

"Made. Past tense. Zarro is dead." Ash raised an eyebrow. "Now what?"

"Then we are without guidance."

"Where are the others leading Dragonborn?" Ash asked.

The man grunted. "There was only Zarro and the Oracle. The others were old, and they died many years ago. Zarro never appointed their replacements. There is no chain of command. Our numbers here dwindle, can't you see that?"

Ash glanced across the courtyard again. The Guard had never been so sparse.

"Take me to my friends."

"In exchange for *what*, exactly?"

Ash handed back the guard's sword and raised both his palms to show he was done fighting, and had no intention of arguing any further. All Ash wanted was to survive the day, and to see Kite and Reverie healed of their trauma. If the Guardsmen listened, maybe the egg would hatch for Reverie's baby, and everyone could leave Dragonborn knowing there would be a tomorrow.

Ash relayed this to the three men. Two of them retreated down the stairs to speak with their comrades, while the leader, now armed with the sword Ash initially confiscated, guarded him. There was no point, because Ash had already made up his mind. All these years, Zarro had governed Dragonborn alone, and in that time he had destroyed everything pure about the oath each man there took.

"Alright," someone called, suspicious, "this way."

The guard led Ash along the walkway and down the stairs into the courtyard. The small crowd parted and allowed them to walk through; each gawped and a few pointed at him, whispering. He heard the word 'Tetrad' several times, and noted not everyone seemed pleased to be working with him. Unfortunately for Ash, that suggested there were many following Zarro and his backward beliefs. If he convinced the majority to help Kite and Reverie for a chance to birth the last Dragon, they would all need to prepare to face resistance.

They made their way slowly across the courtyard and onto the village's main street. Few changes had been made since Ash was last here. The dirt road seemed smaller, but he was ten years older now, and the many humble shops selling clothing, weaponry and 'luxury' foods such as preserves and imported fruits from overseas were still in business. The doorways were stooped and barely wide enough for Ash's frame to fit through, unless he shimmied sideways, and most only fit one or two customers at a time, making trade days busy and wait times sluggish. Today was not a trade day, it seemed, because most were closed as they passed by, heading to a fountain in the centre of a modest square, with wooden benches at the edges facing inward.

They took a sharp right, walking at a brisk pace through the wall walk's archway and past the barracks. Ash noted their increase in speed and wondered if they were trying to hide something. It seemed, however, there wasn't much to conceal. Other than the men in the courtyard—Ash estimated roughly two hundred—the village was deserted. The wall that circled the main facilities and lined the coast was unmanned.

"Is something wrong?" he asked.

"Not wrong," the guard said. "Just... limited."

"Limited?"

The Guardsman stopped and Ash almost crashed into the back of him. He turned, level with Ash, their faces too close for comfort. He reminded Ash that Guardsmen were few these days, and since Zarro had taken over, men considering joining had then decided a life of servitude to a flame they would never see wasn't ideal. Nine out of ten recruits had returned home on the last pilgrim ship.

"I see." Ash hummed. "What did Zarro tell you about his plans for this island?"

"Nothing," the guard replied. "Absolutely nothing."

They continued walking until they reached the building where the holding cells were. Inside, there were three thin wooden cages with a four-person capacity in each. When Ash entered behind the guard, he was pleased to see his friends were not all crammed in together, rather separated across two with the book in the centre, out of arms reach through the bars. A single Guardsman sat on a wooden chair, keeping a close eye on the prisoners.

"I'm here to relieve you of duty."

The guard scowled and tilted his head around the leader's frame to look Ash up and down, then nodded and gathered his things. Once he had left the room and the door latched behind him, the leader threw Ash the keys.

"Am I going to regret this?"

Ash replied, "Your gut instinct says I'm telling you the truth. That should be enough."

Kite and Reverie were nearest the door, so he unlocked their cell first. He let Deerbolt and Sarronious out next, then retrieved his book. Hanging on the wall beside the guard's seat was Ash's satchel (in which he crammed the book) and their other belongings.

"Why are you helping us?" Reverie asked.

The guard chewed his thumbnail as he mumbled, "Curiosity."

"What about Zarro's orders?" Ash asked, handing Deerbolt back her longsword and Kite his bow and arrows. "Are you saying you trust us?"

"Captain Deerbolt brought me to this island," he said, making eye contact with her and smiling. "You were kind, and you wished me luck. Since then, life here hasn't been what I expected it to be. I know Cage and Crane. They are good men. If they'll vouch for you, so will I."

"What is your name?" she asked, returning the smile.

"Riley," the guard said.

He sat, waiting for them to gather their things and re-dress in confiscated clothing. Their hats, coats and boots had been taken alongside their holsters, any baggage and even belts to prevent suicides and attacks not only on the guards, but each other.

"Zarro ruled this place. To tell you the truth," Riley said, now speaking to Ash, "I'm glad he's dead." He lowered his head, ashamed. "*Never* have I wished death on any soul before, but Zarro could be merciless, and he was secretive."

"You have no other leaders he confided in," Sarronious said.

He shook his head. "The Oracle is the only man he associated with in private. Hours were spent locked away in

Zarro's quarters, and the Oracle would emerge exhausted, rubbing his temple or yawning; signs, we recognised, of exhausting his Alchemy as a Seer. He never said what they spoke of or what Zarro's plans for Dragonborn's future were."

Reverie helped Kite with the last of his possessions. "You never asked?" she said.

Riley frowned. "I like my head."

"Zarro was using the Oracle," Kite said as he fastened his cloak around his shoulders with Reverie's help, concealing his bow and arrows. "Did the Oracle ever speak to you directly?"

"Rarely. We avoided contact."

Ash backfilled. "Oracles employed here use Psychometry," he explained. "Most of the men are terrified of physical touch. It's how the Oracle used to keep us in line years ago."

"Still the case," Riley confirmed.

"What's the Oracle's name? I wonder if it's the same man that once terrorised us."

Riley shrugged.

"You don't know his name?"

"You can't ask questions of an Oracle here, and he never volunteered that information. We just call him the Oracle, and he answers to it."

"Why can't you ask him questions?" Reverie raised an eyebrow, puzzled as most Oracles made their living answering questions.

"He's a difficult man," Riley told her.

"Mean?"

"Aye," he replied.

Reverie hummed. "Sounds charming. Can't *wait* to meet him."

Ash sniggered at her sarcasm. "All being well, you won't have to."

"Stay out of his way," Deerbolt instructed her.

"I'll deal with him, Reverie," he said. "Now I'm sure it's the same Oracle, and Riley has a point. He's a horrible being, and quick to delivery what he thinks is justice."

“He's the one that got Ash banished,” Deerbolt revealed.

Kite and Reverie nodded, now understanding Ash's predicament. But Ash would have to wait to get his revenge, because the Oracle was most likely still in contact with the God of Universal Energy, if not re-possessed already. Killing him now? Unwise. Insight into that dilemma and how he'd escaped Akasha was valuable, and something they were currently in short supply of. If the Oracle could answer a few questions first, under torture if necessary, Ash might then take his life knowing he'd done everything possible beforehand to help the Land's chances.

Riley spent the next half hour telling Ash and his companions about the Oracle's quarters, and his daily habits. He admitted after hearing Ash's story from the night of his banishment the Oracle was seen acting strangely—sometimes, he argued with himself when he thought nobody was around to hear, or he'd stand facing the mirror and study his reflection. Oracles were not usually vain, and few of the men on Dragonborn even owned a comb, so it wasn't down to improving his image.

“Do you think the God of Universal Energy is controlling him, Ash?” Kite asked.

He gripped Reverie's hand tightly and pulled her in. If the God had returned somehow, trouble was to be expected. Having his sight back before the showdown would allow him to offer Ash some support. With a sword, he was skilled, but with his bow and arrows, he was an expert. From a rooftop or with a clear line of sight, even at a distance, Kite could be Ash's secret reinforcement and strike when the Oracle least expected it, or if he thought he had the upper hand.

“Sounds that way,” Sarronious answered for him.

He rolled up his shirt sleeves, revealing his dark tattoos and chunky arms.

Riley swallowed hard. *Wouldn't want to get on the wrong side of him,* he thought.

“How can I help?”

Ash placed a hand on the guard's shoulder. “You already have. We can't ask any more of you. It's too dangerous.”

“Can I at least take you to your friends? They don't live far from here.” Ash thanked him, and Riley added, “Then I'll make up my mind. The men of Dragonborn are still loyal to its cause, and once they know Zarro's intentions were tainted, you'll have an army behind you.”

“Some are not so eager to trust me,” Ash told him. “I saw it back there in the courtyard. Tetrads are never welcome here for obvious reasons.”

Riley grinned. “Sounds to me Zarro was a greater threat to our sacred flame than you will ever be.”

CHAPTER EIGHTEEN
DRAGONBORN

Chapter Eighteen: Dragonborn

Riley led Ash, Sarronious, Kite and Reverie to a small apartment just outside the village. It was above a closed bakery, but they picked up on the lingering smell of warm bread, cakes and yeast. They hadn't realised how hungry they all were until then, and Ash's stomach grumbled loudly.

"Crane and Cage will offer you supper," said Riley.

"Sorry," Ash said, blushing. "I forgot how long it had been since we've eaten anything. I hope the Guardsmen have fed the crew, and they are not worrying about us. Reverie, are you feeling alright?"

Reverie smiled. "Aye, but I wouldn't say no to some soup and bread."

"Zarro will have sent those men only to detain and observe your crew," Riley explained.

Ash sighed. "Nothing we can do now if not."

Riley gestured at the staircase leading up to a thick wooden door, engraved with the letters CC. Ash thought back to his Guardsmen days, when personalising an apartment of your own was unheard of. Then, they survived in shared barracks, where it seemed only the lower-level recruits and newbies inhabited now. Those in a higher position and their leaders lived alone, but Ash was pleased this wasn't the case for him. He enjoyed having brothers and friends to socialise with and rely on. They supported one another, complained together, but celebrated together, too. Birthdays were really the only time Ash and his brothers threw parties on the island, because celebrating other holidays was forbidden. Dragonborn was a place of dedication and service, and distractions for religious events or personal circumstances were unnecessary. But, when a Guardsman did reveal it was their birthday, the leaders allowed them an unplanned break. Particularly if the Guardsman had served many years, another birthday meant another year on duty, which the island and the egg appreciated. Allowing birthdays to go ahead as normal was Dragonborn's way to say thank you.

Ash imagined birthdays would be banned too under Zarro's reign, but he decided not to ask Riley. Now wasn't the time for such trivial issues.

"I'll take you up, but then I must go."

"Are you on watch?" Ash asked Riley.

He shook his head and gave Ash a pat on the back. "Once Crane and Cage give me the thumbs up, I will rally some allies and meet you in the morning."

"Will we have that long?" Deerbolt asked, fearful word of their escape would have already travelled to the Oracle.

Without a current leader or any other right-hand men to step up in the meantime, the Guard would be at a loss regarding how to deal with a Tetrad's presence on the island. So if Riley could convince as many men as possible to join Ash in the rally against Zarro's wishes (and the Oracle), they'd be in a better position to overthrow him and the God within his psyche.

"Zarro was not a popular man," Riley said, "but the men here are loyal to their government. The sooner I can spread word of your intentions the better."

Ash and his friends followed Riley up the stairs and

hammered on the door. It was Crane who answered, and when his eyes locked with Ash's, the Guardsman let out a roar of laughter and pulled him into a tight, warm embrace.

"Ash, you scoundrel. It has been too long!"

Deerbolt grinned at the nickname—so it was not only she to refer to Ash as such. It made her smile how others had recognised Ash's darker, cheekier side, and honoured rather than feared it the way she did.

"How are you here? Why are you here? Quickly," he said, dragging Ash inside by his doublet, "come inside. You cannot be seen."

Riley waited for the others to follow, then closed the door behind them. Once inside, everyone seemed to relax a little in front of a warm fire, burning fiercely. Plumes of smoke filtered up the chimney and filled the air with a sooty and harsh familiar scent. There was wooden furniture facing it, and in one chair sat Crane's brother, Cage. His hair shimmered in the orange glow, and his face lit up too when he saw Ash's wide frame filling the window behind him.

"Ah ha!" He burst to life and hugged Ash, holding onto him for a moment longer than Ash was comfortable with, feeling so unwell. "We have missed you, friend."

Ash slapped his arm and beamed. "And I you." He turned to Riley and outstretched a hand. "Do we have an alliance?"

Without hesitation, Riley shook Ash's hand. He pulled Crane and Cage aside to explain all that had happened and asked if they might feed and shelter the outlaws until Riley had chance to rally additional Guardsmen.

"For Ash, anything," Cage said. He turned to Ash, grabbing everyone else's attention at the same time. "My friend, I am sorry we did not do more when you were—"

Ash interrupted. "No apology needed. Everything turned out well in the end." Then he cleared his throat and corrected himself. "I suppose it is not yet the end. We have serious work to do tomorrow, but so far I'm alive."

"And well," Deerbolt added quickly.

"That's not *entirely...*"

She winked to cut Ash off; it would be best, she thought, if the brothers did not yet know of Ash's plight. Already, they were feeling guilty for being unable to save his position on the island ten years ago, and it would only distract them from helping the group to achieve their goal if they knew Ash was a dying, suffering man.

"Ash has thrived on the mainland, though he has told me how much he missed you."

Crane shook Deerbolt's hand, recognising her as Captain. The crew once delivered a special birthday order for the brothers many years ago, including ale (which they hid beneath the floorboards in the barracks at the time to avoid the Oracle's prying touch). Though she wasn't sure she recognised either of them from her trade days with the island, she warmed to their personalities and their response to Ash's return. He needed friends like these who were pleased to have him around, and who felt safe and honoured by his arrival, not threatened.

"Have you and Ash known each other long?" Crane asked Deerbolt.

Rather than respond, she winked again and the brothers chortled in unison. They pulled Ash to the fireplace and immediately got talking about the old times, almost as if Ash had never been away. Deerbolt watched from the curtained window, at ease. They'd made it. Ash was with friends now, and whether Kite's sight could or could not be restored, in her gut she *knew* they were all going to be alright.

That included Ash the Elemental.

Ash the Tetrad.

Overnight, loud voices and stomping footsteps could be heard beneath the apartment window, heading to the village where the cells were. Ash struggled to sleep and kept a hand securely on the strap of his satchel, feeling more confident having the book in hand. At short notice, Dragonborn Guardsmen following Zarro's wishes and hoping to avenge his murder could burst through the door and arrest them all, including the brothers for harbouring treasonous fugitives. The thought of getting the only friends he had left killed sent shudders down Ash's spine.

Laid on the wooden floor with only a thin blanket for comfort aggravated Ash's failing body. Aches and pains plagued his limbs and put a crick in his neck. If he sat up too quickly, his balance would throw him over again, so he'd chosen a spot at a safe distance from the fire's embers.

He wriggled his fingers, wondering if he still had the strength to manipulate his Salamander Alchemy, or if that, too, was under threat. On the ship, he'd hoped being back on the island would ignite what little remained within him and fuel its resurrection. So far, only regret and fear travelled his veins.

"You're awake?" Sarronious whispered.

Ash rolled on to his side and glanced across the room at the First Mate who sat by the stone fireplace. He jabbed at the greying lumps of coal with a long metal poker, seemingly in deep thought. Slowly, Ash got to his feet, using the edge of a wooden table for support. Confident he was steady, Ash willed his stiff legs to move. Deerbolt, Kite and Reverie were fast asleep across the room, but Ash tiptoed; they needed their rest, because when the sun came up, there would be panic and fighting to face.

"Are they looking for us?"

Sarronious raised his chin toward the window. His eyes were yellow and sparkling in the fire's din. Ash used them to navigate through the room and sat beside him, cross-legged.

"They have been searching for hours," he said, "but I don't believe they are going room-to-room yet. I peeked out about forty minutes ago, and a few armed with longswords were patrolling the streets."

Ash warmed his hands in front of the fire. "There's nowhere to go," he said. "We know it. They know it. Sooner or later, we'll make our move, and if they patrol the public areas, they'll catch us with minimal effort once it's light out."

Sarronious grumbled. "We should move now, while it is dark."

Ash threw a thumb towards Reverie. She slept beside an empty bowl of broth—only a few crumbs remained of the bread.

"Rest," Ash said.

Sarronious nodded. "Aye." He sighed, then turned to Ash suddenly with a solemn expression. "There is nobody here capable of healing Kite, is there?"

Ash narrowed his eyes. "What makes you say that?"

"Oh, come on, Ash. Do you take us for fools? You know as well as I any man powerful enough to reverse a curse like Kite's is dead, has returned to the mainland, or is the very Oracle we are hoping to defeat!"

Ash hushed him and wrung his hands together. "Aye."

"Is that all you can say?"

"What do you expect?" Ash snapped, but in a low voice as not to startle the sleeping Seer. "I travelled here assuming the island would be teeming with dedicated Guardsmen, all under the orders of leaders who are long gone, replaced by a selfish follower of the Order. Believe me, I am just as disappointed with our findings as you. Even more so." He rubbed his eyes with his warm palms, trying to relieve some pent-up tension and a building headache. "When I worked here, Sarronious, this island was *incredible*. We were proud. We were loyal. We were undefeated."

"It was all a lie, Ash," Sarronious said, seriously.

"Then? No."

"Aye, you've been deceived. How can you not see it? Zarro's influence has been poisoning this island far longer than your curse has tormented you on the mainland. He and the Oracle were planning this when you served, I guarantee."

Of course he was right. Zarro banned him for that reason, knowing as a Tetrad Ash could stand in the way of his climb to power. If he extinguished the Dragonborn flame, Alchemy across the Land would die along with any chance of the Dragons returning. If Ash destroyed the egg too, these plans would still have been thwarted, but the Gods would no longer be imprisoned (however, still weakened, he hoped).

"I'm glad I knew little then," Ash said, "because I wouldn't be here now to do something about this."

"I think Zarro would have had you killed."

"By his own hand," Ash said.

Sarronious nodded. He was about to ask Ash what serving as a Guardsman had been like, when more boots drummed past, this time followed by shouting and the clang of metal on metal. Ash hushed him and crawled on his hands and knees to the window, then peered through, lifting a corner of the sheet pinned over it, which acted as a single dreary curtain. Finding his strength, Ash jumped to his feet and drew his longsword. The sound startled Deerbolt awake.

"The Guardsmen are fighting in the streets!" he announced, then tugged the full sheet off its nails to get a better view. "It's Riley! We have to help him."

Ash set off enthusiastically toward the door. Deerbolt stopped him with the flat side of her longsword.

"If we do this, Ash, there's no going back."

Ash flicked her blade down and grabbed Deerbolt by the waist. He pulled her toward him and kissed her, and they stood, heads resting against one another, until Deerbolt sighed and opened her eyes.

"Go," she told him, smiling. "We're right behind you."

Ash ran for the door and flung it open, then charged down the wooden staircase and straight into the centre of the men. Deerbolt hammered on Cage and Crane's bedroom doors, and rallied the others.

"Reverie, stay here," she instructed. "Kite..."

"On it," he said, drawing his arrows and setting them by the doorway. "I'll cover you."

He crouched at the top of the wooden staircase and listened intently to the battle below. But it was difficult to determine who was on their side unless Ash himself called for him to target somebody specifically; Kite would follow Ash's voice, then let loose an arrow. Without his sight, it was impossible to judge if men would step in the way—trust in one another was vital, and Kite trusted Ash would guide his aim. Everyone wore the same armour, and everyone carried the same weapons, so even for Ash, determining allies was difficult. They were all equally matched, but divided by what Ash told Riley about Zarro's plans for Dragonborn. Some still followed his idiocy.

Deerbolt nodded at her First Mate. "Sarronious, grab your halberd."

"Aye, Captain!"

With Reverie safely inside, though peeping anxiously through the window at the bedlam below, the others joined Ash in the fight. They clashed swords with any who swung at them, hoping they were foes and recognised their party as outsiders. Deerbolt was almost stricken with the butt of a huge axe dripping at the other end in someone's blood, but another

Guardsman stepped between her and its force, using his blade to block the attempt on her life. She hollered and ran at another man attacking Cage, but Crane was already on the assailant's back, choking him from behind and crushing his ribs with his strong thighs. So, Deerbolt chose another course, and followed Riley out of the main street, chasing a small group of stragglers making a run for safety.

Out of breath, Riley paused and put his hands on his knees. He pointed between two thatched buildings and Deerbolt nodded.

They went that way.

Unable to tell her more, Deerbolt slapped him between his shoulders and took off. She picked up the pace when she caught sight of one up ahead. The group made haste through the trees and disappeared into foliage, through a wall of deep greens and glints of emerald in the sunlight. Deerbolt followed them without so much as a backward glance to check Riley had caught up, and she bolted through and leapt over anything and everything in her way. Dew and twigs mangled her hair, tearing at her braid and her clothing. But, she didn't care. These men were leaving via this way for a reason, and she prayed they were about to lead her to the most sacred place on the island. By heading to protect it they had inexplicably given away the egg's location.

Ash ran his sword through one last Guardsman. He scanned his surroundings but couldn't see Deerbolt anywhere.

He called to Sarronious who huffed, “That way, behind you,” as he was still in an intricate halberd-sword fight.

Behind them were only a few buildings, then nothing but the jungle. And the terrain was a steep, uneven incline. Ash left the clang of metal and drum of boots behind and set his sights on a small pathway between two buildings on the edge of the village, which led to the trees. He didn't remember the road from his days as a serving Guardsman, but in ten years they had rebuilt and added many new huts and shacks. He was lucky to still have his bearings.

From memory, Ash knew at the top of the hill, though it was approximately one mile away from the village, was an ancient structure resembling a temple with two smooth marble pillars framing the entry, one black and one white. On the door, Ash pictured a beautiful woman beneath a huge full moon. Howling in the distance behind the woman were two unrecognisable beasts, one darker. The door was wooden but thick and heavy, and carved with other pretty borders and symbols—Ash mostly remembered there were stars and trees in the background, too. Ash had never entered the temple, because it was a sacred place where only the Oracle and the leaders of Dragonborn were permitted to go. Sometimes, they would post a guard or two on the door, but they were never advised what was inside. Ash assumed Dragons used to meet there, or it was where the Oracle slept, having not been assigned quarters in the village or with the other men at the barracks.

He continued his chase, identifying Deerbolt's path by the flattened ground, the occasional muddy boot print and some snapped bushes. Somebody had been through here, if not her. At his speed, he couldn't be sure if the prints were her size or a Guardsman's.

Halfway, Ash felt the strain on his limbs and his pounding heart wanted to burst from his chest. It drummed and pumped furiously, sending adrenaline through his veins to spur him on. But the curse was definitely getting the better of him; his vision doubled and he had to catch his breath, but he struggled on. Deerbolt was alone out there, *somewhere*.

He staggered into a small clearing and found Riley, listening for Deerbolt's shouts, or the clang of metal on metal. Nothing.

"I lost her," he told Ash, racing to help him sit. "You look... terrible."

"Thanks, I *feel* great."

Ash re-adjusted the satchel's strap to prevent it from cutting into the skin on his neck. The book was leather-bound and very heavy, but he didn't want to hide it or leave the only weapon he had against his enemies with a Guardsman he had only known for a day.

"What happened back there?"

"Rebellion," Riley explained, offering Ash a drink of water. "I did as I promised and spread the word, but not all the men believed me."

"How many are on our side?" Ash asked.

"Enough."

"We hope."

"I *know*," he said confidently. "Can you continue in your state? The temple isn't far."

"Deerbolt can handle herself, and I'm fine," Ash assured him.

He struggled to his feet and gestured for Riley to lead the way. It wasn't far, and when they arrived on scene, Deerbolt was examining the temple's intricate etchings as if nothing else existed around her. One of the men she had been chasing lay motionless at the bottom of the stone steps leading up to the temple's entrance, but the others were nowhere around.

"Are you alright?" Ash asked.

Deerbolt jumped, then grinned. "You scared me! I'm unharmed, don't worry about me."

"He put up a fight?" Riley jabbed a thumb at the unconscious Guardsman; he noted he was still breathing and there wasn't any blood.

"Aye, but he got distracted. I hit him over the head. He's alive."

Riley scowled. "Distracted by what?"

"Something in there," she said, placing a palm on one of the marble structures.

Ash stood back and looked up. There were no windows or vents above them, no keyholes or handles of any kind. The surface was shiny and cool. The white pillar on the right was laced with black from the pillar on the left, where Ash was standing, observing their surroundings. From here, they were unable to see the village, but they could hear echoes and cries from the valley occasionally when the birds ceased chirping. The Cerulean Grace was surrounded by fast-moving figures, and a second ship flying the Order's seal was moored off-shore.

"The crew are fighting the Guard, and the Order have found us," Riley said. "We should get back and join them."

"Not yet; not if what's in this temple could help Kite and Reverie. But, how do we get inside?" Ash asked Deerbolt.

"My crew can hold their own. These doors are bolted and there doesn't appear to be any other entrance. Focus on getting us inside."

"Didn't you see where the other men went?"

"Sorry," she said, "they were long gone. I think that guy was their lookout, or a straggler. I searched his pockets before I came up here, and he didn't have any papers or hidden weapons. All I could find were a few clear jewels. I didn't realise Guardsmen were paid for their service."

"We're not," Riley said. "Everything is provided. Our service is payment for our lodging, food and the occasional tankard of ale."

"No keys, either. Have *you* ever been inside this temple, Riley?"

He turned to Ash, equally as puzzled. "It is forbidden!"

Deerbolt grinned. "Then there must be another way in. We have to find it, and quickly. Kite and Reverie are still in the village, and I don't know how long Sarronious and the others can fend off Zarro's Guardsmen. My crew are strong but outnumbered. We need to move quickly."

They split up—Deerbolt and Ash searched to the left of the temple and Riley went to the right. They agreed to walk the perimeter, examine any windows and doorways, then meet in the middle at the other side. Luckily, it seemed someone walked these paths frequently, because the ground was firm and clear here, and the trees had been cut back to allow enough room for Ash and the Captain to stride alongside one another. So far, though, there were only walls without grooves or foot holes to climb.

They rounded the corner to be met by Riley, who sighed and asked, “Anything?”

Ash grunted. “Nothing. Keep going, we may have missed something.”

They agreed to work their way back, retracing the others' steps, until they met once again at the pillars.

“There must be a way in.”

Ash walked up to the door and pressed his palm to it, defeated.

“Wait, someone's coming. Hide!”

Suddenly, the front of the building rumbled. The wooden doorway slid open. Ash drew his longsword and waved for Riley to duck. The door took several minutes, and it ground against the floor; Ash knew how old the temple must be and it was down to a lack of maintenance or decay in the mechanism. Once open fully, Ash glared into the dark abyss within. From outside, his eyes couldn't adjust, and he dare not light a fireball to risk giving away their location.

Deerbolt stifled a gasp when she saw the Oracle emerging. His face was stern, and his eyes narrow. Robes in brightly dyed colours adorned his skinny frame, but it wasn't his attire that startled her or his bare feet, nor seeing, potentially, the only being connected with the God of Universal Energy for the first time. In his frail, bony hands, the Oracle was carrying an emerald-coloured, scaly Dragon egg. Ash's eyes widened too at the sight. It wasn't the egg he thought he once saw, so he couldn't be sure if this, too, was a decoy. From afar, he studied it—the way the Oracle cradled it made Ash wonder. It certainly looked precious and delicate. But his teachings always said Dragon eggs were sturdy and impenetrable to keep the creature inside safe and warm. If it was true, though, where was the flame? Surely without it, the Dragon would die?

Ash and Deerbolt's gazes moved swiftly from the egg to

Riley, who had decided to challenge the Oracle for its possession without warning. He stood before the Oracle at the base of the stairs, pointing his longsword.

Ash sighed and rolled his eyes. "Fool."

"Take it back," Riley ordered.

The Oracle said nothing, but his fingers curled tightly around the egg's rough surface. Control of the egg and the Dragon inside was his primary objective, and handing it over to a lowly Guardsman who had no authority over his actions seemed... unlikely. On closer inspection, Ash saw the Oracle's fingers were reddening and slick with sweat.

"Put it down, Oracle," Riley ordered again.

"This does not concern you, boy." His tone was gruff but quaky.

Ash recognised it immediately; this was the same Oracle he'd faced ten years ago on the coastal wall. Older now, he still held his head with pride and power, and Ash was sure he'd rather die than accept defeat and be taken prisoner by his own men.

"So, this is where you and Zarro were hiding it," Riley said, walking toward the Oracle.

He took the first step with caution, then moved up the second and third. Closer to the egg, he could see its intricate details—no two scales were the same, and it shone when the light reflected off its surface, casting pretty green patterns across the stone and the Oracle's attire.

"You are interrupting an important ceremony. Get out of the way."

"I can't," Riley said. "We have to return the egg to the flame or soon, that Dragon will die. It is our job."

"No, boy. It is *your* job."

"But... I... I don't understand! You're a Guardsman just like me. Why would you want to murder our last chance for a new Dragon age? Why risk the existence of Alchemy?" When the Oracle didn't respond, Riley added, "You're a Seer! You don't believe in the Order's creation story; you know with that

Dragon egg's death or by extinguishing its flame all Alchemy will disappear from the Land. Your powers..."

"Will no longer burden me," he said. Slyly, he grinned. "His torture is too much for me to bare, boy. This is the only way. Now, stand aside!"

"NO!"

Ash leapt from the shadows and joined Riley. They climbed another step together and raised their weapons.

Deerbolt slammed her fist in the dirt and cursed Ash under her breath.

Not you, too, she thought, *we should have waited and followed him.* Ash had jumped the gun to save Riley's life, because he wouldn't allow the Oracle to pass. It was move out of the way or die by the Oracle's creepy hand. If he fought, the egg might come to some harm.

Ash had weighed up the lesser evil, and chose to defend Riley.

"You!"

Ash's mouth upturned as he gave a bow. "Surprise!"

CHAPTER NINETEEN
LEGACY

Chapter Nineteen: Legacy

The Oracle seethed when he saw Ash's broad frame appear from the foliage to join his comrade. Ten years ago, he thought he'd dealt with the Elemental by telling their leaders of his secret abilities, then causing his banishment. Not a day went by when the Oracle didn't think of Ash; in his mind, he'd taken the life of an innocent Guardsman to protect his own secret—something he no longer wanted.

Despite all that, the Oracle now wished the God of Universal Energy gone from his body and consciousness. No matter what he did or how hard he tried, his soul always returned to plague and control him. For a while, he'd be able to fight off the mental and physical torture of having one so powerful share his existence, but no more. The God's influence was strengthening every day, therefore weakening the Oracle's.

He wished he could apologise to Ash and even beg for forgiveness and help. Perhaps a Tetrad wasn't only capable of extinguishing a sacred flame, but could permanently extinguish a terrifying God? No, Universal Energy would sense his intentions and punish him.

"How are you still alive?" the Oracle grumbled, more through shock than anger at Ash's return. "I cursed you. I banished you!"

"Evidently, you could not kill me. Now put the egg back, Oracle. You know this is wrong."

"My hands are tied," he said, glaring at the egg's surface. His palms were now turning purple against the heat, and sweat coated his brow.

This must be the real egg, Deerbolt thought as she witnessed their argument from the treeline. *He's taken it directly off the flame with his bare hands. Who would be so reckless to cause themselves great pain, and why?*

"Give it to me," Ash said, "and I'll put it back where it belongs." He reached out, but the Oracle flinched and stepped back toward the temple's doorway. "If you won't give me the egg, then at least tell us *why* you're doing this."

The Oracle's eyes flashed to the side, assessing how far the safety of the temple was from his position on the top step. Though they were now obscured by moss and other vegetation, the stone stairs wound further down the hill and deep into the jungle, ending beneath a large archway, tall enough to accommodate a Dragon's horns and wings. Once, the path had been trodden only by Dragons, heading to the temple to worship the Gods who gave them life and Alchemy. Some of the lower steps were dented by their weight, and others were cracked. Though, to the Guardsmen, it appeared they were simply old and unkempt.

Ash sheathed his sword and reached out to the Oracle.

"Please," he said gently, "we only wish to understand."

"You could never."

"Let us try," Riley said, "because we can help you fulfil whatever duty you're bound to *and* save the egg."

"What were you doing in the temple? Why do you have the egg? Is the flame still burning?" Ash asked.

"My hands are tied, boy," the Oracle snapped.

His eyes widened then, and Ash narrowed his in response.

It sounded like the Oracle he once knew, for sure. Stubborn. Argumentative. Selfish. Arrogant. But, that expression was one of pleading, and of vulnerability.

"Tied how? By whom?" Ash quizzed, slowly and carefully moving further up the stairs to avoid spooking the Oracle into a retreat. "By the God of Universal Energy—he's controlling you, isn't he?"

"I am blessed by his presence," the Oracle said.

His mouth moved, but his eyes were fear-stricken and panicked. His arms were shaking beneath the weight of the egg now, and his slippery fingers were wriggling to keep tight hold of the precious cargo. Ash wanted to reach out and relieve him of the burden, not only to save the egg but to aid this frail old man before him.

"You are not the man you were," he said.

The Oracle said nothing in response, so Riley sheathed his sword too and together, he and Ash walked forward against the Oracle's orders and protests. He backed up into the temple doorway and stood just inside; the door didn't close, nor did he seem to attempt to close it. Suddenly, the key down Ash's shirt illuminated. The electric blue light shone through his layers of clothing and brightened the gloomy, cavernous space they faced.

Seeing this, the Oracle turned and ran. He fled into the temple. The door began to close once again. Ash lunged and squeezed through, grazing his back and chest, leaving Riley and Deerbolt outside.

The key lit Ash's path. The temple wasn't a place of worship at all; when he looked around and examined what appeared to be stone monuments and statues of past Dragons, he was stunned to find they were actually graves, where the bones of powerful Alchemical creatures and their families had been laid to rest. The original four Dragons birthed from the original eggs were inside, somewhere, and Ash longed to find their tombs to pay his respects. But there were more imminent problems at hand.

"Oracle," he called out, and his voice echoed. "You don't need to fear me. I only want to help you."

He paused and retrieved the key from his shirt to allow more light to guide him. Along the walkway, Ash saw large bowls filled with what looked like the ashes of coal and twigs.

"I wonder," he whispered.

Using one of the most basic Elemental incantations he knew—one the book promoted as a starting gesture for all Elemental abilities—Ash birthed a blue flame flicking his wrist from the key to the first metal bowl. Sparks flew when his flame hit the substance, and an explosion of lava blasted upwards, forming a warming pillar from the bowl to the ceiling. Ash gasped and staggered away, shielding his face from the intense heat. Then, he grinned and lit a second and a third. By the time Ash was finished, a total of twenty pillars had been birthed from the key's strange and unexplained Alchemy. They acted as a comforting guide to the back of the temple where an altar had been built with rocks and dirt, and atop it burned the Dragonborn flame.

Like any other, it was hot and flickered. Embers spat across the marble floor and fizzled at Ash's feet as he approached and bent to one knee. It seemed to him a small campfire. The flame's fingers curled around another metal dish in the centre of the pit, where the egg should be cradled safely.

It was missing.

On either side of the flame were two black onyx stalks—thin and glowing in the flame's light. Clear, colourful crystals decorated the tops of each one. They were uncut and natural, in green, white, red and blue from left to right. Ash studied them, seeing his Elemental gifts saturated in these crystals, and in the key's warmth against his skin.

"Oracle," Ash announced again. "Please. Show yourself."

"You should not have come," a voice sounded, bouncing off the walls. "Your kind are persecuted here."

"I'm not here to commit treason," Ash said, then added, "unlike some. You were fleeing with the egg to hide it from us."

"Aye," said the Oracle.

Ash span to see him standing a few hundred yards away, still clutching the egg. In the midst of the lava columns, which ran into an overflow trough, then under the building and down the mountainside straight to the ocean, the Oracle's pallid face warmed and he looked younger somehow. His eyes reflected the golden glow of the Dragonborn flame behind Ash, occasionally stealing a glance at it.

"Give it to me."

"I can't," the Oracle replied.

Ash realised then what the Oracle had been trying to tell him. Physically, the God of Universal Energy would not allow him to uncurl his fingers from the egg's surface. He was paralysed; controlled by the God sailing his consciousness like Deerbolt steered her ship. Its weight pained his muscles, and though the God insisted he grip harder, burning his fingers where it had rested on the metal bowl, the Oracle's strength couldn't take it.

"You're going to drop it."

The Oracle tilted his head. Careful not to let go too soon, he knelt and placed the egg on the marble at his feet, swishing his robe around the base to stop it rolling away. He wiped his palms and inhaled, relieved to be unburdened.

"I know you're in there," Ash told him. "I've been speaking to the God of Universal Energy all along."

"Clever Elemental."

"*Tetrad*," Ash corrected, and smirked.

"Why are you here?"

Ash drew his longsword. He didn't want to have to strike the Oracle, knowing he'd be injuring or killing the innocent man beneath the God's shadow, but he had to put on a show of strength and willingness to defend Alchemy's future.

"My friends need help," he replied flatly. "They are in the village. She is pregnant and he is blind. A Shaman tricked them. I promised to bring them to Dragonborn to find one capable of reversing their curse."

"Is that the only reason?"

Ash shrugged. "You tell me."

"You are a Tetrad yet you do not wish to extinguish the Dragonborn flame. It is within your power, you know. So, why not join the Order and help me bond with the final Dragon egg, then do what you were born to?"

Ash lifted the sword to the Oracle's head height and held it there, firmly. He followed the blade to meet his opponent's gaze.

"Because there's a way for everyone to get what they desire without having to commit treason or murder."

"Everyone except the Order, the rightful rulers of the Land."

"Says who?"

The Oracle straightened. "Says I! They have been most loyal!"

"And what influence do you have over your people, anymore?" Ash challenged. "You know as well as anyone as soon as the Order fulfils your wishes, their magic will die along with everyone else's. Only *you* will retain Alchemy in your new, scaly body. Once you extinguish that fire, there can be no Dragons after you, and no one else capable of assisting you in Alchemical matters. You will live, exist and die alone in that Dragon's exterior."

The Oracle's eyes narrowed. Ash could no longer see or feel the influence of the man beneath the God. He had been swallowed whole. Ash hoped he was alive, somewhere, even if only in the Lingerverse.

"Mine was the most powerful of the gifts," the Oracle began. "I possessed power my siblings only dreamt of."

Ash listened intently.

"Reaching into the Lingerverse and pulling fractured souls from the depths was a fun game. Sometimes, I'd free them, only to see them re-birthed to the Land and tortured by Humans as we are all tortured here." He nibbled his nails playfully, casting his gaze everywhere but at Ash. "Mostly, I'd absorb them, when I wasn't busy bending them to my will for other reasons. My siblings could not break the barrier between Akasha and the Lingerverse, though we all frolicked now and then as animals to see what Humans were doing, and experiment with ways to influence them. Then, my father got involved."

The Oracle rolled his eyes and revealed the egg, flinging his robes aside in the blink of an eye. The key around Ash's neck brightened in its presence.

"I needn't tell you the rest," he said, "because you've all heard the variations of our creation story. The God of Magic banishes us to Akasha and steals our Alchemy—enough of it to keep us there, anyway. He gave it to these disgusting creatures. Why? So you petty mortals could learn from them to govern yourselves peacefully. How naïve. Humans have never been capable of peace, even when they had everything handed to them and the tools to co-exist without a need for war or possessions, jewels or cults. Dragons this size were supposed to intimidate you and baffle you; you were supposed to worship the ground they walked on out of fear, so you could be governed. That is, until you realised you were all capable of governing yourselves in more violent ways."

"Your followers ruined it," Ash mumbled.

"My followers simply initiated the natural order of events because they were inevitable. Why wait? They hunted these Dragons and their offspring knowing their Alchemy would spread to Humans and infect them."

"They created chaos. Dragons were order and freedom; they bore Alchemy's burden, and your people released it. Now, they want nothing but to be the sole bearers of Alchemy, despite this bedlam being their fault to begin with!"

"They were not to know killing those beasts would plague the Land with Alchemy at first. When they did, could you blame them for continuing? It is only during the past hundred years they have grown to realise how superior my powers are, and how the Order are the rightful rulers of this Land. The Land can live without Elementals and Seers," he concluded.

Ash snorted at his delusions. "Elementals *are* the Land. We grow and we enrich, we build and we nourish. Without us, the Order would have burned and dried our crops decades ago. They dominate the West now, and do you know what's in the West, Oracle? Nothing. Desert. It's all that's left of our glorious Land. They have sucked it dry of all resources and driven out anyone and everyone capable of replenishing it because of their taxes and genocide."

"You would banish all Astrals from the Land, given the chance?"

Ash considered this, then replied, "I would banish the Order."

"Then you are no better than we!"

"I wish to prevent your cult from destroying everything good about the Land. You wish to end Alchemy completely to suit your own selfish needs. And what makes this worse, Oracle, is that your followers are blind to your true intentions. They believe you'll grant them permission to keep their Astral Alchemy when, in fact, you wish to strip everyone and everything of all that is special about them and be the sole ruler. It sickens me."

"You forget, Ash, I would be powerful enough to heal your friends and save your life."

Ash threw down his sword. A blade would never be enough to rid the Land of this monster, and so it was pointless trying to slay him with metal. The God of Universal Energy knew only Alchemy and dominance; he was devious, making promises he had no intention of keeping and doing business with those less fortunate, spreading hope that by following him, their lives would be enriched. What a snake! What a liar!

The only way to defeat a being like this was with his own magic.

"I won't let you do this, Oracle. There's an innocent soul worthy of that Dragon egg, and it's here on the island just waiting to meet its destiny. You're insane if you think I'm going to use my Tetrad Alchemy to help a man like you, if that's even what you are."

"It would sear your soul to gaze upon my true form, boy," the Oracle hissed.

"I'm a Salamander," Ash said, wringing his hands. "Try me."

"No Dragon will ever grant you eternal life!"

"I'll settle for a few more years, then," said Ash.

Eternal life had never been his wish. The Land was a harsh place. The idea of remaining here forever to witness another cruelty and another sent shivers down his spine. Ash simply wanted to see Deerbolt again, and to ask for her hand in marriage given the chance. He longed to sail the open seas with her, to go beyond the Land's waters and explore what else could be out there; to meet new people, see stunning landscapes, and perhaps sire a child of his own before his time was over.

But first, he wanted to fulfil his original goal: help Kite and Reverie.

"To defeat me, boy, you have few options."

The Oracle sneered and placed a boot atop the egg's surface, threatening to crush it. Ash gasped, then steadied himself. If a Dragon could be killed with the force of a man's foot, Tetrads and the flame would not be necessary. He would be lucky to scuff a scale.

"Oh, I'm aware. I could simply imprison you myself until my friends are healed, then follow my original plan to offer their unborn baby to the Dragon egg. Who knows? Perhaps he or she will be worthy of an Alchemical future, and the Land can rejoice beneath a Dragon's reign once again. I'm sure a Dragon would be capable of conquering the Order. Perhaps I will live to see it; if not, at least I'd have done my duty. I suppose I could find a way to kill the Dragon without extinguishing the flame, too. I'd definitely die. For as long as Alchemy exists, so does this wretched curse. And let me guess, you're above lifting it for me, right?" The Oracle growled. "Fair enough. Can't blame me for trying." Then, Ash concluded, "Or, I could use my Tetrad Alchemy to light these four posts here, and draw its energy first into me, and then onto that flame to extinguish its warmth. This would kill any chance of the egg hatching, and therefore eliminate Alchemy from the Land entirely. I would live, Kite's curse would also be lifted... and you? Well, the Gods' collective Alchemy would perish, too. Akasha or no Akasha to protect you."

"A Land without Dragons," the Oracle uttered. "You would really commit such a treasonous act, simply to torture *me*? Is that what you want your legacy to be?"

"Killing you would also kill our government's influence. As Humans, we would learn to live in harmony again. Ask any of the Guardsmen: that's a legacy we'd *all* die for. We swore an oath. And the poor Oracle you've been harassing would be freed, too."

"But it would not kill your Gods," he argued. "It would not kill me!"

"That wouldn't," Ash agreed. "But, it *would* make you Human again. And believe me... I know a thing or two about killing those."

The Oracle didn't move, but his expression wavered in a flash of trepidation. Ash knew he had solved a puzzle only a Tetrad like he could enact—he had figured out the only way to kill the God of Universal Energy once and for all. To return equilibrium to the Land.

But, at what cost?

"Then what are you waiting for, boy?" the Oracle said, offering Ash the room by stepping away, arms outstretched.

His eyes glazed. It confirmed the God was in full control of the Oracle's body. Did he know something Ash didn't, or was this a risky game to test the Elemental's bravery? It would be easy to perform the ritual if he could only remember what the book had said.

"I'm not like you," Ash said. "The decision is not mine to

make."

Ash tucked the luminous blue key down his shirt once more and picked up his sword. The light dimmed beneath his clothing, then went out, sensing Ash's intentions. Confused, the Oracle moved back toward the egg. To take him by surprise, Ash dived forward, retrieved his blade, and slashed between the Oracle and the egg, creating a deadly boundary and warning him away. The Oracle turned and bolted, weaving between the pillars in case Ash had been concealing arrows, or planned to throw his weapon. When he neared the door, the entry automatically responded to allow his exit. Ash pursued, remembering how tired and achy his body had been at the First Watchtower as he sprinted to save the book, and how lame and clumsy he was at the marketplace. Though his body was still not what it once was and failing with each hour, as he chased the Oracle with his Land and Alchemy-saving purpose, Ash's energy was renewed. The key was warm against his chest, and Ash knew, somehow, it was boosting him. Perhaps, even, keeping him alive so he could fulfil his spiritual task.

Just as the Oracle made it to the doorway, Deerbolt and Riley stepped into his path to catch him. Ash skidded to a stop and bent, his hands on his knees. Out of breath but feeling proud of himself, he helped Deerbolt and Riley to tie up the Oracle, warning them not to touch his skin or his Psychometry might be activated. The last thing any of them needed was an all-knowing God of Universal Energy, set on ruining their individual lives, too.

Before they marched him downhill to the village to end the fighting and declare their success, they had to decide what to do with the Dragon egg and its flame.

"The Oracle knows its whereabouts now. He could direct his followers to it, or if he escapes, he'll come straight here," Riley told Ash.

"We'll take it with us," Ash decided and scratched his chin. "We can roll the egg downhill, carefully, and set it safely in

Crane and Cage's quarters until I've had a chance to speak to Kite and Reverie."

Deerbolt placed a hand on his shoulder and guided him away from the Guardsman and the Oracle, out of earshot.

"What happened in there, Ash?"

He relayed the events within the temple. "I'd like to know how he escaped Akasha before we do anything," he added.

"Me too. I'm so glad you didn't extinguish the flame yet," she admitted, half-smiling.

"I almost did, but I couldn't remember what the book said to do." He shrugged.

"You read that far?"

"I wanted to be prepared. A lot of good it did me! Besides, the egg has always been protected by the Dragonborn Guardsmen," he said, lowering his head. "It should be their decision."

"And if they agree with you?"

He inhaled sharply. "Then I will do my duty. And when I die, it shall be my legacy."

CHAPTER TWENTY
ASCENSION

Chapter Twenty: Ascension

With care and ease, Ash and Riley rolled the Dragon egg downhill to the village, where the Guardsmen were still fighting over Zarro's orders. It was light enough for one man to carry, but not for long, because of its uncomfortable texture and the retained heat from the Dragonborn flame. Ash carried it down the first few stairs, then together, they were able to guide it around sharp rocks and sticks, Riley in the lead to control the egg's speed, and Ash behind to control its direction with his boot. In his hands, he carried further precious cargo.

Using his Salamander Alchemy, Ash had whipped some of the flame into one of the metal bowls in the temple first. He wasn't sure if it would work, but being a Tetrad had it's gimmicks—everyday Elementals would have failed, to prevent the flame being replicated and transported. It was easy enough to move it, but would not be such a breeze to extinguish it later. The bowl was scorching to touch, even for Ash, so he stripped the Oracle of his cloak and created a pillow of sorts for it to sit on.

"Move!" Deerbolt ordered and nudged the bound Oracle forward.

She led the way, and Ash told Riley to follow their path as it would already be flattened for the egg to roll over. Every few minutes, Ash used a short Salamander incantation to flick tiny fireballs from the bowl onto the egg's surface to keep it warm, and then the foursome continued until they reached the village.

When they saw the Oracle bound with rope and the two Guardsmen in possession of the last remaining Dragon egg, the fighting stopped instantly. Half dropped to their knees and lowered their heads to pay respect to the Alchemical beast within, and the other half—in awe and stunned by their defeat—remained still and silent.

"The battle is over," he announced. "Drop your weapons."

The men did as Ash ordered and surrendered their swords, bows, and arrows to the ground. The Oracle jumped at the sound. Deerbolt steered him through the crowd, unsympathetically, and gave him a shove when they were in the centre of the group's gaze.

"Your Oracle is not who he claims to be," she announced. Her voice carried across the square in the breeze, and the audience hung on her every word. "Zarro misled you. He was working for the Order, and they were plotting to insert the soul of the God of Universal Energy into the final Dragon egg to rule the Land, forsaking all others."

Gasps and mild chattering surrounded them. She squeezed the Oracle's shoulder blades until he took the hint and collapsed on his knees.

"This man, the one you all feared would read your thoughts and use them against you, is that very God masquerading as Zarro's advisor," she explained, "and what I'm sure we would all like to know, before we serve justice, is how you escaped Akasha and survived for so long in the Lingerverse."

Many of the Guardsmen nodded and chattered amongst themselves, and some threw their fist angrily in the air and called for the Oracle to be punished immediately.

"Lock him up!"

"Murderer!"

"Traitor!"

Those still following him scowled, but held back their comments and awaited his admission of guilt. Curious by Deerbolt's outburst, it confused them to hear they were potentially the bad guys in all of this, despite their leader being the only man they'd ever trusted enough to take orders from. He'd misled them. He'd driven them to commit crimes nobody had registered as such—all in the name of protecting the Dragonborn flame and its egg.

Deerbolt drew her longsword and held it to the Oracle's neck, tugging back his hair with her balled fist. He struggled and grumbled.

"Talk!" the men demanded.

"Who freed you?" Deerbolt asked.

"You can't kill me, only this body."

"You want your followers to watch you die? To lose respect for you? Tell me who!"

She ragged his head to the side and pressed the blade tighter against his skin, drawing a thin line of blood.

He raised his tied wrists. "My sister!"

Deerbolt snapped her head to Ash, who scowled. Both of Universal Energy's sisters were imprisoned alongside him. To free him, one of them must have also escaped. The question stood.

"You lie," Deerbolt said. "Killing this body will push back your cause."

"You lie and you die!" one man shouted, and a few around him joined in the chant.

Deerbolt hushed them. "Your siblings are locked up. Tell us the truth; how did you escape Akasha? Was it your father?"

"No," he grunted, shuffling uncomfortably on his frail knees. "Lower your blade. It was my mother, the God of Ascension."

In unison, everyone in the square gasped.

Then, silence.

"There is no such God," Ash insisted. "A God of Ascension would total six Alchemical rulers—seven including your father, the God of Magic."

"How can it be we did not know of a sixth?" Riley asked Ash, who shook his head in response.

There would be scripture, he thought.

The Land's texts had always described the Gods being gifted to Human mothers, who birthed and fed them until they were old enough to return to Akasha with their father. He took them away knowing no Human woman could ever understand or meet their Alchemical needs. They were too strong, and too dangerous. Who those women were remains a mystery.

Perhaps even the God of Magic himself has forgotten? Ash pondered.

"The God of Ascension is your mother? Who is she? Where is she?" Riley quizzed.

The Oracle struggled to his feet, unable to use his wrists to support his weight. Once steady, he raised them.

"Free me, and I'll tell you everything you need to know about her. She is powerful—too powerful."

"More powerful than your father?" Ask asked.

The Oracle raised his restraints higher. But Deerbolt laughed and shook her head. If he was lying, the men of Dragonborn would hold her responsible for freeing him.

She asked, "Upon your release, what would you do?"

"You'll never have to see me again. I'll return to the mainland and live amongst the Humans."

"So you can corrupt other law-abiding Astrals, or hop from this Oracle to one with greater influence and begin this ordeal again? No!"

Men in the crowd shouted, "Aye!" and cheered with Ash for the Oracle to be punished.

"We can't risk you escaping—you want to inhabit that Dragon's body yourself. Tell me, what of its soul then?"

"A return to Akasha," the Oracle lied.

Everyone there knew its soul would go straight to the

Lingerverse. But, there was no way to *really* know exactly what would happen; if its soul merged with the God's, there would be no stopping his reign of terror upon the Land. It crossed Ash's mind.

"Enough!"

"Kill him!"

Deerbolt hushed the Guardsmen. None of this mattered if the majority couldn't agree on a course of action. They were guests on the island, there to help two innocents to heal and live a better life. Ash cast his glance through the crowd to where Kite and Reverie stood hand-in-hand, silently, beside Sarronious. Reverie's eyes were tear-filled. Kite still gripped his bow tightly. Rightly, he did not trust the fight was over yet and had to protect his pregnant wife. Sarronious hadn't taken his eyes of Captain Deerbolt since they entered the square, and Ash's stomach tightened with jealousy. He gave him a nod to thank him for his efforts—some in the village had been killed, many bled. Sarronious included. Across his chest, a thin red line soaked through his shirt, and a trickle painted his left cheek from a wound on his forehead.

"If there is a God more powerful than the God of Magic, we'd have seen her by now. We'd know of her Alchemy. Why haven't we seen or felt her?" Riley asked the Oracle. "He's lying, Ash. And everyone knows their mothers were Human."

"Aye!"

"Snake!"

"Liar!"

There was nothing more Ash could do to probe the Oracle. Faced with being made Human and a death as final, the only way to gain solid answers was to extinguish the flame and kill all Alchemy.

"My fellow Guardsmen," Ash began, raising his sword to draw their attention from the Oracle's crumpled frame to his own. "My name is Ash the Elemental, and ten years ago, the Oracle banished me from the Isle of Dragonborn for being a Tetrad. Familiar faces will know I am a Salamander; until now, I did not know of my true inheritance." Ash pointed the sword at the Oracle. "I was loyal to the Guard and had no intention of extinguishing the flame. The guard was *all* I had."

Sensing his vulnerability, Deerbolt wanted to step forward and comfort him, but she resisted. A public display of her affections right now wouldn't help his cause. They needed to see his independence and strength despite all the Oracle had done to him.

"For ten years I've suffered. Cursed to live a degenerating existence in Open Country amongst thieves and outlaws. I have been chased, and starved, withering away until my Salamander Alchemy offered barely a flicker in the darkness. I stand before you as a dying man on borrowed time." Ash removed the key from his shirt and knelt beside the egg. At the proximity, it illuminated, sending a wave of awe through the crowd. They stepped back, gasping and chuntering.

"What is this Alchemy?" one man asked, fearfully.

"It unlocks *this*," said Captain Deerbolt, retrieving the book from Ash's satchel and holding it high above her head. "It's one of a kind. It belonged to a Tetrad."

Ash turned suddenly to face her. *Raven was a Tetrad?*

Banking his shock, he said, "I believe I came here to free you of Zarro and the Oracle's imprisonment. They've been using you for so long to prepare for the God of Universal Energy—him!—to inhabit the egg and rule the Land. I was tasked by an Oracle on the mainland to help a poor, innocent couple to expel an unfair curse."

Kite released Reverie's hand and allowed her to weave through the crowd until she took Ash's. He squeezed her palm and pulled her to his side. Her gaze found the egg and she smiled, placing her free hand on her stomach.

"This is Reverie—she's willing to offer the egg her unborn child," Ash told the Guardsmen.

"The egg hasn't hatched so far," one man shouted. "What makes you think it will hatch for Reverie?"

"She's innocent," Deerbolt answered. "Pure of heart."

"You came here for your own benefit too," said another, scowling.

"Did Zarro tell you that?"

The man shrank into the crowd. *One of his supporters,* Ash assumed.

"Aye," Ash told the man, "I came here hoping I could save my life. I'd like to restore Kite's sight first," he added, nodding at Kite in the crowd, who lowered his bow. "At heart, I am still a Guardsman."

"But you possess the Alchemy to extinguish our flame," the man argued. "Why would we trust you?"

"Aye, he does," Deerbolt interjected, "and he could have used it up there in the temple, where your egg rested. He chose to wait and to ask you all how you'd like to proceed."

Ash began, "This egg is alive now *only* because I took it from the Oracle's possession. He planned to relocate it, but hadn't given thought to how he would transport the flame, too. I'm feeding it with this," he said, sitting the bowl beside the egg but continuing to douse the surface.

"I wouldn't have let the creature die," the Oracle interjected, "because I need it."

"Irrelevant," Riley shouted. "A few minutes more and that Dragon would have died."

Ash hushed him, and Riley stood down. "So I put the question to you, men. What would you have me do now? Here I stand, capable of preventing the Order from continuing in the Land's government by extinguishing the flame and killing the Dragon. That book," he said, gesturing at Deerbolt, "holds instructions only I can perform—at least, so I thought," he grumbled, glaring at the Captain for withholding Raven's true nature from him.

"What would that gain?" the man asked, "other than fewer taxes?"

"You haven't been back to the mainland in a long time, have you?" Sarronious spat, startling him.

The man moved away as Ash said, "The God possessing

the Oracle would be made Human, and therefore, mortal." He raised his brow.

The man studied Ash, then whispered to his comrades. Tempting though this seemed, he was sure they would rather spare the life of the Dragon for its potential. Thankfully, they had a backup offer.

"Or," Ash said, "we force this God to heal Kite, and in return he will offer his unborn baby to the Dragon egg. If it hatches, you will promise to raise and protect that child alongside its parents. After all, being chosen as the next Dragon Rider would make them the Land's saviours—the only soul the Dragon deems pure enough to lead us past the Order's reign."

Another man suddenly asked, "But what of you, Tetrad?"

Ash shrugged and replied honestly, "My days are numbered. I've made my peace with that."

He cast a sideways glance at Deerbolt, but purposely avoided direct eye contact. The thought of leaving her to the Land as he moved on to the Lingerverse, or Akasha, was too difficult to bear.

"If the Dragon refuses the child, then what?" the Oracle groaned, prompting Deerbolt to squeeze the back of his neck until he squirmed.

"Aye!" one man shouted, and soon others followed.

"Then at least my friend's sight would be healed, and the Oracle imprisoned. We will take our leave, and you will never have to see any of us again. Govern yourselves; protect the egg until a soul worthy of its return arrives on the Isle of Dragonborn." Ash paused and, when nobody responded, he asked, "Do we have a deal?"

"It would not banish the God of Universal Energy," Deerbolt reminded them, "but he will be unable to do further harm if he's behind bars."

"Will you comply?" Ash said, nudging the Oracle's ribs with his boot.

He grumbled 'Aye', so Riley widened his eyes at the man

who seemed to have taken the role of spokesperson for the group. *Agree*, he willed him, frantically nodding, for those unwilling to follow Zarro's original orders.

Riley escorted the Oracle to Crane and Cage's quarters, and after a few words with the Guardsmen, Kite and Reverie followed them. As it was a Seer—Echelon, Shaman of the Deeds—who cursed Kite several months ago to lose his sight, they determined a Seer like the possessed Oracle could undo it. Ash told Kite to take his bow and arrows, and keep them pointed at the Oracle until he complied. It wasn't difficult to know where in the room he was. Kite's exemplary skills and lack of sight heightened his other senses, and he heard the Oracle's shuffling feet and heavy breathing. He could also smell the oils on his skin, and feel his body heat whenever he passed close by.

"I need a Necrosis flower," the Oracle told him as they climbed the stairs to their apartment.

Craven and Cage directed Sarronious to a place not far into the jungle where they grew, and within an hour, he had retrieved a bunch. They couldn't be sure how many flowers Echelon used originally. Sarronious thought it best to overestimate. After Kite had explained the deal he made to the Oracle, the God of Universal Energy temporarily allowed him to regain control of his body in order to perform the ritual. But, in the background, Reverie could see the God was still present, watching and studying their actions. It unsettled her, more so than the new curse, which involved Reverie once again touching the cursed petals. This time, the Oracle enchanted them to *give* sight rather than steal it.

While the couple, the Oracle and Riley performed the ritual behind the closed door, Ash and Deerbolt gathered the Guardsmen to discuss the egg.

"You should be up there," Deerbolt told Ash, smiling.

"I know, and I wanted to be with them, but the egg needs my Alchemy."

She grinned and led him to the square where the men were waiting. Ash still carried the bowl, resting upon the Oracle's folded robes, and occasionally he flicked a flame at the egg which was surrounded by inquisitive Guardsmen. Some stroked its surface, then pulled back and hissed when it burned their skin. Others kept their distance, afraid the Dragon would hatch or the mere presence of unworthy souls would kill it—a rumour Zarro had started a few years ago to keep them from prying into the egg's location, or discovering his intentions.

The spokesman greeted Ash, and immediately quizzed him about his book and the glowing key. When Ash was close enough to the egg, it seemed to reach out and float a few inches from his chest, similar to when Ash had unlocked the book for the first time.

"Is it sentient?"

Deerbolt answered for him. "We don't know but another Tetrad gifted him the book and the key so he could harness the skills of the other elements."

"I'm a Salamander by day," Ash told them, "which is why it's so easy for me to keep the egg alive. This flame was transferred from a pit in the temple, and there were four pillars there with Elemental symbols and crystals. In the book, there are incantations I can perform to activate each one in a particular order. Once I've done that, I can bring their collective energy together and that will extinguish the flame."

"Why did you bring the egg here, then?" the man asked.

"Some of the Oracle's men got away from us, and I was afraid they'd return to the temple and move it."

Deerbolt added, "We also wanted to show you how real it is, and let the Oracle face you himself."

"But he's not really the Oracle. He's a God masquerading as the Oracle."

"Aye," she said, "and I'm sure we don't have to stress how diabolical it would be if he achieved his goal."

"To transfer his soul to the egg?" the man asked.

Ash nodded. "The God of Universal Energy—the cruel, destructive influence the Astrals of the Order worship—would be the single, most powerful creature this Land has ever seen. His father gave the Dragons the Gods' power for a reason. They were too reckless to rule us. Of them all, Universal Energy is the worst."

The man turned to discuss Ash's story with his comrades, and they agreed the Oracle should never be allowed to roam the island without supervision again, especially if they were unable to banish the God from his consciousness. Ash relayed what happened to him on the wall that night, and how the Oracle convinced the Guard to banish him from the island, cursing him to die.

"If he can remove Kite's curse, can he not remove yours?" the spokesman asked.

Ash sighed. "He will claim not." He wished it was that easy. "I've tried many times," he said. "Oracles across the Land over my ten years in Open Country have attempted to lift my curse, but I'm afraid I can only be saved if Alchemy itself no longer exists. Kite's curse, though unpleasant, isn't life-threatening. It's torture in another form. To curse someone to death is something else entirely."

The man couldn't console Ash but he understood. Some curses weren't meant to be lifted.

"If the Oracle is successful, Kite's blindness will be returned to Echelon," Deerbolt explained.

"Where is he?"

"We don't know. Probably the Gravelands."

"It's brave and noble of you to return to the Isle of Dragonborn, Ash. We could have shot you on sight."

"I think a small part of me prayed you would," he admitted.

"Aye, it would be a kinder fate," the man agreed, then gestured at the egg. "So, what are we going to do about the Dragon?"

Deerbolt smiled. "Allow Kite and Reverie to try. They are willing and grateful for your help. Imagine if the Dragon accepts their baby's soul!"

"Would any harm come to the child?" Ash asked the Guardsmen, who confirmed it wouldn't be painful or fatal for the unborn baby to bond with such an incredible creature.

"Of course, we haven't witnessed something so magical in hundreds of years. We are looking forward to the miracle." He bent to examine the egg and said, "But, we are realistic, and won't get our hopes up."

"Aye, good idea," Ash said.

Deerbolt turned to Ash and asked, "Do you think its true about the God of Ascension? Surely, we would know of her power or have seen drawings of her? Scripture speaks of Human mothers."

Ash put the bowl down for a moment and took Deerbolt by the shoulders. "Why didn't you tell me Raven was a Tetrad? He could have travelled with us, trained me himself."

She lowered her gaze, ashamed she had withheld such a secret, but it wasn't her secret to reveal. She explained as much to Ash.

"They persecuted Raven for many years just for being a Slyph. Like you, for so long he didn't know he could manipulate other elements and I don't think he really wanted to. He crammed his knowledge into that book and locked it, hiding everything about himself he despised within its pages and shoved it on a shelf in his library. He only finished writing it a few months before I met you."

"And the key?" Ash asked, fingering it. "Its energy is far from anything the Land has seen before. Almost like the magic of a Dragon urges it. If I hold the book or touch the egg, it comes alive. It frightens me," he said, sighing.

"Raven wouldn't have gifted it to you if he thought you'd be in danger. He knew of your plight, and he loves me like a daughter."

"Aye, he wouldn't risk you coming to harm through me," he agreed. "I long to understand it, though, and I think when we are finished here—if I survive, and if Alchemy is still shared amongst us—that we should return and ask him about the key's glow."

"I have a few questions for him myself," she said.

"I imagine the God of Universal Energy's mother to be beautiful. Like that carving in the temple door, but blonde and blue-eyed," Ash told her, worried about the possibility of a seventh God like everyone else.

"That image spoke to me," she told him, meeting his gaze and smiling. "The image of the moon is inspiring. Perhaps that's her?"

"Well, just as there is no evidence of her existence, there is nothing to suggest she was imprisoned with the others if she *is* real. She may have tried to free her son from Akasha out of pity, and was overpowered by him. Being the son of two Gods explains his unique strength. Anything is in the cards."

"Aye," Deerbolt said, "and pray she is merciless and kind, unlike him"

Crane and Cage's apartment door opened and Sarronious led the Oracle out with his wrists tied behind his back. Reverie took Kite by the hand and followed them to the top of the stairs. They kissed one another, then she threw fistfuls of black petals up in the air and watched, smiling, as they fluttered into the square and tumbled at Ash's feet.

CHAPTER TWENTY-ONE

Chapter Twenty-One: Fire, Earth, Air, Water

It took more of them to roll the egg back up the hill than it did to bring it down, and Ash hadn't given much thought to how they'd return it to the temple. One-handed, Ash stood behind the egg to stop it rolling backward, and was still able to transfer the flame's heat to it.

As far as they knew, Ash's actions were enough to keep the Dragon alive, but nobody had ever seen a dead egg, so they couldn't be sure. Perhaps it had died when the Oracle removed it from the flame earlier that day. Collectively, they agreed only a cold egg was a dead egg.

They reached the bottom of the stairs, leading up to the temple's carved wooden doorway. From the base, the marble pillars reflected the sunset's dwindling light and appeared ethereal. Ash handed the bowl to Captain Deerbolt and bent to pick up the egg. The others held their breath, stunned that his fingers didn't burn at its touch.

"I'm a Salamander," he reminded them, and took the first step of one hundred until he reached the top without incident. "I'm sure that would have been easier if I'd mastered my

Gnome or Slyph Alchemy," he said and wiped the sweat from his forehead with the back of his hand. "But the key's energy helped."

Ash touched the doorway. It slid open, and Riley wrung his hands together, pleased they had finally figured out how to activate it.

"A Dragon's presence?"

"Then how did the Oracle access it?" Deerbolt said.

"He's not really an Oracle though, is he?"

"No, he's a God," Ash said.

"But then, how did *you* access it earlier?"

Ash frowned. Riley had a point. He thought about the first time they'd approached the doorway. Deerbolt had been ahead of him, standing between the carving and Ash. Riley was in the trees. The second time, Ash had placed his palm on the door to examine it for keyholes before he heard a noise inside and retreated to the jungle. Could *he* have prompted the doorway to open, and if so, how? So far, the rule had been that only Dragons or Gods were permitted to enter, and Ash was neither.

"The Oracle was on his way out," Ash suggested, "so maybe he opened it?"

But he didn't believe his own theory—the key around his neck was baffling enough, and drew its power from somewhere or something outside of himself. It fed him energy and answers, and responded to his needs before he knew what he wanted himself. Like a spirit from the Lingerverse was steering him and, as an Astral uses those souls to boost their own Alchemy, this key did so for Ash without consequence.

Its glow was constant when lit, and it never wavered. Whatever its source, there was unspeakable power inside.

"What about this?" he said without thinking and lifted the key. "I don't know exactly how it works, but it's helped me in unexpected ways."

Riley reached out to touch it, then thought better of his actions. The men in their party all stepped back; it did look like a plain metal key. If fancier, perhaps. But none of the other keys on the island were alive.

Instead, Riley said, "You might be right, Ash. But, I see no keyholes anywhere. None of us have entered the temple before—only the Oracle and Zarro came here. So, maybe it's cursed?"

"Raven gave this to me," Ash said to himself, then turned to Deerbolt. "Along with the book. Do you think he knew it would unlock the egg's location, given he was... you know?"

Deerbolt chewed her lower lip. She thought Raven had told her everything there was to know about his past and why he'd written the book. Unable to openly use his Tetrad abilities, and terrified to speak of them, Raven collected every incantation he had learned and noted each slither of advice to store them safely for the next Tetrad he met to take advantage of before he settled in the north. Raven hadn't forged the lock and key himself; he had it made by a capable locksmith at the First Watchtower when he finished writing. He'd worked with an excavation team in the Gravelands just before Deerbolt met him, and they sold most of what was found in exchange for jewels to pay the Order's taxes. All except the key, which he asked the locksmith to create.

"I suppose he could have," she admitted, a little puzzled. "But, I'm pretty sure he found the key in a chest beneath the desert when he worked in the West."

"Well, something happened. I'm assuming the key wasn't in the chest's lock." Riley said. "He must have known it was special, even if he couldn't explain why."

Ash's fingers tightened around it. *Something happened to it*, he echoed. *Then someone buried it for a reason.*

Kite and Reverie made it to the top step and lingered behind them, a little out of breath.

"That was much easier with my sight back," Kite chirped.

"I bet it's wonderful to see how Reverie's body has changed," Deerbolt told him, and the couple beamed in response.

"Right," Reverie said, "let's get this over with, shall we?"

"You can back out of this at any time," Deerbolt reminded her.

"We made a promise," she said, "as a thank you for healing Kite. We can't turn away now, not when we are so close to knowing if our child is the key to the next Dragon age."

"Either way, you will never lose us," Kite assured her.

Holding her hand, he led Reverie through the open doorway and into the temple. The pillars of lava continued to burn and light the way between bowls like Ash had been carrying. Deerbolt allowed Ash to pass next, so he could return the egg to its pyre at the far end of the walkway, which he enhanced with the sparks he'd taken earlier. Once settled safely again, everyone let out a sigh of relief, and a collective weight seemed to be lifted.

"Does anyone know how we go about this?"

Riley shook his head and turned to the spokesman, who he'd learned on the way uphill was called Sweets after his original employment on the mainland making candies and baked goods somewhere in the Sleeping Reeds Valley. Nobody knew his real name, but Sweets seemed to suit his young, unshaven face and short but prominent presence.

"Sweets, did Zarro or the Oracle tell the Guardsmen anything about how this works?"

"Sorry," he said, "but we were kept in the dark. Personally, I thought the egg would simply sense when a suitable soul was present, and respond in its own time."

"Perhaps it doesn't work in the womb?" Kite said.

Deerbolt elbowed Ash in the ribs and threw her head in the direction of his satchel, where she had safely secured the Tetrad book. Then, she cast her gaze to the four Elemental pillars guarding the egg's resting place.

Ash already knew what he needed to do next. He pushed through the men standing ahead of him, ignoring their protests. Everyone wanted to be at the front to witness the Dragon's miracle. Some dare not blink in fear of missing the first signs the egg was responding.

"Sweets, I have an idea."

He allowed Ash to step up onto the platform, standing beside the first Salamander pillar with the red crystal atop it. Carved into the front was a flame sitting in a bowl. *Fire*. Ash remembered what Raven had written in the book about how to create embers from nothing. Normally, a Salamander required an existing flame in order to use their Alchemy, but according to Raven's notes, there was a way for confident Elementals to birth fire themselves. Supposedly, using their body heat and their will—the fire in their hearts. Ash would need to recreate the symbol by forming a horizontal figure eight, then swinging his arms out to either side, representing the bowl.

Ash then looked across to the second pillar with the green earth stone on top, and carved into that were three circles, which Ash would have to mimic by swirling his arms in rings. On the other side of the egg, the white air stone glistened, allowing Ash to catch sight of the carving for Slyphs. A crescent moon shape, followed by three wavy lines, which Ash knew was probably the easiest to demonstrate with his body. He could draw the C-shape, then move his arms and upper torso to form the wind. Finally, the blue water crystal and its paired symbol sat at the far end, and though it was faded, it looked like a wave made of three circles, which Ash would have to build one at a time using his hands and a swirling motion in the space in front of him.

Together, Ash would have to perform the most complex incantation he had ever attempted, and get it right first time. If not, who knows what he could accidentally summon? Then, rather than draw the energy from all four above the egg in order to extinguish the flame, he wondered if it might awaken the Dragon to Reverie's presence.

"Do it," said Riley. "Sweets, you're with us, right?"

Sweets nodded, and the men around him urged Ash to give it a try, waving him forward and smiling. Suddenly, he felt supported and appreciated—in ten years, nobody had made

Ash feel so important, not even Captain Deerbolt or the marketplace Oracle.

Reverie knelt before the egg and waited patiently as Ash prepared himself. He paced back and forth, wrung his hands together, and took a few deep breaths. This was a lot of pressure.

What if I get it wrong? If I die, will Raven make the journey to try in my place? Or, could I blow our only chance?

"You can do this, Ash," he heard Deerbolt say amongst the whispers and chattering. "This is your legacy."

She's right. I've got this.

Ash began. He formed the symbol for fire, then send a fireball to the crystal, causing it to glow cherry red and burn. He side-stepped to the earth pillar, which trembled through the incantation before glowing green and sprouting a Necrosis flower. Reverie turned away and swallowed hard at the memory, but it was over now. Kite had been healed, and they were on their way to forming the future of Alchemy.

She felt Ash's presence move behind her as he shuffled to the air pillar and performed the necessary incantation. He sent a gust of wind to the crystal, illuminating it like a star against the black backdrop. It twinkled, and the air surrounding it cooled. Finally, Ash moved to the water pillar, sending droplets to ignite the blue crystal, which seemed to then produce its own. It trickled down a groove to pool in a crevice below.

"Now what?" he grumbled.

Reverie groaned and folded forward. The only thing within reach she could use to steady herself was the egg, and when her palm touched its scorching surface, the crystals exploded. Fragments splintered and rained on the Guardsmen; they shielded their eyes as multi-coloured pieces scratched the skin on their arms and faces. Reverie gasped, wondering why the egg wasn't burning her and tried to back away. But her skin was fused to the scales and she couldn't get up.

"Ash!" she called, but Ash couldn't hear her above the

shouting of the Guardsmen.

Kite pushed his way through and quickly loosened two arrows at the egg to try to pierce its shell. They ricocheted off. Everyone ducked and complained.

"Ash!" he screamed until he got his attention. "What's happening to her?"

When he was near enough to offer aid, the key around his neck illuminated again and floated between them. Slowly, he ducked out of the ribbon and let it hang mid-air, then shimmied around to free Reverie's hand. With both Kite and Ash tugging and Reverie pulling with all her might, the egg refused to budge.

It never crossed his mind someone could reach out and steal the key. If they did, they would likely have been killed. From it, a flash of light and a crack of thunder shot, connecting with the egg and sending colourful veins up and down Reverie's fingers to her bump and back again.

She panicked and thrashed but to no avail.

"Am I going to die?" she asked Kite.

Kite cuddled her. He wrapped his entire frame around her body to shield her from the egg. Ash covered her palm with his—whatever was about to happen to Reverie, he wouldn't let her suffer alone. They were in this together. This was his doing; if anyone deserved to perish, it was Ash.

The men in the temple fled, leaving Sarronious, Deerbolt, Riley and the brothers Crane and Cage huddled together at the base of the podium.

"I'm sorry," Ash told Reverie, and they all squeezed their eyes shut.

Beneath Reverie's palm, the egg cracked. Scales dropped from its surface onto the marble floor beneath, and Reverie was able to wriggle her palm free. The three of them rolled backward and scampered to join the others, blinded by the key's electricity.

"Something's happening," Riley mouthed to Ash, who reached out to wrap an arm around Captain Deerbolt.

Were they all deaf? Not a sound escaped, except for the cracking of the egg's shell and the jingle of its scales against the floor beneath, like jewels being dropped against metal. Ash stole a glance in time to see the key's light cut out and it fizzled, as if someone had doused it with water. But, within the egg, a rumbling and grumbling could be heard. It vibrated, sending shock waves across the temple, shaking the lava pillars and knocking a few of the bowls over, spilling the contents and forcing areas of the temple into darkness.

"We can't stay here," Deerbolt said, grabbing Reverie by the hand. "This building is about to crumble!"

Sarronious helped Deerbolt to pick Reverie up off the floor, then ushered everyone out through the wooden door and onto the steps. They crashed to a halt against the tree line and spun to see the walls of the temple creak and sway. After only a few more seconds, the roof caved in, and the temple fell. Dust and debris filled the air. Everyone coughed and spluttered.

Ash formed the air incantation again to get a clearer view of the destruction and to make the surrounding air breathable.

Reverie stroked her belly and said, "The baby is kicking a LOT. Whatever that was, it's unsettled us."

Standing in the centre of the chaos, Ash carefully approached the remains of the temple, wondering if the egg had survived the explosion. Smoke plumed where the Dragonborn flame had been, and as he navigated chunks of stone and wobbly slabs, he made it to where he thought, roughly, it had burned.

Relieved to see a tiny flicker between two pieces of marble, Ash exhaled. "It's here!" he called to the others.

Sarronious shouted back, "Can you see the egg?" and the group held on to one another, tense, as Ash searched for evidence the Dragon hadn't been killed.

When he thought all hope was lost, Ash spotted green scales beneath debris. He rummaged until his fingers felt a sharp, scaly sphere. But, it was only part of the egg. Around it were scattered pieces of the shell, littered with scales and a slimy, pink substance. He wiped it on his doublet and turned to tell the others.

"You won't believe this, but I think—"

The ground beneath Ash's feet gave way, and threw him. He landed on his back, winded, with an *umph*. Pieces of the temple peeled away as something underneath rose from it. Rubbing his eyes, Ash rolled onto his side and crawled out of its way.

"ASH, LOOK!" Deerbolt screamed.

Towering above him, glaring down with brilliant blue eyes and sharp, white quartz teeth, was a Dragon. Before them, it grew in size and width until it stood ten metres tall, and flexed its gigantic wings. From head to toe, it was spiky and solid, with a pronged nose and two deadly horns. It's four-toed feet crushed the stone beneath, turning it to sand.

Ash tried to escape, but he couldn't find his footing. His arms were grazed, and every time he fell, he tore another part of his clothing. He never thought to draw his sword. Subconsciously, he knew it would do no good.

Deerbolt cried and set off to help him, but Sarronious held her back.

"ASH!" she called. "Let me go!"

"Get her out of here!" Ash yelled at him.

"Deerbolt, it's no use," he said, wrestling her to the ground. "You'll get yourself killed. Let him go."

Deerbolt burst into tears. "Run, Ash!"

Despite his fear and the Dragon's advantage, it did not advance toward him. It leant to nuzzle him with its long snout, and puffs of grey smoke escaped its nostrils. Ash swallowed hard, closed his eyes, and waited to be squashed. But the Dragon pulled away.

"It..."

Everyone turned to face Reverie.

"What?" Deerbolt asked her. "It what?"

Reverie smiled. "It... I mean *she*... says... *hello*."

Ash gulped. "Uhm... hello?" he said, and the Dragon

snorted. "Reverie, do you know what the Dragon is saying?"

"My... baby... does," she said.

Ash fought to a stance and staggered until he reached the others, feeling with his boots for rocks he could topple over. At first, the Dragon didn't move, but once Ash was back in the welcoming arms of Captain Deerbolt, she followed. His thirty steps, to her, were only four, and the ground shook with every bound.

"She hatched," Sarronious said, "and bonded with Reverie's baby!"

"Aye," Reverie said, beaming.

The Dragon lowered her snout and allowed Reverie to pat her scales. Stunned, Ash and the others moved cautiously away, but Kite remained by her side with his bow raised, and an arrow drawn.

"No need," said his wife, resting her hand on the tip of the arrow to lower it. "She won't hurt us."

"What of the flame?" Riley asked Ash.

"It burns, but it's weak."

Reverie gave the Dragon a final pat, then turned to him. "It doesn't matter. Because when it goes go out, only she will remain to rule over us. There can be no future Dragons, though, but the Gods will remain imprisoned until her death."

"I can't believe she's here, and she's *real*," Kite said, blinking through tears. "And I can see her!"

"She's beautiful," Deerbolt uttered. "But... how?"

The Dragon snorted and bowed her head, as if to prompt Reverie to tell the story because she couldn't. Behind her, a thin streak of smoke rose to the sky—the flame was about to go out for good, and Ash had not had to initiate it himself. Somehow, he still felt accomplished. This was something the Guard could never blame him for; they'd agreed to allow Kite and Reverie to try for this miracle—as far as Ash was concerned, it was their doing, and it was blissful, remembering how they'd banished him to keep the Dragonborn flame from falling victim to a Tetrad when it was the Guard themselves who did the deed. Rather than feeling angry or spiteful, Ash was calm.

"When Ash lit the crystals, the energy woke her from slumber."

"You mean, all this time she's been sleeping?" Riley grumbled. The Dragon scraped her claws in the dirt, and he cringed, then held up his hands. "Sorry, sorry."

"She sensed my baby was near, and accepted the offering of the innocent soul. But in order to hatch through such a tough, scaly shell, she had to use the crystal's energy. She didn't mean to destroy the temple."

"We weren't overly attached to it," Riley told her, hoping she'd forgive him.

Through Ash ran an extreme amount of adrenaline. He'd waited for ten years to be rid of his symptoms. Imminent death took the fun out of anything and everything he did. No matter where he went or who he met, in the back of his mind, he told himself none of it mattered. He'd be dead soon. Why waste time befriending, falling in love, earning and spending jewels, or travelling the Land, when at any moment, his body could fail him?

As his limbs shook and his chest tightened, Ash wondered if finally, the shock of seeing the Dragon would finish him off. He'd lost the key in the rubble somewhere. He didn't know if it would still work without the flame to power the Land's Alchemy, or if it was actually the key that had kept him going so far.

Ash shuddered and crumpled to his knees.

"Ash! Are you alright?"

Deerbolt caught his armpits, and eased him to the ground. His head pounded, and he could hear the drumming of his pulse in his ears. All colour drained from his waxy face.

"*Our* Alchemy is dead," she replied, maintaining eye contact with the Dragon. "Without the key, his body has returned to its current Human state."

Deerbolt realised it was no longer Reverie talking, but the

Dragon. She clasped her hands together and knelt, begging her to save his life it if was at all within her ability.

"If Alchemy is dead," she said, "then why is the curse still killing him? Please, you can stop this. Please," she said, sobbing through her words. "I... love him."

Through Reverie, the Dragon explained the curse had been affecting Ash's physical presence on the Land, as well as his spiritual. Killing Alchemy could not undo the damage done to Ash's Human form beneath, which is all he was now the Dragon had taken over Alchemy's responsibilities.

Ash groaned and set off on his hands and knees across the rubble, occasionally slipping and smacking his nose or forehead on the stone.

"What are you doing?" Deerbolt said, following him.

She tugged his shirt collar, but he bat her away. With the last of his energy, he clawed at the dirt and debris, searching for his missing key. Sarronious ran to Deerbolt's side and held her.

"He's gone mad," she said, nestled in the First Mate's shoulder. "Oh, Sarronious, I don't think I can watch him die."

"You... won't... have... to," Ash moaned, and stuck his hand between two sharp chunks of marble, which slashed at his wrists and drew blood.

Riley ran to Ash's aid, tripping a few times, but remained

upright. He felt down the side of Ash's arm, taking the sting of every slash and nick from the shards of marble, and tickled the ground beneath.

"Got it!" Riley said, revealing the ornate key, still attached to the ribbon.

It was dirty and fraying now, but otherwise intact.

He handed it to Ash, who held the key in both hands. It was dull and scratchy to the touch—nothing at all like it had been when alive and bursting with energy.

"Reverie, what is he doing?"

The Dragon nudged Ash, flopping him onto his back so it could look him in the eye. Through unspoken words, they seemed to understand one another, and Reverie beamed in response to their telepathic communications.

She sang:

"Bless all who watch o'er the flame,
Where loyal guards are duly sworn,
For here they are re-birthed to new name,
So unto pledge their hearts to Dragonborn."

The others in the group listened intently, then one man in the Guard joined in, followed by Sweets and Sarronious, Crane and Cage. Some were not in tune, and a few stammered or coughed between words, inhaling the dust from the temple's ruins. But, they persisted. Soon, everyone in their party was singing, including Deerbolt, Reverie, and Kite.

As if coaxed from a coma, the key flickered. The Dragon swayed along with the song, unable to sing itself. Deerbolt thought she saw her smile, though.

If Dragons can *smile*.

Ash strangled the key until his knuckles turned white. He willed the light to soak through his skin and into his bones. He willed it to save his life.

Unexpectedly, the Dragon slammed her foot down hard beside Ash, who jumped and threw the key into the air. She caught it delicately on her tongue, holding it in place with her front teeth, which were flat and straight like a Human's. Ash's eyesight was failing, but through a haze he saw her chomp down, hard. There was a sharp crack, and Ash felt the *thud thud* of two pieces hitting his chest.

She had destroyed it.

"NO!" Deerbolt cried, and threw herself at Ash, nuzzling his chest with her teary cheek.

The Dragon roared and stepped aside to reveal a young blonde woman, no older than Reverie, with sapphire eyes that twinkled like starlight. She stood still, surveying the scene, and tilted her head, curious.

"Who are you?" Deerbolt sniffled.

Reverie gasped. "She is a God," she relayed. "The... God of *Ascension*."

With Kite to steady her, Reverie walked to where Ash and Deerbolt were laid, overlooked by Sarronious who seemed so broad and mighty in comparison. She knelt and placed her cool hands on Ash's face. His eyes were closed and his breathing laboured—he didn't have long.

"Ash the Elemental, you have finally pledged your heart to Dragonborn," Reverie said.

Deerbolt lifted her head and blinked, glaring up at the Dragon. Her chest heaved, and she squeezed Ash's hand tightly.

"I... I have never..." Ash struggled, wheezing, "pledged... my life... to... anything," he said.

The God of Ascension seemed to float over the debris, but was beside them in the wink of the Dragon's eye. She said nothing and did nothing, only watched them.

Ash's eyelashes fluttered and his dry lips pursed as he struggled to say something else. Reverie leant to hear his whispers. She smiled.

"What did he say?" Deerbolt asked.

Ash coughed.

"He said... only to loving you."

Deerbolt balled. Sarronious lifted her and hugged her close, begging the Dragon and the God of Ascension to ease Ash's suffering or end it now—take away his pain.

"All this time," Kite said to the God, "you were trapped in there?" He pointed to Ash's key, and she tilted her head back the other way.

"Aye," Reverie explained. "She missed her son, and vowed to free and rehabilitate him to lead his half-siblings by example to *help* the Land. But, he deceived her, and trapped her Alchemical soul in a key." *To what?* Reverie asked, and the God replied through her, "A key without a lock has no purpose, and so is discarded. Therefore, *my* curse was never supposed to have been broken."

She lowered her gaze. Deerbolt was now buried deep in Sarronious's neck, sobbing, so she didn't see what happened next. The God of Ascension stood above Ash. Using an incantation similar to that of an Elemental, she cast a curse. Her lips mouthed the words and the group strained to hear, but it was beyond their capabilities; as if they were unworthy of hearing such a melodic voice.

The Dragon snorted, and Reverie nodded. It was her job to translate.

"She says to tell you that to live upon this Land is, in itself, a curse. A Human existence is... difficult." Reverie repeated, "Unforeseen by my son, I was given the opportunity to unlock Ash's Tetrad Alchemy, and so with the right amount of physical force," she said, blinking at the Dragon, "I could finally be free."

Ash couldn't move. He couldn't speak. All he could do was cough and grunt and wriggle his fingers, which he did to the best of his ability. Seeing his attempt to acknowledge this truth, the God of Ascension granted his wish. She called every fragment and particle of the shattered crystals to her in a cloud by raising both hands to the sky. Her eyes illuminated, reflecting in them the power of the key. She opened her mouth and appeared to scream without sound. Ash flinched, and

Deerbolt turned to see what the fuss was about when Sarronious gasped at his reaction.

The crystals reformed. She guided them carefully to sit on Ash's body. The red rested on his groin, the blue at the base of his throat, and the green over his heart. She took hold of the white crystal and placed it carefully in her mouth until it had been absorbed. Together, they glowed.

Ash took his final breath.

"NO!" Deerbolt screeched. "NO!"

Reverie told the group, "In return for freeing her soul from her prison, she gives a piece of herself to Ash the Elemental." She beamed.

Captain Deerbolt clasped her hands together, too amazed and grateful to speak. The crystals dissipated and sank through Ash's clothes. Suddenly, his eyes opened and he coughed, shaking his tousled hair.

"Wh-what was that? Where am I?"

"ASH!"

Deerbolt flung herself at him, kissing every inch of his filthy face until he pulled her away, laughing.

"Oh, I thought you were dead. I thought I'd lost you!"

"H-*how* am I here?"

His eyes then found the God of Ascension, and he swayed as if he was about to pass out.

Reverie assured him, "She's here to help you. She was imprisoned in your key, and the Dragon freed her. In return, she revived you."

"I was dead?"

Sarronious grunted. "Only just."

Deerbolt backhanded his chest. He smirked. And Ash smirked back.

When he turned to thank the God of Ascension for her kindness, she was gone.

EPILOGUE

Epilogue

Ash stood at the temple's ruins and tried to practise his Elemental incantations. No matter how hard he concentrated, he could no longer summon his Salamander Alchemy.

Deerbolt wrapped her arms around his waist from behind. “Struggling?”

Ash exhaled and chortled. “Strangely, I don't miss it.”

“Well, you lived for long enough without using it in Open Country. Can't be that different.”

Ash nodded. “Feels weird to be officially Human.”

“*Good* weird?”

“Aye,” he said, and turned to kiss her. “And now the God of Ascension is free and the flame still burns, there is potential for her to convince the God of Magic to bestow new eggs upon the Land. I hope they both banish Universal Energy to suffer as a Human.”

“Why, so you can kill him?”

“Without my Alchemy, it's the only thing I'm still any good at!”

From where they stood, they could see the entire island. The village nestled at the base of the hill and the temple's ruins halfway down. The Cerulean Grace in the distance, and tiny ant-like figures milling about the dock, loading and unloading supplies, and the stillness of their behaviour now the fighting had ceased as the Order was suddenly without their Alchemical influence. They couldn't see where the Dragon was through the trees, but they heard her growling and both were filled instantly with pride.

"Let's hope there can be peace now," said Deerbolt.

"Kite and Reverie are staying here, then, in case there isn't?" Ash asked.

"They want to be near the Dragon."

"Did you offer them passage?"

"Of course I did! I'm glad they're not returning with us. The mainland will be chaotic. Nobody will understand why their Alchemy is gone, and there will be fighting against the Order."

"Looks like your crew resolved that for us," he said, gesturing downhill toward the dock. "Being blessed by the God of Ascension, Riley offered me the leadership of the Guard," he told her, smirking, then immediately added, "but I rejected them."

"*Why?*"

"The offer stands," he assured her, "but I think I should be where I can best serve people. Right now, that's the mainland—a lot of confused, lost ex-Alchemists, and a crumbling government. I'm going to miss our new friends, I admit."

"Me too. When the child is born, she'll want to be close to her rider—she's going to have an amazing, world-changing life, that kid, and witness it all from the clouds." She inhaled deeply, imagining the experience.

"*She?*"

"Didn't Reverie tell you?" she asked, surprised.

Ash scowled. "Nobody tells me anything."

"They're having a girl, and they're going to name her after me." She smiled from ear to ear. "Her name will be *Artemis*."

ASH

DEERBOLT

~ What's Your Signifier? ~

AUTHOR'S NOTE

I would like to dedicate this book to my son, OFS, who I am hoping will love reading magical adventures like this when he grows up as much as I enjoy creating them. But this book is also dedicated to my family and my bookworm friends, who are the solid support system I couldn't live without.

I'd specifically like to thank SM for being the first to volunteer to BETA read this novel and for helping me with the title. But I owe her sister EM an apology. I'm sorry this wasn't another Arriette Monroe story (you can hate me if you want, though I'm sure you've enjoyed Elemental Ascension just as much).

A lot of research went into this book, and I loved attending psychic events, reading about Tarot, and even trying my hand at interpreting a deck of my own. I purchased *The Light Seer's Tarot* because the artwork spoke to me—it is colourful and feminine, multifaceted and simply beautiful. If you'd like to check that out, you can visit www.lightseerstarot.com.

I must thank DC for checking this research against her own

experience and knowledge of the cards, and for attending festivals with me to gather information from speakers including spiritual leaders, mediums, and authors. Because of her, I also purchased my own deck of *The Mythic Tarot* cards by Juliet Sharman-Burke, which came with a hardback guidebook and a cloth. This helped me to learn the positions of the Celtic cross traditional spread, which Ash's reading also follows in *Elemental Ascension*.

I appreciate everyone reads and interprets tarot cards in their own way—we all see and understand the images and their stories individually. Whilst I have done my best to read as many books on tarot and how to read them as possible—in particular the major arcana for the purpose of this novel—I would like to apologise in advance to anyone who would have read Ash's spread differently.

I love writing about magic and I absolutely adore world-building. Since creating the Arriette Monroe stories, which I combined in *Finding Pandora: The Complete Collection*, I've had a real taste for the creative freedom high fantasy allows, and the depth of the complex sub-plots that always enrich young adult and teen fiction. Between writing that, my post-apocalyptic adventure, *Aeon Infinitum: Run For Your Life*, and my visionary & metaphysical duology, *Noah Finn & the Art of Suicide* and *Noah Finn & the Art of Conception*, it is safe to say I adore writing (and reading) speculative fiction.

While writing this novel, I learned so much about myself. This truly is a blessing, and something I know fellow writers will appreciate; when we write about spirituality, we look inward—though we don't always understand what we find, it allows us to both grow and *glow.*

Bless all who watch o'er our flames.

Rachael x

ABOUT THE AUTHOR

I'm an Amazon international #1 bestselling author from Bradford, UK, and the founder of Curious Cat Books, offering professional author services in the UK.

As a speculative fiction author, I believe in entertaining my readers by offering a temporary escape from reality. Whilst I aspire to write fun, addictive adventures with characters my readers can relate to, I need to write meaningful and emotive stories alongside them to explore the depths of what it is to be human—in doing so, I can encourage people to also look within.

I feel through writing we face our darkest fears, explore infinite new worlds and realise our true purpose. Creative writing helps me to understand what my purpose is.

I have diplomas in Successful Self-Publishing and Journal Therapy, alongside a university Business Studies qualification and many other writing-related achievements. I'm also a trained copy-editor and publishing coach, and now run Curious Cat Books, freelance services designed to help overwhelmed debut authors.

***

Curious Cat Books is a small independent service; it has been carefully designed to meet the needs of new writers looking to produce their debut titles.

CCB hopes to prevent new authors from feeling lost or overwhelmed by the industry by offering straightforward advice alongside professionalism and affordability. This is based on the experiences of its founder, bestselling author E. Rachael Hardcastle, who self-published for the first time in 2010.

Now, publishing a book in 2023 doesn't have to be complicated or expensive—with the correct tools and guidance, we can all maintain more creative control and see higher royalties in exchange for our hard work.

Curious Cat Books encourages writers to invest passion and hope into their manuscripts. This small but energetic company promises personal service—always there to cheer you on. Whether you're looking for copy-editing, formatting, or cover design services, Curious Cat Books can help.

"Bless all who watch o'er the flame,
Where loyal guards are duly sworn,
For here they are rebirthed to new name,
So unto pledge their hearts to
Dragonborn."

www.erachaelhardcastle.com

DID YOU ENJOY THIS BOOK?

PLEASE CONSIDER LEAVING AN HONEST REVIEW THROUGH YOUR FAVOURITE RETAILER'S PLATFORM.

ALSO BY E. RACHAEL HARDCASTLE:

YA
POST-APOCALYPTIC

YA
HIGH FANTASY

MIDDLE GRADE
(DAVID HARDCASTLE)

ADULT
VISIONARY &
METAPHYSICAL

ADULT
VISIONARY &
METAPHYSICAL

WRITING AND
PUBLISHING
REFERENCE